Not Quite Forever

Also by Catherine Bybee

Contemporary Romance

Weekday Bride Series

Wife by Wednesday

Married by Monday

Fiancé by Friday

Single by Saturday

Taken by Tuesday

Not Quite Series

Not Quite Dating

Not Quite Mine

Not Quite Enough

Paranormal Romance

MacCoinnich Time Travels

Binding Vows

Silent Vows

Redeeming Vows

Highland Shifter

Highland Protector

The Ritter Werewolves Series

Before the Moon Rises

Embracing the Wolf

Novellas

Soul Mate

Possessive

Erotica

Kilt Worthy

Kilt-A-Licious

CATHERINE BYBEE

Not Quite Forever

Montlake
Romance

Text copyright © 2014 Catherine Bybee

Published by Montlake Romance, Seattle

www.apub.com

Amazon, the Amazon logo, and Montlake Romance are trademarks of Amazon.com, Inc., or its affiliates.

ISBN-13: 9781477825891
ISBN-10: 1477825894

Cover design by Anna Curtis

Library of Congress Control Number: 2014940354

Printed in the United States of America

This one is for Angelique.

I admire you more than words can express.

Chapter One

"We're sitting in the back of a police car! This isn't my idea of research!"

"Lighten up!" Dakota knew Mary ignored her words. "There isn't any way we'll be charged with squat. You didn't say we *had* a bomb . . . you simply said the *word* bomb."

Mary's less-than-happy face reminded Dakota of her own mother when she wanted to bury her with a look.

"I repeated *your words*, Dakota."

"Repeated in a *not so soft* voice. Even I know not to yell the word bomb in an airport."

Outside the squad car, uniformed policemen were talking among themselves while the temporarily misplaced airport passengers were let back into the terminal.

"I didn't yell." Mary tossed her head back, a curly lock of blonde hair moved away from her eyes in the process.

Dakota let loose a snarky laugh. "The ol' lady next to us did."

Yeah, the blue-haired crone managed to hear one word from their conversation, pointed her crooked finger in their direction, and you'd have thought they were both walking through baggage claim with an AK and an Uzi. In an effort to calm her friend, Dakota made the remark that everything that happened could be used for research. From the moment airport security showed up and put them in hand-cuffs to feeling the palms of the *not so friendly* guard running down their legs, Dakota tried to spin the experience.

They were visiting Florida for a writers conference. OK, it was more convention than conference. Plenty of parties, lots of fans . . . and tons of fun. Fun that didn't normally involve the police. Handcuffs, however, were optional.

Dakota would have liked to find the arresting officers worthy of a chapter in one of her books. Unfortunately, the woman who cuffed her wasn't amused and her partner wasn't any kind of hero Dakota would profile for her next novel.

Unable to help herself, she looked around the tiny backseat of the squad car, noted the cage separating the front seat from the back, and all the radios and toys the police used.

Who'd sat in the car before her? Her shoes stuck to the surface under her feet. She couldn't remember ever being in a car without carpet. A combination of bad musk, cigarettes, and something that sadly reminded her of vomit filled her nose.

Research only went so far. The thought of a night in jail—sleeping in the same space the previous occupants of the backseat did—churned her stomach. The longer they sat there, the worse her head started to spin.

"Oh, God," Mary said.

Dakota rallied. "Relax, Mary . . . and for God's sake, when they open the door again, let me do the talking."

Mary, bless her heart, didn't have the stomach, or the street smarts, to talk her way out of a gay bar full of lesbians. No, she'd try to ask said fictional lesbians about their childhood and try to determine if they were truly attracted to women or if they were just trying to piss off their parents. Mary spent her days, and sometimes nights, with a private client base that paid her to listen to their problems. With a master's degree in marriage and family therapy, she was a huge sounding board for Dakota. Right now poor Mary was probably wondering if she could continue to practice if she ended up in jail.

Mary jumped when Dakota's door opened and one of the officers leaned over and addressed them. "Which one of you is Dakota Laurens?"

Dakota swallowed. "That would be me."

Without even a hello, the overweight, balding man pulled her out of the car. Her Lakers cap fell from her lap as he marched her to a second car where two more officers stood. Next to them, the female officer that had cuffed her seemed to have loosened the bun on her head, and she offered a smile.

In an effort to ease the tension, Dakota lifted her eyebrows and tried to grin.

"This is all such a huge misunderstanding." Dakota let a little bit of the South slip into her accent.

Mr. Baldy held up a hand, stopping her, and nodded toward the female officer. "Is this her?"

The woman stepped closer, tilted her head. "Who are Mathew and Cassidy?"

For one brief second, Dakota's brain short-circuited. "What?"

The woman simply stared.

"*Surrender to Me?*" The title of her last bestseller fell from Dakota's lips and the officer's eyes lit.

"I think it's her," the female officer murmured.

While the officers exchanged glances, Dakota kept talking . . . after all, outside of writing, it was what she did best. "My friend and I are here for a conference. The Morrison is hosting Booklovers Unite. That sweet little old lady simply misheard my friend. There's no bomb." She whispered the word *bomb* and looked around them.

Dakota's gaze met her luggage, which was strewn, panties and all, across the sidewalk with more than one dog sniffing the contents. *Now that has to go in a book.*

"Ms. Laurens, you do understand the severity of yelling the word *bomb* in an airport, right?"

Dakota met the dark eyes of the only man not in uniform. "Well of course I do. My friend and I didn't *yell* anything."

"Mrs. Leland said you pointed to a bag and—"

"I'm a writer, Mr. . . ."

"Hansen."

Dakota smiled. "Mr. Hansen. As a writer, I tend to let my muse wander a little more than the average person. My friend and I seemed to have our luggage in the very back of the plane, and for a few minutes, we didn't think it was ever going to appear down that chute. As a writer, I thought, and whispered, 'I suppose it could be worse . . . there could be a bomb in here somewhere and we'd have to evacuate and wait even longer to get to the hotel.' Well, my friend Mary shoved my hand away and told me to be quiet about bombs. Next thing I knew, Mrs. Leland, bless her little ol' heart, started yelling we had a bomb. That's all there is to it. I swear on Nana's grave." Dakota lifted her right hand and hoped her Nana wouldn't be pissed if and when she ever learned that Dakota buried her prematurely.

From the corner of her eye, she spotted Mary talking with several officers.

So far . . . the Florida conference was sucking ass!

———

The Lakers cap caught his attention when she walked into the room and settled at the bar. As if knowing she wasn't anywhere near Lakerland, the brunette removed the cap almost the moment her butt hit the cushioned seat. Her sleek, dark hair wore a kink where the hat had creased it and she didn't wear a stitch of makeup. She was beautiful.

Walt sipped his whiskey and glanced at the never-ending pamphlets of patient care that were in constant need of revising, made a note, and glanced back to the bar.

From where he was sitting, he didn't hear what she ordered, but the bartender brought a short glass with a few cubes of ice and a nice amber liquid. Walt stared into his own drink and grinned.

Kink-haired Laker Girl tilted the drink back, taking half of it down with one swallow.

Nice!

The bar was busy for a Wednesday due to the conventions hosted by the Miami Morrison. The question was, what convention was Laker Girl attending? Walt had arrived at the hotel earlier in the day to find massive banners and the entire second floor of the conference hall filling up with pictures of half-naked men and women embracing. At first, he thought the competing conference had something to do with adult film. When he asked, he was told a writers convention was dominating the hotel for the weekend. By comparison, the number of people at the conference he was attending was a drop of water in the ocean. Soon the hotel would be filled with writers, readers, publishers, and agents. The genre of choice . . . romance. Books written with nothing but happily-ever-after in mind.

Walt had a hard time picturing any conference featuring romance books filling the hotel. Time would tell.

He glanced up to find Laker Girl pushing earbuds into her lobes and fishing a notebook from her overly large purse. Nothing said *don't try to pick me up* more than earbuds.

Yet Walt kept watching her. She sipped on her second drink as men and women made their way to and from the bar. Her shoulders folded in and she started to laugh quietly. She made a note and then held perfectly still, only to laugh again.

Walt pushed his attention back to his work and tried to concentrate. He doodled on the edge of the paper, found his eyes drawn away from his work.

She was laughing again, this time with her head in her hand as if she was trying hard to keep her mirth in. Walt had no idea what amused her, he found a smile on his lips and wanted to laugh along.

He folded the binder together and moved from the booth to one of the available stools at the bar. From his perch, he ordered another drink and discreetly watched as Laker Girl tucked her hair behind her ear and made another note. On impulse, Walt glanced at her left hand and found it bare.

Not that it meant anything . . . he'd met plenty of women in bars who were married but didn't wear rings when they were attending conferences. More than one woman, or man for that matter, used time away from home to troll.

If he had to guess, laughing Laker Girl didn't fall into that category simply because she wasn't making eye contact with the bartender.

Two seats down, an attractive blonde parked her shapely butt into a seat and ordered a glass of wine.

Laker Girl noticed the woman and twisted her way. Within seconds, a man moved to the space between the two women and struck up a conversation with the blonde. Beside them, Laker Girl wrote frantically and sucked in her bottom lip. Though she was trying to keep her laughter to herself, she captured the attention of more than one set of eyes.

She met Walt's gaze from across the bar, briefly, then returned her attention to her notepad. Nearly as quickly as she turned away from him, she looked again.

Even in the dim light of the bar, Walt could see the exotic gold spark in her brown eyes. He imagined her with a little bit of makeup accenting those eyes, maybe a ruby red lipstick. The room grew hot. He noticed the laughter inside her spread to her eyes, making her even more attractive. He knew he was staring, and didn't care.

She kept his stare as she lifted her glass to her lips and finished her drink.

Walt couldn't remember the last time he'd picked up a woman in a bar. Probably in college. Pickups in bars left a bitter taste in his mouth, but he was half tempted to do so now. Bitter be damned.

"There you are!"

A familiar voice redirected his attention and brought a smile to his lips.

Monica Fairchild, newly minted nurse practitioner, stood beside her husband, Trent, her arms open in greeting.

"Mo!" He accepted her hug and stood back to shake Trent's hand. "You're early!"

Monica nudged her husband's shoulder. "On-time flights are easier when you're behind the controls." Trent Fairchild and his two brothers owned and operated Fairchild Charters. A private air charter company with a fleet of jets, big and small, not to mention more helicopters than one could count, which was why they were attending the conference of International Emergency Medicine . . . a conference where professionals worked to improve the emergency response to natural disasters all over the world. "Is Glen with you?" Glen was Trent's brother and liaison to the fixed-wing portion of air travel for the sick and injured.

"He's flying in later," Trent told him.

Monica glanced around the bar and motioned to an empty table that would hold all of them.

After they settled, Trent flagged the waiter.

"Looks like this place is gearing up for quite a week." Monica's words mimicked Walt's thoughts.

"What are all the posters for?" Trent asked.

Walt explained the second conference taking place and Monica's eyes lit up. "Really? Romance novels?"

"Don't tell me you read that garbage," Walt said with a roll of his eyes.

"Don't judge. There's enough blood and guts in the world. Books help me escape."

Trent shared a glance. "Everyone has a vice. Besides, it helps her midflight."

How a pilot and a woman phobic of flying ever managed to get together . . . Walt would never know.

"Reading is not a vice," Monica corrected.

Trent pulled her close in the booth and kissed her cheek.

Walt's gaze moved to the end of the bar and he realized Laker Girl had moved on. Only an empty glass sat at the bar.

Chapter Two

Walt moved past the hordes of women standing in line in front of the conference room door and couldn't help feeling a dozen eyes rolling over him. He knew, without a doubt, that the women in this line weren't there waiting for his riveting conversation about improvising medical tools in the field of emergency medicine. Between the canvas bags hoisted over their shoulders sporting half-naked bodies and the names and accolades of an author's achievements printed on T-shirts, Walt knew he was walking into the wrong room.

Scanning his itinerary, he confirmed the time and room before he pushed inside the double doors.

Chairs were set up in rows of ten separated by a middle aisle, giving the capacity of over a hundred places for an audience to sit. In the front of the room was a single table where two women, one blonde with massive curly locks rolling down her back, and another with long, straight dark chocolate brown hair, stood with their backs to him. The women were speaking with a heavy-set man wearing a three-piece suit. *Management.*

The man turned as Walt approached and clutched his notebook to his chest. "You must be Dr. Eddy."

He set his briefcase on the table. "I am."

"I'm Robert Cruise." The man extended his hand.

At that moment, the brunette turned on her pointed heel.

Walt found himself drawing in her appearance in slow and measured degrees. The sexy arch of her foot should have looked ridiculous in four-inch heels. Did she know how bad it was for a woman to wear spikes on the ends of her feet? That thought was brief, and then *hell yes, there is a god and he loves a woman in strappy shoes* swamped his brain. From there, tanned, smooth skin slid up shapely calves until they met a skirt with a slit that gave sight to the perfect amount of thigh.

Her maroon skirt hugged her hips, cinched at her waist, and fanned up to a white silk button-up shirt that wasn't quite secure right above her creamy breasts.

Walt blinked, twice, and tried to remember he was at a conference and not in a nightclub.

"There seems to be a conflict."

Walt snapped his eyes to the lips speaking. Her voice was dark honey that should have been reserved for a professional phone operator for the truly desperate, or the sick. Yet nothing . . . absolutely nothing looked ill about the woman standing in front of him.

Her dark eyes laughed, even when her crimson lips hardly held a grin.

"It appears we've double booked a few rooms this week," the hotel representative explained. "With two conferences going on at the same time . . . things like this happen."

"My session begins in ten minutes," Walt told Mr. Cruise.

"We're searching for another room to accommodate you."

For one brief moment, Walt thought Robert might be speaking to the woman and her blonde companion, who seemed to have taken a few steps back.

"To accommodate me?" He pointed a finger to his chest.

"Yes, Dr. Eddy. We're very sorry. This entire wing was only supposed to house the guests of the novel convention. All the medical professionals were supposed to be based on the third floor." Robert pulled the back of his hand across his forehead and shuffled his feet. "There was a computer glitch . . ."

"I understand," Walt told him. No need for the man to have an MI over the ordeal. Considering Robert's girth and sudden onset of perspiration, a heart attack might already be in progress.

The brunette's half grin moved on to a full laugh.

Walt tilted his head and brought her into focus. She stepped around the presenters' table and kept a giggle close to her lips. As she attempted to control her mirth, Walt recognized her.

Laker Girl. Remove the hard-on-inducing clothing, the heavier makeup, and all the polish that went with it, and there she was. The woman who'd sat at the bar last night sucking back whiskey and listening to other patrons' conversations moved in front of him . . . competed with him for the very space they stood.

"You find this amusing, Miss . . . ?"

Her eyes met his and she leaned over the table, planting both hands firmly in place. "Laurens. And yeah, I do."

The blonde rapped her knuckles on her friend's arm. "Dakota!"

Dakota . . . snazzy, a national landmark more than a name . . . a beautiful woman full of life. Yeah, the name suited her.

"What?"

"Maybe we should move to another room." The blonde was in a much more agreeable state than Miss Laurens.

"I'm guessing there are more women out there here to listen to me than professionals here to listen to the good doctor."

Walt envisioned the women standing in line, knew without a doubt Dakota was right.

In any other situation, Walt would have simply smiled and left the room, but something about Dakota Laurens sparked something inside him and made him want to get under her skin. Something made him want her to stop laughing and to take notice . . . of him.

Robert turned away from them when the phone in his hand buzzed, and he talked in hushed tones.

"You're part of the romance convention?" Walt asked, already knowing she was.

Dakota removed a stack of papers from her bag and tapped the edges together to align them. "You say 'romance convention' as if it's a disease, Dr. . . . . Eddy, is it?"

"Walt. And I didn't know they had conventions based on bodice-ripping novels."

The blonde's agreeable grin slid and Dakota blew out a sigh. Her lips kept her snarky grin, but Walt knew his words dug deep. His own mother wore that look whenever his father said something just to piss Mom off.

"What are you presenting today, Dr. Eddy?" Dakota stood tall, her shoulders back with a chin out in defiance.

"I'm sharing the art of improvising medical tools and equipment when all you have is dental floss and a toothpick. What about you?"

Her eyes would be classified as brown, but damn they looked nearly black when she was ticked. And although Walt didn't know her well . . . he knew enough to know she didn't look happy. In a second, those eyes took on a softer shade, almost liquid chocolate mixed with honey. A wicked smile tilted one side of her lips.

Walt had to remind himself not to lick his own in response.

"The art of crafting a gratifying sexual love scene."

Walt did lick his lips . . . blinked twice, and drew his brows together. "Excuse me?" He pulled on his collar, knew the room wasn't warm.

Dakota relaxed a hip against the table that separated them and leaned in just enough for him to see the depth of her cleavage.

"I write *bodice rippers,* as you so eloquently labeled them, Dr. Eddy. Safe to say there are a couple of satisfying ripping of bodices in them . . . don't you think?"

He pointed to the door. "And all those women are in line to hear you talk about that?"

Instead of answering, Dakota Laurens lifted one eyebrow and smiled.

For one brief moment, they stared at each other.

Stalemate.

Or maybe it was just her way of holding power . . . didn't matter, and Walt wouldn't call her on it. He'd probably say something that would embarrass him eternally.

Robert returned to their side, shoved his phone in his pocket. "We found a room . . ."

The doors to the room opened and women shoved inside to capture a front-row seat.

Fascinated, Walt stood back and watched as a few women nudged past him and shoved books on the table in front of Miss Dakota Laurens.

"Can you sign this?"

Dakota pulled away from the table and scooted into the chair. She scooted the book into her hands while the blonde beside her handed over a pen.

"What's your name?"

Walt didn't hear it . . . he only noticed when Dakota glanced at him and squeezed her eyes together as if to say, *you can kiss my ass.*

Damn if Walt didn't want a chance to try.

———

Walt? Was that short for Walter? And what parent named their kid Walter?

Stuffy, Dakota decided. Parents that were stuffy and stuck on tradition. She would lay her next advance on the line to say that Dr. Walt Eddy's parents were doctors themselves . . . or at the very least, pompous elite who named their son after some long-dead beloved grandfather. Probably both.

Make that her next two advances.

What was that upper-crust lip about bodice rippers?

Screw him. And his strong-jawed, short-haired, hazel-eyed loveliness. Didn't matter that he filled out the suit he wore as if he weren't a stuffy doctor, but maybe a closet bodybuilder instead. Shoulders like his should come with a warning label.

She knew better than to be attracted to a man like him. The night before in the bar she noticed him briefly before he was joined by a beautiful blonde and a man who had to be her husband or at the very least an attentive lover.

What would his pickup line have been? She wondered then . . . wondered it even more now.

Damn if he wasn't fun. Getting under his skin had been invigorating.

After her class on the fine art of crafting meaningful sexy intimacy concluded, Dakota signed more books and moved along with the stream of women rushing to their next class, to meet their next author-crush in person.

She had two more appointments for the day . . . a meeting with her editor, another with a boatload of her author friends to get pissing drunk in the hotel bar. But that wasn't until much later.

"Dakota?"

Behind her, Mary called her name and Dakota slowed her steps.

"You're in an awfully big hurry," her friend said as she hoisted the conference-issue bag up onto her shoulder a little higher.

"I need coffee." She did. Not the watered-down stuff the hotel liked to give in the massive urns stationed at a few watering stations along the convention floor. A shot or two of espresso might help fight the fatigue nipping at her eyelids. The Starbucks on the ground floor was calling her name.

Mary fell in step alongside Dakota as the halls emptied, the women at the conference streaming into individual rooms like water in a multitude of funnels.

"I don't know how you manage any sleep with all the caffeine you consume at these things."

Dakota offered a short laugh. "That would be the whiskey chasers with dinner." They rounded the corner to the escalators and she stepped on the one leading up to the third floor.

"I thought you wanted coffee." Mary stepped alongside her and glanced at the level they'd just left.

The third floor was much quieter and less crowded with advertising. Dakota twisted her name tag around so the back side faced out.

"You're checking out that doctor." Mary looked around and lowered her voice.

"You're smarter than all that blonde hair implies."

Mary pushed her shoulder and offered a playful frown. Dakota was always giving Mary crap about all her hair. The snarky comments stemmed from sheer jealousy. Mary might complain about how her hair took on a life of its own, but every inch of it was beautiful and the envy of many.

Two volunteers sat behind a small table with a slew of packets and registration sheets.

Dakota offered a practiced smile and turned to the women at the table. "I've lost my itinerary," she told them.

Without question, the woman picked up the doctor conference pamphlet and handed it over. "No problem, Dr. . . ."

Dakota didn't offer a name, simply took the material and thanked the woman.

"How do you do that?" Mary asked as Dakota led her friend away.

"Do what?" She opened the conference schedule and scanned the list of doctors . . . focusing on one name. Walt stuck out like a cat in a room full of dogs.

"Make people think you belong when you don't?"

Sure enough, Dr. Walt Eddy's first scheduled class was in her room . . . but where had they put him? She glanced around, found a handwritten *change in venue* billboard along the main hall.

"I belong." She twisted and started toward the room to which the hotel had moved Dr. Eddy.

Dakota found the room and turned. "This won't take long. Meet you downstairs for a double shot latte in ten?"

Mary eyed the door with a frown. "You were kind of mean to him, ya know."

"Which means I need to kiss some ass."

Mary laughed. "You don't kiss anyone's ass."

If it's cute enough I will.

"Ten minutes, at the coffee shop."

"Fine!" Mary twisted on her heel and waved behind her. "Be nice, Dr. Laurens."

With a laugh, Dakota opened the door and slid inside.

The room was a postage stamp, and it appeared that Dr. Eddy had quite a following. The chairs were filled and several people were standing along the walls.

". . . are you saying we should use duct tape to stop the bleeding?" The question came from a man in the fifth row.

Dr. Eddy stood leaning against the desk. His hands clutched the sides, his eyes met those of the man asking the question.

"I'm saying that if you're the only one there and duct tape will keep your patient alive, then you damn well better use it."

"But if the removal of the tape—"

"Skin issues don't mean a whole lot on the dead, Doctor."

The door behind Dakota squeaked as one of the conference volunteers entered and signaled that Dr. Eddy's time was up.

His hazel eyes skidded past the volunteer and landed directly on Dakota.

He paused and the fierce passion he had for the discussion started to fade.

"That's all the time we have now. I'll be available to answer individual questions outside and throughout the conference."

Funny, he was addressing the class, but looking at her.

The hair on Dakota's arms stood on end.

Just like during her classes, some people moved from the room while others lingered.

Dr. Eddy stood where he was and pulled his gaze away from hers, directed it to those who approached him.

She eased her way to the front of the room, smiled at those who passed her and offered an appreciative glance.

"Thank you . . ." one of the conference attendees said while shaking Dr. Eddy's hand. "One of the things that worried me most about joining Borderless Doctors you just blew out of the water."

Dakota stood back and listened to the exchange.

She knew Dr. Eddy watched her out of the corner of his eye as he gathered his material and shoved it in his briefcase.

"Why did you choose emergency medicine, Dr. . . . ?"

"Daniels. Sounds cliché but I wanted to help the helpless. The ones in severe crisis."

"Let me guess . . . politics, insurance . . . malpractice . . . everything gets in the way of you doing the right thing for the patient?"

Dr. Daniels let loose a long sigh. "Exactly!"

Dr. Eddy met Dr. Daniels's eyes. "You're no different than anyone else in the room. A few weeks of your life a year and you'll remember why you lived on coffee during your residency." He slipped the younger doctor a card and shook his hand. "We have our own set of politics, but it's nothing like it is in your paying job."

Dr. Daniels glanced at the card and walked away with a smile.

Another suit-wearing man, probably another doctor, lifted his hand to Dakota so that she might have her turn with Dr. Eddy.

Walt stood, snapped his case together, and waited.

"I believe I owe you a drink, Doctor."

Somewhere behind his eyes, a smile grew . . . but it had yet to make an appearance.

"It's a little early for alcohol, Miss Laurens."

He remembered her name. The thought had her holding back a smile.

Beside them, the man waiting to speak with Walt watched, and Dakota wasn't oblivious to the scene and how it might play out to an unsuspecting audience.

All of it . . . every second recorded in her brain as a scene from one of her novels.

Sometimes life did imitate art.

"Coffee is a drink."

There was his smirk.

Damn it was beyond sexy.

"You're talking about coffee?" He didn't look convinced.

She made a motion of looking at her watch. "I have a meeting with my editor . . . perhaps something with more punch . . . later?"

His full-watt smile brought fire.

"You do owe me."

Dakota lifted her chin. "Seven?"

Dr. Eddy agreed with a mere tilt of his head and Dakota turned and walked away.

Chapter Three

He needed to know . . . couldn't stop himself from taking a little walk through the second floor.

The hallways and corridors were overflowing with massive posters featuring authors and their work. Tables lined the walls with bookmarks, pens, and postcards. Walt dipped his hand into a basket and pulled out colorful condoms with an author's website printed on the packaging. *Sexy Swag to Live By.* He found himself pocketing a couple of giveaways, telling himself it was for the guys he worked with back in California. Lip gloss, emery boards, squishy stress balls, colorful trinkets of all sizes and flavors . . . romance authors had healthy imaginations. He turned down another hall to find it filled with the same.

This was Dakota Laurens's world. The overload of half-naked bodies had a strange way of turning up the heat in the room. From five yards away, Walt zeroed in on her name. The *D* scrolled on the page, the ass of a naked woman, her head tossed back with dark hair flowing down her back while a man leaned over her, lips to neck, filled the cover. "*New York Times* Bestselling Author" blasted above the banner.

Surrender to Me.

He read the title and had a strong desire to find the nearest bookstore to grab a copy.

Women, and a few men, slowly trickled from the conference rooms and began to funnel into the hall.

"Dr. Eddy?"

He heard his name, twisted toward the voice calling him.

"Did they mess up your room again?"

The blonde, Dakota's friend, glanced behind him and began to grin.

He was so busted.

"No . . . ahh, I'm sorry, you have me at a disadvantage. I didn't catch your name."

"It's Mary," she said, not offering her last name. "It's a great cover . . . don't you think?"

Walt turned toward Dakota's banner. "It certainly catches the eye."

"It's her best seller to date. And that's saying something."

Someone bumped into him and he moved aside for the women passing.

A heavy-set fortysomething stopped midtracks and turned a smile his way. "Oh, are you one of the models?"

"Excuse me?"

"Alice!" she said to the woman at her side. "Take my picture with him." She juggled her bag and removed a cell phone from her back pocket.

"He's not—"

Alice shoved in and suddenly Walt felt the woman's arm slip around him. The impromptu paparazzi moment was met with a flash.

"Thanks," the woman managed right as he felt a distinct pinch just south of his waist.

He blinked, repeatedly, and stared at the women as they disappeared around the corner.

Mary began laughing, the chuckle started low and built. Walt felt himself smiling right along with her. "What the hell was that?" he asked.

"Entertaining! That's what that was. Dakota isn't going to believe it."

"No, really? What?"

Mary stepped closer. The hall was neck-to-neck women now, some pushing in between them to reach the free swag on the tables.

"There are about a dozen models running around, brought in by the magazine hosting the convention. Cover-model types that pose with the women for pictures."

Someone beside Mary turned when she heard the word *picture*. A redhead with more aggression than the previous woman and too much makeup for Walt's taste turned her attention his way. "Oh, what's your name?"

"Walt," he said on impulse as he tried to ignore her lean body as she pressed it against his.

She squeezed her eyes together as if his name made her look twice. "You have the businessman-suit thing going. Very sexy." She leaned in, snapped a picture herself with her cell phone, blew a kiss, and walked away.

All the while Mary laughed.

"I think I need to get out of here." He said the words aloud but his feet didn't move.

"Hey, Mimi," Mary called over her shoulder.

"Can you take our picture?" She handed Mimi her cell.

Walt lost his smile while Mary glanced behind him, pushed him to where she wanted him, and posed. "Smile, Doctor," she told him. "Your friends back home are going to want to see this."

They would.

He smiled.

———

Dakota's phone buzzed right as her editor, Loretta, ordered a salad. "Is it too early for wine?" the woman asked.

Dakota laughed and turned to the waiter. "We'll have a bottle of champagne and two glasses."

"We have several to choose—"

She waved her hand in the air, cutting him off. "Your most popular under a hundred fifty bucks."

"One of the many reasons I love you," Loretta said as she pushed her beyond-petite frame into the plush seat.

"How many times do I have to tell you . . . when the publisher is paying the bill, tell them I asked for the wine by name. What are they going to do . . . say no?" Dakota knew they wouldn't rack up half the bill on a lunch date as they would a dinner. Loretta was a young mother, a kick-ass editor who simply "got" Dakota and didn't cut loose often. In the beginning of their relationship, it was Dakota who worried about stepping on toes. Those roles reversed when her sales blew through the ceiling and every publisher and their brother called her agent and asked for her next three books. Mumford Publishing topped her last advance with a special seven-figure deal that kept her and Loretta in a working relationship. A publisher willing to part with that many zeros wasn't going to complain about a bottle of bubbly.

But because Dakota really valued Loretta's friendship, she leaned in and said, "You let me know if there's ever *any* pressure to cut back on these lunch dates."

"Oh, Dakota."

Loretta was corporate to the core but as easy to read as a diary with a paper lock.

Dakota's phone buzzed again, but she ignored it.

"*Succumb to Me* has officially been accepted. Not that there was any question."

Dakota broke off an edge of a cracker. "I never assume."

"Are you kidding? Your fans are clamoring for the end of this series."

They were. The question was what was next?

"Mumford would like to see you extend the series."

Dakota released a sigh. She knew this was coming. Desi, her agent, had told her as much in an earlier conversation.

The waiter arrived with the wine, poured them both a glass. "To *Succumb*," she toasted. "May it be as successful as the others."

Loretta tilted her glass back, drained half of it. "About the next book."

"This series is finished. Mathew and Cassidy are solid . . . a baby on the way." God knew they screwed enough in the books to warrant another generation.

"Your fans . . ."

"Half would be happy it continued, the other half ticked that I'm squeezing another book out of the series."

"You know we'll work with you and Desi to make it worth your time."

Dakota lifted a hand. "Stop. OK . . . I get it. Sex is the new vampire and you want more. It would be almost impossible for me to write outside of erotic right now . . . but I want to work on new people. New characters. Who knows . . . they could be even bigger than Mathew and Cassidy."

When her phone buzzed again, she took the diversion and pulled her phone from her purse.

Facebook had lit up . . .

Mary . . . in all her blondeness stood beside a very sexy Dr. Walt Eddy with *her* banner poised behind them. The caption in the picture tagged Dakota and simply stated, *Found a doctor in the house checking out our favorite author.*

Her mind that took in everything went into overdrive. A single doctor . . . a volunteer . . . what makes him tick? Why is he single? He's gotta be in his thirties. Mid or earlier . . . a little reserved but not the private practice type that lived for billing codes and top dollar.

"Earth to Dakota."

Loretta waved a hand between them.

"Sorry." She picked up her glass. "Where were we?"

Dr. Eddy became the *where's Waldo* of the convention. Dakota followed the Twitter feed with the hashtag #sexydoctor and found several images snapped by convention attendees. Because Mary had linked her name to the picture, she had easy access to the gossip following the doctor at their conference.

Two steps into the bar and Dakota found herself surrounded by friends, colleagues, and faithful fans who she only saw at conventions. She allowed herself a good thirty minutes before she was to meet up with Dr. Eddy for the obligatory drink.

Unlike the night before, tonight people were three deep at the bar, and getting said drink might prove difficult. There were plenty of suit-wearing doctor types with their ties missing and their wedding bands stowed in a pocket.

Do they really think we can't see the tan lines on their ring fingers?

Dr. Eddy didn't have that tan . . . yet his skin tone told her he lived somewhere with plenty of sun. The *I'm married and stepping out* vibe just didn't fill Walt's aura. Not that she was a huge fan of the aura, but there was something to be said about the energy surrounding people.

"Did you hear about Jen Adkins?" her friend Cherry asked.

"A little something." Dakota inched her way closer to the bar.

"She hosted a small party in her suite and damn near got kicked out of the hotel for making too much noise," Cherry told her.

"Last night?"

"No . . . like an hour ago."

"It's early." Who bitched about a party in the early evening?

"I know. That's one for the books."

Dakota squeezed between the fray and waved down the bartender as he sailed by. "Whiskey on the rocks."

The only acknowledgment was a quick wave.

Mary slid up beside her, wine in hand. "There you are."

"Hey. You've been busy today."

"You saw that?"

"Did I see an overwhelming thread of a certain doctor . . . yeah, I saw."

"Walt was such a good sport." Mary turned and gave Cherry a quick hug.

"It's Walt now?"

"That's his name. He doesn't really like being called Doctor. Said it reminded him of his dad."

I knew it! His dad was a doctor. Walter Sr. perhaps?

"Miss?" the bartender handed her a drink and a bill. She signed, placed her room number, and moved away so another needy conventioneer could take her place.

"What was Walt really doing on the second floor?" Dakota tilted the glass to her lips, savored the warm flow down her throat. *Nice.*

"I found him staring at your banner." Mary lifted two fingers. "Scout's honor."

What woman didn't like the thought of a man working hard to figure her out?

"Then random women stopped him, snapped pictures. You know how it is up there."

"Some of those women are crazy," Cherry added.

Dakota raised her glass toward Cherry's. "With enough of these, you are, too."

Instead of denying anything, Cherry lifted her glass in salute. "Who is he?" Cherry asked.

"One of the doctors from the other conference," Mary offered. "The hotel mixed up his room with Dakota's this morning."

Mary went on to explain the morning's mishap. "Oh . . ." she nudged Dakota, nearly spilling her drink. "And get this. He has some *in* at the hotel. Special guest or some such thing."

She wasn't surprised. Doctors had a way of making people bend to their will. Or so she thought anyway. "How so?"

"As he put it . . . he knows somebody who knows somebody." Mary waved her hand in the air, the drink in her hand already hitting her empty stomach. "Staying in a suite on the top floor. How cool is that?"

Dakota found her eyebrow lifting. The hotel was one of the best in this part of Florida. Top-shelf never sucked in a place like this.

Cherry wandered off with another group of friends, leaving Mary and Dakota.

"Excuse me?"

Dakota felt the hand on her arm the same moment she heard the voice. Behind her, a blonde, somewhat familiar, flashed a huge smile and let her arm drop. "Are you Dakota Laurens?"

She twisted toward the woman. "I am."

"I knew if I hit the bar early I'd manage to run into someone I've read."

A fan. "Easy to do at a conference. Are you a writer . . . reader?"

The woman shook her head. "No. Well, a reader, but not part of the book convention."

The blonde wore a black dress, just short of her knees, with small straps and a pleasing dip to her cleavage. She looked the part of someone going out to paint the town instead of hanging in a hotel bar. Dakota glanced at herself, realized her red dress wasn't exactly hotel-bar ready.

"Trent?" the blonde called over her shoulder and caught her companion's attention. Together Dakota realized how she recognized them. The night before, from across the bar . . . sitting with Walt. "I want you to meet someone."

Turning a practiced smile on the couple, Dakota extended a hand to the handsome man. "Dakota Laurens," she told him.

His face was blank. No shock there. He obviously didn't read her books. "Trent Fairchild."

"I'm Monica," the blonde said. "Sorry."

"A pleasure," Dakota said, meaning it. Fans and all their tongue-tiedness never got old.

Monica nudged the man at her side. "You remember, Barefoot. Our last trip to Houston . . . the layover."

His face remained blank until Monica leaned in and whispered something private in his ear.

The grin on Trent's face slid into something much more wicked. "*That* Dakota Laurens?"

Monica lifted her hands, nodded. His cheeks turned pink.

And *that* reaction never ceased to amaze Dakota either.

"I have a strange need to thank you," he said. The laughter came easy.

Monica hid her face, but her embarrassment didn't last long.

"Are you here with the doctor convention?" Dakota asked.

"We are. This is the first time there's been such a lively crowd in the bar."

Mary leaned in. "Romance writers love to party."

Dakota introduced Mary and eased into small talk. "Are you both doctors?" Mary asked.

Trent placed his arm around Monica, pulled her closer.

"Nurse practitioner. Trent's a pilot."

"How does a pilot fit into your conference? Isn't it about medical crisis or something?"

Before Trent could answer, another man, slightly taller, strong jaw with the same unmistakable DNA as Trent's, moved beside them. "There you are. This place is a madhouse."

Dakota looked around. It was a complete crush of people. The noise level made talking nearly impossible.

The newcomer was Trent's brother, Glen. His gaze lingered on Mary a little longer than anyone else in their small party. The feeling was apparently mutual. Mary turned away slightly and fanned herself.

When Glen looked away, Mary caught Dakota's eye and mouthed the word *hot*.

Looking out for her friend, Dakota asked a few pointed questions. "Are you a pilot, too, Glen?"

"Yeah."

"Is your wife here with you?"

Glen lifted an eyebrow. His gaze fell on Mary. "I'm not married."

Dakota finished her drink, set it on a nearby table, and winked at Mary before turning toward the party.

The hair on the back of Dakota's neck prickled. Awareness that only a man could deliver from across the room shivered up her spine. Was he watching her? Did his gaze linger on the curve of her butt . . . the very curve of her body where she felt heat swimming along the surface?

Dakota let her eyes drop to the ground and feather over her shoulder.

He stood still in the entrance of the bar, women walking around him, eyeing him. His eyes swept her frame, his bottom lip sucked in between his teeth in a way that said a hell of a lot more than any words could.

Walt wore a button-down silk shirt and casual pants. His hair was still wet from a recent shower. Someone attempted to stop him as he moved toward them, but he brushed them off and kept moving forward.

"Hey," Monica said the moment he made it within earshot. "I was wondering if we were going to see you before your date."

The word *date* had Dakota lifting her eyebrows.

"Drinks, Mo. Not a date."

Beside her, Mary chuckled.

"Drinks can be a date. I'll bet some of your books have drink dates . . . right, Dakota?"

"I can think of at least one book that starts off with a drink date."

Walt actually shuffled his feet. And was that a blush?

Adorable.

Monica glanced over their heads. "So where is she?"

Mary's giggle turned into a laugh.

"I won't embarrass you," Monica continued.

"Too late," Mary mumbled.

Dakota knocked an elbow into her friend's side. "Getting a quiet drink in here isn't going to be possible," Dakota announced.

"I can see that."

By now, the bar was four people deep and the temperature shot up several degrees.

"There are a couple of bars just down the block," Walt suggested.

"Sounds good to me," Monica said.

Looked like quiet drinks with just the doctor were going to have to wait.

"Let's go." Dakota took the liberty of latching on to Walt's arm.

He didn't miss a beat, just held on and started walking away.

"Wait. You're Walt's date?" Monica asked.

Dakota shook her head. "Nawh, it's just drinks. Right, Doc?"

He laughed.

Heat and humidity always accompanied Florida. The forced air conditioning of the hotel really didn't let those inside understand the oppressive weather outside the doors.

Gray clouds blocked out the sun, but didn't drop the temperature below eighty.

"Feels like a storm," Trent said behind them as they ducked into the comfort of the air-conditioned bar.

"I'm glad we're not flying," Monica said.

"I love a good storm. We don't get enough of them in California."

"Is that where you're from?" Glen asked Mary.

"Yeah. We haven't had rain in so long even the tumbleweeds are becoming extinct."

They found a table big enough for all of them and staked their seats. Walt pulled out Dakota's chair and the gesture told her two things. One, he *did* think of this as a kind of date, and two . . . his mother taught him how to treat a lady.

Mary reached for a bar menu and started flipping through it. "I hope they have something other than fried food. I'm starving."

"You haven't eaten?"

"Convention food."

Monica laughed. "Cheese, crackers, and fruit if you get in line first."

"Exactly," Dakota said.

Monica glanced at her husband. "I wonder if Jack is open to suggestions on convention menus. I know he doesn't deal with them directly, but there has to be something better than cheese and crackers."

Mary reached for the peanuts on the table, cracked a shell. "Who's Jack?"

The question sat on the tip of Dakota's lips.

"Morrison. Jack is my brother-in-law."

The connection didn't click immediately.

Walt leaned forward. "Jack Morrison, as in the owner of the hotels."

Dakota found herself holding her breath. "Seriously?"

Monica confirmed with a nod while one of the servers approached the table.

After they ordered drinks, the conversation picked back up. "So where do all of you live?" Dakota asked.

Trent, Monica, and Glen lived in the Northeast, and surprisingly Walt lived about thirty miles from Dakota's Orange County condo.

"How do you know each other?" Dakota asked.

"I used to work with Walt in Pomona. We both volunteered in the relief effort in Jamaica, which is where I met Trent."

Dakota had an overwhelming desire to find a pen and start taking notes. Something triggered a memory . . . a story . . . "Fairchild and Morrison. Wait, are you the two who were trapped and thought dead?"

"That's them," Glen told her.

She'd read the story, heard about them on the news. A nurse and a local went missing, their names famous because of their connection to the hotel family and some airplane charter company.

"I remember the news. Wow, you guys are lucky to be alive."

Monica grasped her husband's hand. "We are."

"They survived and eventually married. That's a romance novel right there," Glen said.

"Romance is everywhere," Dakota reminded her friend.

Their drinks came and a live band slowly trickled in and started to set up.

Dakota was incredibly intriguing to watch. Walt could practically hear the computer in her head typing away a new story while she learned about the lives around her. She talked about herself, but only briefly, even though Monica attempted to pull more information from her.

At first, Walt had been disappointed that their party of two turned into a party of six. But here, he could learn much more about her because of the curiosity of others. She became a writer "because it was the only thing she was good at." Yet the more he listened, he knew she was probably omitting certain truths, or simply downplaying her success.

She was confident in a way few women achieved, but most wanted.

Hot! She was so sexy in her red slim-fitted dress with stiletto heels, dark almond-shaped eyes that sat against tan skin only achieved by someone living in a sunny climate, that he had a hard time sitting still. She didn't look at you . . . she absorbed you with a glance, devoured you with her eyes, made you hers with a stare.

Dakota Laurens was the kind of woman he most definitely wanted in his bed, but didn't dare go there. Walt always considered himself a strong man . . . self-sufficient, well respected . . . a damn good doctor. This woman could consume him. He knew that fact instinctively. No memo needed.

Yet he knocked back another drink and listened to her colorful tale of airport police and smelly cop cars.

"Wait!" Glen held up his hand. "You two are the reason I had to circle Miami for almost an hour instead of landing?"

Dakota giggled when she drank, and the South blossomed in her voice. "Blame Blondie here. She's the one who yelled *bomb.*"

Mary had a hard time containing her smile. "I didn't yell." She lowered her voice and tried again. "I didn't yell, Glen. Just so happened a little ol' lady overheard us at that very moment."

"We were in the back of a squad car for over an hour. I thought they were going to strip-search us."

"It wasn't funny." Mary was laughing. "It wasn't."

"It was kinda funny." Dakota continued to laugh until everyone at the table joined her.

The band hit the stage, welcomed the room that had managed to fill in the hour it took them to set up. Their first song brought a few people to the small dance floor and drowned out most of the conversation.

Walt pushed his chair closer to Dakota's, leaned in since conversation with everyone else wasn't possible with the volume in the room.

"I hope drinks with friends is working for you."

"Your friends seem like good people." She looked behind her and they both noticed Mary laughing at something Glen said in her ear.

The band hit a higher note, and Monica and Trent moved from the table and joined the dance floor.

The song swiftly changed and Walt noticed Dakota tapping her foot. He nodded toward the floor, and she agreed with a smile.

Dakota liked to dance.

He loved the smile on her face. Loved the way she closed her eyes, felt the music, and embraced it.

For over two hours they drank, ate . . . danced. None of the dances were slow, which probably was for the best. The crowd didn't seem the type to sway on the dance floor, though Walt would have loved an excuse to hold something other than Dakota's hand.

Against his better judgment, he was about to order another round of drinks when the lights in the room flickered and the PA crapped out with a loud squeak.

The lights returned but it was obvious that some of the power wasn't back up.

The lead singer onstage tapped the mike only to move away and raise his voice from the useless amplifier. "Looks like that tropical depression is a little closer than the weatherman said."

Walt remembered the news saying a low pressure system was headed over the Gulf, but he didn't think it was anywhere close to Miami.

When it became apparent the power wasn't going to come back up, Monica suggested they return to their room.

The hotel didn't appear to have any power problems, but it did seem the volume on the main floor had dulled to a low roar.

"Holy cow!" Mary hummed as she stepped into the suite. "This is your room?"

Monica tossed her purse on the coffee table and crossed to the kitchen. The main room was nearly a thousand square feet, complete with a kitchen, dining room for ten, living room, piano, and foyer. Three bedrooms splintered off from the space, giving full panoramic views of the city. The penthouse was built for a family. Glen took one of the two additional rooms in the top floor apartment. Walt's room was down the hall and half the size. Still, a penthouse suite wasn't something he would ever spring for and yet couldn't say no to when talking with the Morrisons.

"I told my sister we didn't need this," Monica said with a sigh.

"It's bigger than my condo," Mary exclaimed.

Dakota adjusted quickly. "It's very nice."

Trent moved to the massive window and opened the blinds. Outside, rain started to spray against the glass. Trent shoved his hands in his pockets and rocked back on his heels.

Walt moved to his friend's side, looked at the ominous rain-filled clouds. "Looks bad."

"I lived through my share of storms in Jamaica."

"You think this is one of them?"

He shrugged. "The path of the storms don't often veer off course by too many miles. They do pick up strength, however."

"Honey?" Monica called from across the room.

Trent turned toward her.

"Want another drink?"

He waved her off. "I'm good."

A denial of a drink this early in the evening made Walt pause. He'd taken care of many disasters after they'd happened, but hadn't been a huge part of one while it was occurring. The second earthquake in Jamaica was as close as he came.

Walt was about to ask Trent if he thought the weather was going to get worse as a gust of wind and pelting rain slapped the window.

"Looks nasty out there." Dakota walked up behind them.

"Weather like this seldom leaves behind anything good."

"I suppose you'd know that better than most," she told Walt. "How long have you volunteered with Borderless Doctors?"

"Little over five years."

"You love it." It wasn't a question, simply an observation from someone he hardly knew.

"Restores my faith in humanity. There are people out there suffering and are willing to take any help they can get. People who've lost everything and want to help others simply because they have it better than the guy in the bed next to them. Those of us that go to do what we can, do it for the basic humanity of life."

Dakota leaned against the large window and sighed. "And there are people like you willing to risk their own safety *to* help. That makes you a hero, Dr. Eddy."

He snorted, was thankful he didn't have a drink in his hand or he'd feel the burn of the alcohol in his nose.

"You laugh," she said. "You know I'm right."

"I get on a plane and fly to crazy places and do what I do. That doesn't make me a hero."

She lowered her gaze to her shoes before slowly lifting it back to his. "I'm the writer, Doctor. A hero is anyone willing to give of themselves without anything in return."

His smile fell. "I get plenty in return." The smiles of his patients, the knowledge he made a difference. It was why he went into emergency medicine.

Noise from the television filled the room and they both turned to see a crew of Florida weathermen and -women covering the storm.

"The tropical depression has now been upgraded to a tropical storm and is spinning off Cuba and picking up speed." The reporter on the news stood against pelting rain, the effect of drops slapping against his otherwise perfect face, dramatic enough for the evening news.

"A tropical storm isn't as bad as a hurricane, right?" Mary asked.

"Just shy of a hurricane," Trent told her. "Makes a difference in smaller countries, but aren't that dramatic here. Unless they linger and cause unexpected flooding."

"Or power outages?" Dakota asked.

Monica moved beside her, placed a drink in her hand. "The hotel is prepared for this kind of thing."

"As much as they can be," Dakota said. "Anything past the what . . . the eighth floor . . . won't have water if the power goes out. It takes power to pump water."

Intrigued, Walt wondered if Dakota's statistic was correct.

"You've been watching way too much of that prepper show, Dakota."

"It's either a fact, or it isn't. Bottom line, here on the twenty-eighth floor, or us on the seventeenth . . . we won't have water if the power goes down."

Walt considered himself an observer in life. He watched, listened, and made executive decisions when the time came. Preparing for anything other than long stints at work wasn't part of his life. If the storm got worse, those in the room could just leave if they needed to. Helped to have a couple of pilots with access to private helicopters and airplanes. Sure, he could add Dakota and Mary to that exiting mix, but what about the others in the hotel?

"We have drinking water and enough food to last awhile in the fridge," Monica told them.

"And flushing the toilet?" Dakota wasn't letting this go.

Walt found himself smiling.

Monica's face fell into a frown. "I didn't think of that."

Dakota lifted her glass to Monica. "Fill the tub now. Worse case, you drain it in the morning."

Glen looked over his shoulder. "That's not a bad idea, Dakota."

Rain continued to pound the massive windows in the suite, Monica disappeared toward the bathroom, and the sound of running water filled the room.

Chapter Four

The water in the tub was drained the next morning and the tropical storm didn't manifest into anything. The power flickered once, forcing Dakota and Mary to take the stairs back down to their room sometime after one in the morning. Their new friends, Monica and Trent, suggested they stay in their suite, but with a room only a few flights down, they decided to take the walk.

A slight edge of discontent sat under Dakota's skin as she made her way through the early hours of the next day. She hadn't managed much of a conversation with Walt outside of a joint one with their small party the night before.

When she found him standing outside the room where she finished her morning class, a smile met her lips and her heart skipped. Today he was dressed in a casual pair of pants and a simple pullover shirt, no suit, no sleek shoes, and no briefcase.

"Hi."

"Hey. Flying home today?" she asked, knowing perfectly well he wasn't scheduled to leave for two days.

"Flying, but not home."

Dakota forced the smile to stay on her lips. "Excuse me?"

"The storm," he tilted his head to the side as if the entire weather event stood next to him. "It's a . . . it provided an opportunity to take a few of us off to triage some of the islands in the Keys."

She blinked, twice. "You're leaving?"

"Trent is flying us down. We'll probably fly back to the West Coast from there."

A twinge stuck somewhere between her brain and her lungs and caught. "Oh."

"I, ah, thought I'd say good-bye before I left."

His gaze met hers and held.

At a loss for words, Dakota sputtered. "The islands? Are they . . . is there anything serious going on there?"

Walt shook his head. "I doubt it. A good training exercise. Something we can use since we have a couple of pilots and plenty of experienced staff with us."

"It's what you do . . . right?"

"Yeah. I thought . . ."

He let his words die off and she thought right along with him. Thought maybe they'd have an opportunity to get to know each other a little better before they both returned to their normal lives.

Dakota reached over to the table outside her room, found several copies of her latest book sitting there. From her bag, she grabbed a pen and opened up the cover.

She handed him the book and offered a smile. "My schedule is more flexible than yours, Doc."

He glanced at the book she shoved in his hands.

She heard his phone buzz in his pocket. To his credit, he didn't acknowledge it. Just stared at her. The heat in his eyes registered and made some of the confidence inside her sizzle and lean toward him.

His phone buzzed again. "They're meeting me . . ." He pointed toward the sky.

"On the roof?"

"Right."

"Then you should probably go."

Only, he didn't move. People walked around them in their rush to get to a class, to move to their next event.

"Walter." She used his full name and he blinked. "Read the book. Call me."

He tapped the paperback in his palm and finally broke away. "Right. OK." He stepped back.

The ball, as they say, was in his court. If he wanted to get in touch with her when he returned to LA, he now had her number. There wasn't anything else she could say outside of good-bye and that didn't feel right.

Dakota hiked her bag higher on her shoulder and took a step back.

"Safe flight home, Dakota."

"You, too, Doc."

"Walt," he corrected with a laugh.

She backed away a couple of steps. "Walter . . . is that Walt the Second or the Third?"

He moved away, both of them speaking through the bodies swarming around them.

"The Third. How did you know?"

She laughed. "A hunch. Was Grandpa a doctor?"

When Walt opened his mouth to answer, she lifted a hand and stopped him. "Tell me later," she told him. "Enjoy the Keys, Dr. Eddy. I hear they're beautiful this time of year."

With that, she turned and left him standing there.

———

Dragging, with his eyes straining to stay open, Walt finished his last verbal dictation for the night. Outside light was pouring in from the ambulance bay. Already the morning was heating up. The California sun's only redeeming quality was the fact that it was dry. Still, anything in the triple digits meant more accidents, more assaults, more chaos. After three long graveyard shifts following his trip to Florida, Walt was ready for a night off. A night of uninterrupted sleep sounded like heaven.

Walt finished his dictation, hung up the phone, and signed off his charts.

"Walt?" the day shift clerk, Nancy, called out as he started toward the doctor's room where he left his keys.

"Yeah?"

"You have a call on 2748."

He lifted a hand in acknowledgment and moved to the private room where he could at least hold his tired head in his hands while he finished any last-minute conversations for the day.

He sat on the unused bed in the private room and clicked into the call. "Dr. Eddy."

"You sound just like your father when you answer the phone."

He loved his mother, but her timing couldn't be worse. "Hi, Mom."

"Oh, you have that *I'm tired and you've called at the wrong time* voice." JoAnne Eddy was a doctor's wife. She knew all about late shifts and the need to sleep.

"I did just finish three nights in a row, Mom. What's up?"

"I knew you'd turn off your phone so I called you at work."

Walt closed his eyes. "You could leave a message and I'll call you back."

His mother sighed. He envisioned her oversprayed hair and perfect makeup. "You know how much I hate playing phone tag. The mother is the last to get a call back. I thought I was a good mother . . . one that deserved more attention from her only son."

Walt was too tired to listen to the guilt trip. "Mom. I'm tired. It was a busy night. You wouldn't want me to fall asleep on my drive home . . ." He'd learned how to place guilt trips from the best.

"Oh, that's just mean. But I'll get to the point. Your father's birthday celebration is in two weeks. You're still coming, right? There hasn't been some silly outbreak of pig flu somewhere that is dragging you away, is there?"

Pig flu? This disgust for how he spent his free time was always a breath away when speaking to his parents. Giving his services away for free somehow mocked them and every dime it took to put him through medical school.

"I'm still coming."

His mom waited a beat. "Are you bringing someone?"

What he wouldn't do to stop the flow of questions he knew were coming. The image of Dakota, and a passage in her book that he'd read from beginning to end, popped into his head. He really needed to call her. Let her know he was back in town. Maybe she'd have some choice words to stop his parents from their constant questions.

The woman did have a way with words.

"No."

"You hesitated."

"I didn't hesitate. I'm coming alone."

"Who is she?"

He yawned. "There's no one."

"You hesitated again."

"I yawned. I'll see you in two weeks." He glanced at his watch. *After eight already?* The traffic was going to suck.

"You promise?"

"Unless the big one hits and airplanes don't fly."

"Don't say that," she chastised. "You know how much I hate you living in that godforsaken place as it is. Colorado has its faults, but we don't have big earthquakes."

Yes, but you're both there, he wanted to say but didn't.

"Good-bye, Mom."

By the time he walked into his apartment, he was more awake than when he'd left the hospital. Between the traffic and the bright sun, his head decided sleep could wait a little longer.

He tossed his keys and his wallet in a bowl by the door and headed to the kitchen. A big bowl of cereal and a glass of milk would give him the right amount of fuel to help him sleep. Or so he hoped. Even a few hours would make the evening better.

His fridge was a void wasteland. The milk was fresh but nearly empty. A few beers and a head of wilted lettuce would keep him from starvation if the big one hit.

Why had his mother placed that image into his brain? Walt didn't worry about things like that. Truth was, if the big one rocked the southland, he'd be in the ER for days. Food would have to come by way of the cafeteria.

He leaned against the counter as he poured sickening-sweet cereal into a bowl. His eyes landed on Dakota's book sitting on the counter. He'd already dog-eared a few pages. Admittedly, one passage was filled with steam and attraction . . . the others, however, were witty passages or ones that made him question her personal past.

He was attracted. So much so she found a way into his mind daily since he left her in Miami. No one woman took that kind of space in his mind since Vivian. Even now, years after . . . Vivian's name in his mind brought up images of their time together.

He didn't want to do that again. Life was fragile, painfully so. Who knew that better than an emergency doctor who watched people lose their battle with life on a daily basis?

Then he'd read Dakota's book. Two people from different lives, different histories . . . both having issues that most would never experience nor understand. Their physical attraction was off the charts.

Walt knew that was probably some of his attraction. How could a woman who wrote words so explicit and emotionally compelling be anything but a passionate wonderland under her Lakers cap and sarcastic exterior?

He needed to know a little more about her before he let the wonder of the woman he knew as Dakota, author of sensual romance novels, walk out of his life.

Walt opened the book and picked up his phone.

She answered on the second ring.

"Hello?"

"Dakota." Her voice had a sleepy quality to it. It brought to mind early mornings and long evenings.

He cradled the phone in his hand and played with the cardboard on his empty cereal box.

"Dr. Eddy. I was wondering if you'd call."

"Wondering or hoping?"

"Eweh . . . such a leading question. Does the woman say with a breathy tone . . . Oh, Doctor, I've just been pining for your call.'" The slight Southern accent he'd heard after a drink licked the edges of her voice. "Or does the woman say in a noncommittal tone . . . 'Doctor who? I forgot all about you.'"

"Do you always play out scenes in your head?"

"You read my book . . . you tell me."

"How do you know I read your book?"

Dakota laughed and something inside him sprouted. "Because it's a long-ass flight from Miami to LA. How did the Keys hold up?"

"Fine. Minor damage, few problems with the local hospitals."

"Anticlimactic and not worthy of the fuel to fly there."

He laughed. "Have you been talking with Trent and Glen?"

"No. But that's something I'd guess they'd say."

"You'd be right."

"I'm an observer of people, Doc. Something I think you and I have in common."

Walt gave up playing with the box and poured milk into the bowl. "You're going to have to forgive me. I'm in need of food and can't seem to end this conversation before I shovel it in my mouth."

"Ah, honesty. Very admirable. Have you been at work all night?"

"I have." He went on to tell her about the last three nights, some of the never-ending sagas that became his patients' lives. He shoveled in a few bites when she offered a comment.

"I'm taking notes," she told him.

"Untold stories of the ER?"

"No, that's been done. I'm going with the jaded doc angle. Character profile. I'm using you, Doctor, fair warning."

"Ah, honesty. Very admirable." His words mimicked hers and her laugh crawled up his spine again.

"My schedule is stupid," he told her.

"My schedule is flexible."

He pushed his unfinished bowl of cereal aside, pulled her book in front of him. "Have any of your stories started with two people simply dating?"

"No. Actually, there's usually chaos and drama."

"Dating is too simple?"

"You might say that."

He would.

"Tomorrow night. I need your address."

She was silent.

His heart sped.

She started spouting off numbers and a street.

He scrambled to write it down, the half-empty bowl of cereal tilted and fell to the floor.

Shit.

"What time, Doc?"

"Six," he told her.

"And how should I dress?"

"Casual." Because he had no earthly idea what they were going to do.

"You're making this up as you go along."

"Maybe."

Her laugh brought a smile to his face. "Again with the honesty. I didn't used to think that was a desirable quality in a man."

"Glad I can shift that character profile for you, Miss Laurens. I'll see you tomorrow night."

"I look forward to it, Doctor."

"Dakota?" He caught her before she hung up.

"Yes?"

"It's Walt. Not Walter . . . not Doctor. Just Walt."

"Whatever you say . . ."

He waited, knew it was coming.

"Doctor." And then she hung up.

Seduced by Pizza might be the title of her next book.

Pizza and bowling.

Did anyone bowl anymore?

"A woman prides herself on her shoes." Dakota glanced at her two-inch heels that complemented her designer jeans and silk shirt.

Walt pushed dollar bills into a sock vending machine. "Bowling shoes are very retro."

She reached into the machine, removed the plain white socks, and tapped them to his chest. "Good thing you're cute."

"C'mon." He pulled her toward the lane he'd just paid for. "Nothing says *successful first date* like a little friendly competition."

"What if I told you my average is two hundred?"

He stopped and she bumped into him. "You just grumbled about bowling."

"Doesn't mean I'm not awesome at it." She wasn't. At least she hadn't been when she last played. That had taken place in college, well over five years ago.

They stared each other down for about ten seconds and Dakota slipped, let a smile spread over her lips.

"You're bluffing."

She moved around him and set her purse on the table assigned to their lane.

"You're so easy."

He blew out a breath as she moved to the rack of house balls and picked out one that fit her hand and wasn't so heavy she'd lose control and toss the thing behind her.

Walt disappeared long enough to get them a couple of drinks and order a pizza. A good ten lanes of the bowling alley were packed with a league of some sort. From the scores on the digital boards, the league was serious about their game.

She picked at the tiny laces that both had knots in them from the previous careless bowler who simply tugged the shoes off.

Bowling shoes really did have a lot to be desired, she told herself once they were laced and she rolled a small cuff at the bottom of her pants to avoid tripping.

The digital display started to flash their names when Walt returned with the drinks.

He wore a pullover shirt and jeans. He had sandy brown hair that looked like it would bleach out if he spent any time on the beach. She couldn't decide if his eyes were a shade of blue green, or gold green. She settled on hazel. The question was, what triggered the color change?

Walt set the drinks on their small table. "Pizza in thirty minutes."

"Everything but fish?"

He flashed a smile. "What one wants on their pizza is important."

Dakota picked up her ball and stepped up to the lane. "Almost as important as what they drink." She knocked down a whole two pins on her first throw.

"When was the last time you bowled?" he asked.

"College. You?"

"Couple years ago."

Her ball rolled up and she knocked down another three before she let Walt take his turn.

His ball flew down the lane at what seemed like Mach speed, taking out eight pins. "I played a bit in medical school. I think it had something to do with cheap entertainment and late hours."

A roar went up to their right where the league players were watching someone manage strike after strike.

"Were you ever on a league while in medical school?"

Walt tossed his second ball, missed both pins. "No time for anything at that point in my life."

"But you wanted to."

There was a slight hesitation and she inched past him to get her ball. "Anything other than golf."

"Avoid the cliché?" The next ball knocked down a few more pins than the last. Maybe by their second game she'd break a hundred.

"Golf-playing doctors . . . not my thing."

"Let me guess . . . your dad plays golf."

His blue-gold eyes turned a little darker. "How did you know?"

"He's a doctor, isn't he?"

Was it her imagination, or did his ball actually crush the pins at the end of the lane?

"Lucky strike," he said as he sat beside her.

She managed a sip of her drink. "He is, right?"

"Cardiologist. Took over my grandfather's practice, built it up."

Dakota leaned forward. "Was medicine a birthright or did you really want it?"

Walt twirled the ice in his drink. "I always wanted to be a doctor."

There was something missing from his statement, she'd bet money on it. "But?"

"Cardiology just wasn't for me. Emergency cases . . . fine. But day in and day out? Nawh . . . not me. Imagine going to school for ten years of your life to learn everything about how the engine on a car works and dedicating your life to the fuel pump when it was all over."

"Fuel pumps are important."

"They are. And eventually every one of them will need to be replaced or overhauled or the car doesn't run. But there's so much more to the car that keeps it running."

"Emergency medicine or bust."

He laughed. "You might say that."

"I'll bet your parents are proud."

Walt sipped his drink . . . didn't meet her eyes.

"They're not?" She was certain her jaw hit the table.

"They wanted the practice to go to me . . . eventually."

She didn't see that coming. "But you're a doctor. You volunteer for humanitarian relief. How can any parent be anything but over-joyed with that?"

"C'mon, Dakota, I'm sure some of your characters come from less-than-perfect parents."

"That's fiction." Fiction based loosely on facts that she'd picked up from people she'd met, research on personality traits.

"My story isn't unique. My dad wanted me to follow in his foot-steps, literally. I became a doctor but not the kind of doctor he wanted me to be. My mom has only ever been his wife. Supported his desires."

Dakota couldn't help but laugh straight out with that. "Really? She didn't exist before him?"

"She lives to be in his life."

Dakota rolled her eyes as she stood and grabbed her ball. She let the ball roll, thought about what Walt was saying.

"Did she go to college?"

"Yes."

"What did she study?"

When Walt didn't say anything she knew he had no idea what his mom wanted before marrying Dr. Walter Eddy II.

Fascinated, she didn't even mind that her second ball rolled down the gutter.

"I'm sure your mother has other things on her mind than being your dad's wife."

Walt shook his head. "She called two days ago to remind me of my dad's birthday celebration and to make sure I was coming. She only calls for things like that. Dad doesn't really call at all."

"So in short . . . you became a doctor because you love it and managed to piss off your family because you didn't follow in the family business. Let me guess . . . your parents don't live close by."

He frowned. "Colorado."

Walt was still frowning when he returned from knocking out another seven pins.

There was obvious tension from the conversation, something she really didn't want and imagined Walt didn't either. "My parents don't approve of me either. You're not alone in that."

It was Walt's turn to let his jaw drop. "You're a successful author. *New York Times* bestseller . . . millions of readers."

She laughed. "You read my bio."

He raised his hand. "Guilty."

"All that and I even make amazing money. Still, my parents are less than thrilled." She turned on her best Southern accent and lowered her voice to a whisper. "'She writes those porn books.'"

"You're kidding."

Dakota shook her head, left a smile on her face but felt her parents' disapproval even at a distance. She might laugh about it openly, but deep down . . .

Walt reached over and took her hand in his. The color of his eyes took on a pale shade of golden brown. Warmth ran up her arm, and some of the noise from balls hitting pins and the shouts of excitement disappeared.

Walt looked at her. "What I read wasn't pornography. More detailed than anything I've read before, but nothing so trite. Your characters were really fucked up, serious issues, and in the end, I was hoping they'd work it out. Of course I have to wait six months until the next book comes out to find out if they do."

A warm laugh shook her. "It's a romance novel, Doc. Everything will work out . . . eventually." They dug into the pizza and had yet to finish one game. They both sucked at bowling. Well, Walt did a much better job, and if Dakota had to guess, his last couple of gutter balls were totally thrown on purpose.

They were both enjoying a second drink and Dakota had to admit that bowling was a great first date. Well, second if she counted drinks in Miami with friends.

"How often do you get home?"

"To my parents?" she asked, snaking a long string of cheese with her tongue.

Walt's eyes caught the movement and he paused.

The attraction, the one that made her say yes to a date, shivered up her spine. She felt her skin tingle, and she knew it wasn't from the forced air in the bowling alley. She had to concentrate on chewing.

"South Carolina, right?"

"Yeah." She chewed quickly. "As little as possible."

"That bad?"

"You have no idea. The South is vicious. And the women. For the love . . . the women gossip about you from two feet away. California is so much easier."

"No one gives a crap here."

"Right!" She pointed her pizza at him before taking another bite. "Or they look right at you and can call you a bitch. So much easier to deal with."

"I can't believe your parents don't approve."

Dakota shrugged. "When my very first book was released, seemed everyone in my hometown managed to get a copy and read it all at the same time. My phone started ringing by the time chapter ten made its rounds. My mother was furious. Some of my close friends, those I'd known since grade school, started talking smack." The memory of that time crawled over her spine. She'd been so ecstatic about her first novel, only to have those she thought would be the most supportive turning their backs.

"Did everyone shun you?"

She shook her head. "Not everyone. But enough negative vibes were flying around to make me leave. I was in an apartment just outside of Savannah at the time. I took my advance and moved here, worked hard to drill away my Southern accent. I go back when I have to. Holidays, that kind of thing. Some of my old friends have come around with the success of my work."

Walt flashed a smile. "I like it when the South slips into your words."

She laughed. "There are times I can't contain it. If you go around talking like this all the time"—she let her accent fill every syllable—"no one would take me seriously."

"And you want to be taken seriously."

She sipped her drink. "I've worked hard to get where I am. I don't want anyone trivializing my efforts because of an accent or a bias because of the genre I write."

"I guess I hit your hot buttons when I called romance novels *bodice rippers*."

Dakota narrowed her eyes and Walt sat back, tossing his hands in the air.

"I'm an educated reader now . . . I'll never make that mistake again."

She shook a finger in his direction. "If you know what's good for you, you won't."

When she stopped laughing, she sat back in her plastic chair and sighed. "We have a lot in common."

He lifted his glass. "To avoiding our parents."

She could drink to that. "So when is this birthday bash for Dad?"

Walt rolled his eyes. "Two weeks."

Dakota found herself groaning for him. "Will it be awful?"

"Oral surgery might be better. Birthdays bring out family."

"You'll get it from all ends."

"Yeah. I'll get off easy if my mother doesn't set me up on a blind date."

Dakota patted his hand. "Oh, Walt, that's awful and deliciously funny at the same time."

"My mother's taste in women and mine couldn't be further apart."

"You have to give her points. If she sets you up with a local girl, you might just move back home and pick up the practice for your dad."

Walt ran a hand through his hair, picked up his drink. "I was trying so hard to think she just wanted grandkids, but you're probably right."

"Not the grandkid guilt. Try being a woman. My mother thinks that if a uterus isn't used before the age of thirty it's going to shrivel up and fall out."

Walt's eyes instantly watered as the drink in his mouth turned into a coughing fit of laughter.

Chapter Five

They never finished their game. They eventually moved to the diner across the street for coffee and pie. Conversation with Dakota never stopped. They snarked on their parents and moved on to those in the bowling alley who were shocked when they got up and walked away from the game.

Dakota didn't have a filter. He liked that. She said it the way she saw it and didn't seem to care if that pissed anyone off.

"You pulled what out of his ass?" she asked, her dark eyes glued to his.

"A cucumber, but I didn't take it out. Poor kid needed to go under and the GI guy fished it out."

"How old was he?"

"Sixteen." Stories from the ER never did bore his friends who weren't in the trenches with him.

"Wow. And his parents just stood there?"

"I don't know who was more embarrassed, the kid or the parents."

"That's one crazy fun job you have there, Doc. Who knew?"

He eventually paid the bill and drove her home.

Five minutes from her condominium, she turned to him with a straight face. They were at a stoplight and he met her gaze. "What?"

"Why aren't you married?"

His heart squeezed in his chest. Instead of answering, he turned her question back on her. "Why aren't *you* married?"

"That's easy. I'm outspoken, opinionated, and if you haven't been told, I write porn. Which is either a complete turn-on for the wrong guys or turnoff for the right ones. Add to that I make more money than most of the guys I've dated and that either intimidates them or makes me wonder if they're around just for the cash."

The light turned green and he moved down the road. "You've given this some thought."

She sighed. "Not really. That's a practiced line I lay on my mom each time she asks."

"A line based on facts?" Because from what he'd learned about her on this date, nothing she'd just said wasn't a fact.

"Some. I guess. I write books where two flawed people meet, fall madly in love, and will do anything to be with each other. I'm not looking for that, not at this point anyway. I'm happy being single."

He turned down her street.

"You didn't answer my question," she told him.

He took his time answering her, parked in her driveway, and opened her door. "I'm happy being single, too," he told her as they stood outside his car.

The light from her porch bounced off her face. She leaned against the car and offered a nod. "No one to answer to." Her words rang true in his head.

"No one to worry about when I have to fly off to third world countries."

"No one to get upset when I'm up at two in the morning writing like a madwoman."

"No one to wake me after a long graveyard shift."

Her smile was weak and all Walt could see was her lips.

"No one . . ." she murmured.

He reached over and cupped her cheek. The warmth and softness of her skin had him stepping closer. Her lips parted and he took his first taste. Apple pie and coffee laced her kiss and mixed with him.

When he melded his body to hers and felt her hand reach around him, the desire to have *no one* started to fade.

A simple first kiss shifted course when she moaned and opened for more. This kiss zinged right past his head, down to his toes . . . oh, it stopped in the middle and made his jeans tight, but he expected that.

It was hard to keep the kiss simple, impossible to pull away. Had they managed a conversation in the hotel that first night at the bar in Miami and ended up like this, maybe he'd already know what it felt like to be inside her. Simple affairs with nameless women were an enjoyable heartless release. The woman in his arms now didn't fit that bill. He knew her too well to place her in *that* category.

Her hand slid down his waist, over his hip.

Walt pulled his lips away. "You're making it hard to be a gentleman."

She didn't remove her hand as her smoky eyes mixed with her sexy voice. "You make it hard to be a lady."

He kissed her again . . . open-mouthed, indecent kisses.

Walt heard her purse hit the pavement before her arms slid over his shoulders.

Four words . . . four words and they could finish this.

Can I come in? He'd said them before, knew without any doubt he'd say them again . . .

Walt captured her head in his hands, enjoyed the way she pressed against him.

She pulled away, breathless. "I want to invite you in . . ." It wasn't an invitation, but an admission.

"I'd want to accept that invitation . . ."

She leaned her forehead on his chest and took a deep breath.

Walt pulled her close and simply held her.

———

Mary ran over early the next morning, letting herself in as she had for the past two years. "He didn't stay the night?"

Dakota looked up from her coffee and frowned. "Do you ever knock?"

Mary moved to the coffeepot, grabbed a cup, and made herself at home.

"We spent time in the back of a squad car together . . . nothing says *a bond that never needs to knock again* like that." Mary shoved into an empty chair at the kitchen table and huddled over her black coffee. "How did it go?"

"We went bowling."

Mary blinked.

"I know, right . . . bowling!"

"So it sucked."

"No. It was awesome. Totally kicked back . . . couple of drinks, pizza."

"And bowling." Mary didn't sound convinced.

"We knocked over a few pins. Did we finish a game?" Dakota glanced at the ceiling as if it held the answers. "No. We left on the eighth frame."

"You didn't finish the game?"

"We were too busy talking. His parents suck, kinda like mine. Loves being a doctor, loves the flexibility of the ER. He lives in an apartment."

A look of horror passed over Mary's face. "Why? He must make money."

"Doesn't want the commitment of a mortgage, home repairs. I don't know."

Mary's shoulders slumped. "Commitment phobic. I see . . . that's why he didn't stay over."

Dakota sipped her coffee. "A night in the sack isn't a commitment, Mary. It's sex. Besides, neither of us pushed."

"Sloppy kisser?"

"Amazing kisser . . . *knock you out of the universe* kisser. I took notes."

"Wow. But you didn't sleep with him."

"You make me sound like a slut."

Mary lifted an eyebrow.

"Oh, God, will I ever live Vegas down? That was almost two years ago and it happened once."

"You didn't get his name."

"He didn't get mine either."

Mary drank her coffee. "You're a woman . . . a woman should have the name of the man she's sleeping with."

"There wasn't any sleeping, Mary. I guarantee it. Either way, it was once and neither of us wanted to repeat it. I've been very selective since."

"Mason?"

"That's low. I liked Mason." The bastard was married. *Married!* They dated a few times and when they moved to the next level, he stayed over once. Then his wife called. Dakota had no idea there was a Mrs.

Bastard.

"Steve."

"I didn't sleep with Steve."

"That's right . . . sloppy kisser," Mary reminded herself.

"Let's not forget his lisp when he was excited."

Mary started to laugh and before either of them could sip more coffee, they were both bent over and mimicking Steve's lisp. Poor sloppy-kissing guy that he was.

"So if Walt's an amazing kisser, not married, and is void of a lisp . . . why are *we* having coffee this morning?" Mary waved an index finger between the two of them.

"I don't know . . . it just wasn't right. I mean, I think we'll be amazing . . . but it's too soon."

Mary sighed and her shoulders slumped while a silly smile crept onto her face. "Oh, Dakota . . . you really like him."

Dakota had awoken that morning alone, under her down comforter with an incredible feeling of hope inside her chest. Hope that most often fizzled out by a third date. She knew Walt had his own reasons for hesitating. The way he didn't commit to another date, only a call, made her wonder if he didn't feel the same way about her kiss as she felt about his. Except he'd seemed on the cusp of asking to come inside. She was only half ticked that he didn't push.

"You're a hopeless romantic," Mary said, as she did after every Dakota date.

"My expectations are too high. Life isn't a romance novel."

"He's a doctor. Your parents would love him."

Dakota rolled her eyes. "That's reason to lose his number right now."

Mary leaned back in her chair. "He's sexy."

"His parents would hate me."

"You say that about any parent that isn't a fan. They'd love you."

"They sounded pompous. Walt avoids them nearly as much as I avoid mine."

"Does he have siblings?"

Dakota dropped her hand on the table. "I-I don't know. We didn't talk about it."

"Has he ever had a serious relationship?"

"I don't know."

"Does he go to church?"

"I—"

"Democrat or Republican?"

"Good Lord, Mary, I didn't have him fill out an application. I don't know. Religion and politics didn't enter in the conversation. And before you ask . . . neither did abortion." Dakota moved to the coffee-pot and filled her cup. Caffeine would be her best friend on this day.

Walt spent the morning huddled over coffee and a computer.

Damn electric bill was past due and he'd all but forgotten he needed to pay for water.

Something told him Dakota had this stuff down. She probably paid everything two weeks ahead of time all while having a manicure.

He'd noticed her finely polished nails the night before as she picked up the bowling ball and rolled the thing down the lane. She really didn't know how to bowl. Telling her his average was well over 180 would have been a mistake. So he threw most of the game and didn't even bother trying to finish.

She had a hard exterior that he imagined stemmed from her parents' disapproval. Anyone as driven as she was had to have some kind of drama motivating her. He'd have to ask her if she had a sister or brother that buffered her parents' issues with her writing. Or did her siblings feel the same way? He couldn't imagine. At least his own sister understood why he had moved away. Brenda was stupidly happy and married to her first love. Or so that's the story he'd been told when she'd announced she was getting married right out of college.

His parents would hate Dakota.

The thought popped into his head and actually made him smile. The opinionated and nonfiltered personality that endeared her to him would make them squirm, especially his mother.

Walt clicked the *Pay* button on his banking site and picked up the phone.

"Good morning," he said when Dakota answered.

"You're up early."

"So are you."

"I could still be in bed . . . lazy morning and all that."

He leaned back, felt the chair tilt a little too far. *Damn it . . . need to fix this thing.*

"You're drinking coffee," he told her. "I'm thinking just sugar . . . or just cream, not both."

Her husky laugh told him he was right.

"Raw sugar. Honey if I'm in a restaurant. Refined sugar is bad for you, Doctor. You should know that."

He pushed away his empty bowl of *nothing but refined sugar* cereal and glanced out the window. "I'm working a midshift today, off a day, then on two mornings . . . have a dinner with the directors of Borderless Doctors after that."

"OK." She paused. "Why are you telling me this?"

"I told you my schedule was stupid."

"Which is easier because you're single."

Right.

"Everything is squished together because of Miami and my dad's birthday—"

"Walt?" she interrupted him.

"Yes?"

"Do you want to see me again?"

He hated how much. "Yes," he admitted.

"Do you and your colleagues ever go out after a shift?"

He laughed, thought of the dive only a few blocks from the hospital. "Joe's."

"Fine. I'll meet you at Joe's for a drink on Tuesday."

This felt too good . . . too right. "Do you pay your bills in advance?"

For a moment, there was silence on the line.

"What?"

"Your bills? Electric, water . . . that stuff. Do you—"

"I understand what bills are. Yes, I do. I hate to think of them stacking up and me forgetting them. Do you?"

He offered a nervous laugh, turned to his computer, and noticed a red "overdue" notice on his water bill. "Of course . . ." He punched in the amount due and hit Send.

"Doctor?"

"Yeah?" He clicked through the bills he normally paid, noticed his cell phone was a couple of days away from being shut off. "Damn," he mumbled.

"You can't lie worth shit. I hope you know that."

He placed the amount due in the empty box, hit Send. "What?"

The rest of his bills were good. Rent was on a monthly payment, cable too—not that he really needed it. He was never home. Automatic credit card, and car payment . . . insurance.

There was silence on the line. "Dakota?"

"I'm still here. Are you done paying your bills?"

"Yeah." *Wait* . . . did he tell her he was paying bills? "I'm busted, aren't I?"

"You're not perfect? That might be a deal breaker, Doc."

He pushed away from his desk, drank his black coffee. "Tuesday?"

"Tuesday at Joe's by the hospital."

He liked that. "Be safe."

"You too, Doc."

Chapter Six

Desi Calloway had been her own boss since she was twenty-seven. The literary agency she'd started after her short stint working with one of the big publishers changed her mind about editing for a living. She wanted to represent authors, lots of authors. She'd set out to be a powerhouse in her field and accomplished an impressive list of authors by her midthirties. Closing in on her fiftieth birthday, she was on her second marriage and had one daughter in college. Calloway Literary Agency now employed a half-dozen agents and an equal amount of ancillary staff.

Whenever Dakota visited the New York office, she was treated with a warmth usually reserved for family. The staff knew her by sight from day one. They answered her e-mails within twenty-four hours and never said no.

"You can't blame them for pushing, Dakota. You've been under one contract or another with them for three years. They want the Dakota Laurens machine to keep dealing out new books."

"I'm not sure I want to write another series right now. I have a single title swimming around in my head."

"Single title, series . . . they don't care. Give me two sentences to pitch to them and we'll get the ball rolling."

Dakota laughed. "I've come a long way from the six-page synopsis." Or as she more frequently called it, suck-nopsis. An emotionless outline of a proposed book that often veered off course during the writing process. Every writer she knew dreaded writing the things.

"Shoot me an e-mail when you have something. We should have your numbers for the last pay period in the next couple of weeks, which might give us more leverage during contract negotiations."

"I'll let you deal with that. I'll play temperamental artist and make stuff up to sell."

Desi laughed and wrapped up the call.

For the next hour, Dakota sat with an open notepad and a pen. Some of the personalities she'd met at the Miami conference floated in her head and started to take shape. For Dakota, writing always started with her characters. Who were they, what were their experiences that brought them to the point in life that the book began? She hadn't been completely kidding when she told Walt that she was writing a character profile on him. Well, not him, but a doctor . . . or maybe a nurse. Perhaps a male nurse and a female doctor . . . she jotted down that idea, asked herself how that would impact the story.

When her ideas crashed to a halt, she'd step into the kitchen and pick a cupboard to clean. Halfway through the kitchen junk drawer her thoughts moved to Monica Fairchild. Without any hesitation, she picked up her cell phone, found the number Monica had given her, and placed the call.

"Hello?" Monica's cheerful voice was accompanied by a bark. "Gilligan, down!"

"Monica? It's Dakota."

"Oh, hey. Can you hold on a second?"

"Sure."

She heard Monica call her pets outside and had to smile.

"Sorry about that. Seems they just love it when I'm on the phone."

"Sounds like kids."

"Bite your tongue. I'm not ready for that." They laughed about kids and phones for a couple of minutes, discussed how unready they both were for parenthood.

"Walt told me that flying down to the Keys was a bust."

"Not a complete waste of time, but yeah, not what we thought it might be."

Dakota started drawing circles on a blank page in her notebook. "Part of the reason I called was to pick your brain a little bit. I'm working on a new book . . . or I think I will be soon. After Miami I thought it would be great to have a doctor or nurse in my next story."

"Really?" Monica's giddy laugh was contagious. "I'm not sure how I can help, but I'd love to."

"That would be great. I can look up facts online, but there are things that happen in every profession that never make it into a book."

"I completely agree. I'm sure Walt can answer . . . wait, did you say you saw Walt since you've been back to LA?"

"Yeah."

Monica hesitated over the line. "As in a date?"

"Is that strange?"

"For Walt it is. Don't get me wrong, I'm sure he has a personal life, but I've never heard about anyone he'd actually say he was dating. Wow."

Suddenly the need to know more about Walt's lack of dating became the driving theme of the conversation and her character profile drifted away.

"So the good doctor doesn't date. I wonder why."

"I always thought he was just too busy to bother. Between Borderless Doctors and the ER there's no time."

Dakota kept drawing circles, filled some in. "He said as much. Still, I can't imagine single nurses looking the other way."

"Take it from me," Monica said. "Hospital romances are overrated. It's more common that the nurses hook up with the paramedics that come in. At least when those relationships fail you don't have to see your ex on a daily basis . . . or if you do it's only briefly."

Monica went on to tell her about a past relationship gone bad and how difficult it was after.

Dakota flipped her page and asked, "So is there an unwritten rule not to date doctors?"

"Not really. A lot of nurses hooked up in nursing school, but again, those didn't last long. None that I know of anyway."

"What about male nurses and female doctors?"

"Now that would be a great book," Monica said. "I don't know of any . . . but I can see the hot factor in a book."

Dakota smiled, placed a circle around the words *female MD, male RN.*

"So are you and Walt going to see each other again?"

"Drinks at Joe's after his shift."

Monica laughed. "Joe's is a dive. Fair warning."

"Good to know."

"Walt's a good guy and a great doctor. He really cares about his patients."

"You don't have to convince me to go out with him, Monica."

They laughed and changed the subject.

Monica gave her the green light to call anytime for nurse and hospital information.

Joe's was the Plaza of dive bars. Dakota knew better than to dress up for a simple drink at a bar she'd already been warned about, but having been raised in the South it was against her nature to leave the house without makeup and a little polish. In short, she looked hot but nothing worthy of the Oscars. She told herself the tight black leggings, long shirt that managed to look like a dress, and three-inch heels were her norm when grabbing a drink.

Lying to herself wasn't a new thing.

Chances were she'd meet a friend or two of Walt's at the bar. Since he didn't date, she wanted to make a good impression . . . and that was a first. Most times, she couldn't care less what people thought of her.

Dark walls filled the bar along with the smell of old beer, smoke-filled ceiling tiles, and musty depression that accompanied dives like this one.

It was seven thirty-five, minutes past the time that Walt said he'd be there. There was a group of twentysomethings in the corner drinking bottled beer. Two sets of eyes from that group found her before she moved her attention away. The bar housed a couple of older men, somewhere in their late fifties, and a couple.

There were tables, but only a few, and a jukebox poured out a mix of contemporary rock.

The place was old, dark, and smelled stale, but Dakota realized when she sat down that it was relatively clean . . . well, except for the ceiling. It might take a California wildfire to take out that dirt.

A table large enough for two sat in the back of the bar where she could keep an eye on the door. She knew there were plenty of eyes on her as she moved through the bar. She chose to ignore them.

The waitress wore jeans and a smile.

"What's the best whiskey you have back there?" she asked.

The waitress replied with a label that might not have been Dakota's first choice, but better than she expected. Before the girl walked away, she nodded over her shoulder. "Those guys over there are already trying to buy you a drink."

Dakota avoided looking over the waitress's shoulder, knew the younger men in the room were eyeing her.

"Are they regulars?"

"Sadly."

"If I tell them I'm married?"

"Like that would matter."

"Big biker boyfriend?"

The waitress was smiling now. "There are five of them . . . does this boyfriend of yours have friends?"

Dakota tossed back her head with a laugh. "Do they have priors? Anyone on parole?"

The girl lost her smile. "You're a cop?"

"Maybe . . . maybe not. I don't need anyone buying my drinks."

The blonde set a napkin on the table and laughed. "I like you. You need Hector to walk you out . . . let me know."

Dakota lifted both index fingers to the waitress and grinned. "You got it."

With any luck, Hector wouldn't be needed.

Fifteen minutes later, Dakota started to wonder. Never going anywhere without a notebook, she jotted down her impressions of the bar and described a character sitting on a barstool watching a recap of an earlier game.

The first two people who entered the bar in scrubs kept her in her seat. Monica had warned her that ER shifts weren't like any other monster. There was no telling what would keep the staff late and no real way to contact an employee if they were knee-deep in a trauma or an equally difficult situation. The two walking into the bar narrowed their gaze on her the moment they hit the door.

"I'm sorry," the petite blonde pulled her long hair over her shoulder. "Are you Dakota?"

Relieved she wasn't being stood up, Dakota lifted her hand. "I am."

"I'm Valerie." The girl was small, but her handshake wasn't wimpy. "This is Nancy. Walt wanted us to tell you he's on his way."

Nancy moved into a chair beside Dakota. "Full moon. Nothing good happens with a full moon." Without a pause, Nancy continued, "I love your books."

Dakota grinned. "Thanks."

Valerie waved at the blonde waitress. "Gina, I'd kill for chicken wings."

So the waitress had a name. "You got it . . . Nancy?"

"Vodka tonic."

With their orders taken, Dakota's two new bar friends turned and stared. "You're really Dakota Laurens."

Dakota took a swig of her drink. "You make it sound like I'm crazy famous."

"You are."

"A couple of bestsellers—"

"At least three that I know about. When is the next Surrender book coming out? I'm dying to know if Cassidy is knocked up." Nancy was clearly a fan.

"The next book will be out after the holidays."

Before the women could continue, two more scrub-wearing employees joined them. "There you are . . . you guys rushed out of the parking lot." The man speaking wore scrubs like the others, his chin sported a slight shadow and a confident grin.

"I'm thirsty," Nancy said.

Valerie made introductions . . . Dale and Maria were the next two to pull a second table next to hers. They ordered more drinks and Gina set a big basket of fried chicken wings smothered with barbeque sauce in the center of the table.

"Never fails . . . end of a shift and someone has to come in all messed up from the freeway." This came from Maria.

Valarie leaned next to Dakota. "Three-car pileup on the Ten."

"I came from that way . . . didn't see anything."

"I think it was from San Bernardino."

Nancy lifted her cocktail. "Which means I might as well relax. Traffic home is going to suck."

"Was everyone OK?" Dakota asked.

"Couple of minors. The passenger took the hit, which is why we're late getting out tonight. She was on her way to surgery when we left." Valerie drank water with lime.

The staff talked about the accident, the day's events. Dakota realized that Joe's dive bar was a place for necessary decompression for the hospital staff. Only a couple of them actually drank. The others ate, laughed, and let the day's events purge out of their systems.

By eight thirty, Nancy was checking the time on her phone. "I wonder what's keeping Walt?"

Valerie kept a closer eye on the door than Dakota. By nine, it was apparent that Valerie needed to leave and Maria kept texting someone on her phone. This small group had a one or no drink maximum and all their glasses were empty.

"You don't have to wait here with me," Dakota finally said.

"I told Walt I would."

Ah! That explains why they're all still here.

Just before nine, Dakota removed her cell and checked her messages. Nothing.

It wouldn't bode well for Walt to stand her up with his colleagues by her side. He probably got caught up. Deflated, she gathered her purse, dropped her phone inside. "I'm going to use the restroom and head out," she announced while she placed a few bills on the table to pay for her drink.

Nancy looked relieved, Valerie blinked several times, and Maria was already headed toward the door.

"It was great meeting you," Maria managed. "I'm sure Dr. Eddy just got tied up. It happens."

"It's all good."

By the time Dakota left the restroom, her new friends were gone.

The crowd in the bar had grown, but not by the one person she'd come to see.

She considered driving over to the hospital but thought better of it. She'd call him, leave a message, and suggest another time.

The cars in the lot were lit only by the lights of the bar. In an effort to keep her car from gathering dings and dents, she'd parked close to the back but found it surrounded by other patrons anyway.

"Hey, baby."

Dakota didn't bother looking behind her. Her hand slid into her purse, grasped the stun gun she always had close by.

"So it's like that, eh? Too rich for us?"

"Not interested," she called behind her shoulder, hoping the guys would get the hint. There were three of them, all wearing black, brown skin, black hair.

Returning to this bar was checked off her list. Her car was five feet away.

"C'mon, babe. Take a chance."

She avoided a panic and then heard footsteps catching up with her.

Dakota slipped the stun gun out of her purse and clicked off the safety. She didn't scare easily, but wasn't afraid to admit to herself that she was out of her element.

"Hey!" She heard the shout right as a hand grasped her shoulder and spun her around.

The self-defense weapon was engaged and screeching with an ear-shattering pitch. The sparks of the device briefly lit the space between her and her enemy. Without looking, she shoved it at the hand holding her.

"Oh, fuck!" The hand dropped and Dakota took a giant step back.

From the bar, she heard laughter. The three men taunting her were still standing there.

Kneeling on the ground, holding his arm, was Walt.

"Oh, God."

Dakota dropped her purse and moved beside him. "Are you OK? Oh, no."

"Damn, woman."

"I thought you were them . . . I'm sorry."

Walt's eyes were closed, and his arm kept twitching.

She'd never actually had to use the stun gun on anyone before. It obviously worked.

"She got you!" One of the guys yelled across the lot.

Dakota flipped the hecklers the bird and helped Walt to his feet. "What the hell was that?"

The weapon was still clenched in her grip. "A girl can never be too careful."

Walt kept rubbing his arm where the electricity had met his skin. "Does it hurt?"

Walt met her eyes. His frown said everything.

"Sorry. Really."

"Serves me right for being late."

He wore scrubs and plump, turned-down lips. "You look exhausted."

"I-I am. I knew trying to hook up after work wasn't the best idea."

Dakota retrieved her purse from the parking lot asphalt. "You're a doctor . . . goes with the territory."

He looked around. "Where's Dale . . . Valerie?"

"They left."

The lines on Walt's face moved deeper. "Dale should have walked you out."

"I'm a big girl, Doc."

He rubbed his arm. "You don't have to tell me that."

She moved his hand and turned him toward the ambient light from the bar.

The angry red welt pulled a small cry from her lips. "Is that going to be OK?"

"Fine. I'm sorry I left you here alone."

She shrugged and the night air made her shiver. "You should probably go home, get something on that."

His soft eyes swept her frame and his frown finally started to shift. "You look great. Too good for this dive."

"It was my suggestion."

"Scrubs or sweats, not stilettos and spandex."

She winked. "Got it. But I don't own a pair of scrubs and only my workout pants are spandex."

He laughed, stepped closer. "I'm sorry this didn't work out." She felt his fingertips push away a lock of her hair and tuck it behind her ear. The warmth of his hand had her leaning into his touch. "Let me make it up to you?"

"I just hit you with a stun gun, Doc. You don't have to make up for anything."

"For the reason you reached for it then."

"As long as it doesn't include a dive bar."

His hand found the side of her neck and held on. "How about you pick and I pay?"

She lifted an eyebrow and held still as he closed the space between them. "I have expensive taste."

He hovered over her lips. "I can handle it."

Dakota lifted her lips to his, let the sensual shock vibrate through her. The long wait in the bar was quickly forgotten . . . that was until the catcalls from the yahoos watching them met her ears.

They both pulled back, laughing. "I won't forget this night anytime soon," he told her.

"Me either." Admittedly, she wouldn't have a burn on her arm from it.

Walt walked her to the door of her car and opened it for her.

She turned over the engine and rolled down the window before shutting the door.

He leaned over the car. "Do you own a gun?" he asked.

"A gun?"

"Yeah, you know . . . bullets?"

She pulled her hair over her right shoulder and looked up at him with a grin. "You snuck up on me."

"I need to know what kind of medical kit I need to have on hand for our dates."

"An almost date. Kissing in the parking lot doesn't count. Not since high school anyway."

Walt tossed his head back with laughter and moved away from the car. "Be safe, Dakota."

"You, too, Doc."

Chapter Seven

Brenda never called. Hearing her voice on his answering machine shot alarm bells off in Walt's head.

"Who is the best little sister in the world?" she asked when the machine gave her time to talk.

"I am, that's right. I just learned through several channels that Mom is setting up not one, but three potential love matches for you when you come over for Dad's party."

Walt groaned.

"Don't you dare flake on this party since I told you this. Larry told me to relay that he's already got a bottle of Crown stashed at Mom and Dad's for you."

Larry was his sister's husband. Poor sap lived less than twenty miles from his in-laws and had to endure a whole lot more than Walt did.

"Take some advice from your younger, albeit wiser, sister. Bring your own dates and this shit will stop. Love you, bro. Can't wait to see you next week."

He'd been running nonstop since he watched Dakota drive away, his arm stinging beyond anything he'd experienced.

He was doing his best to get all his obligations out of the way so his date with her the next night could go on uninterrupted. He'd ordered flowers, and he'd even stocked his wallet with new condoms. That made him either a bastard or thoughtful. He still wasn't sure which. One thing for sure, he was hopeful he'd use them. Dakota, and her stun gun, had invaded his head. He thought of her and couldn't ignore the heat inside him.

The day after the incident at Joe's, Walt took it upon himself to scout the area around the hospital to see if there was a better alternative than the watering hole they were all used to.

Sadly, everything else pushed his limits of dive bar or was so trendy and opposite from everything he and his colleagues looked for in a place to unwind.

Walt set his clean laundry, clothes that really needed to be folded and put away, aside on his sofa. He turned on his TV and opened a beer. He hadn't watched a game in forever, knew he could get the last half of the Dodgers game.

He was cursing a ref's call when his phone rang.

"Hey, Doc."

Damn her voice was sexy. After quickly turning down the volume, he replied. "Didn't I tell you to call me Walt?"

"You did. But I never dated a doctor before so you're just going to have to deal."

"So it's a status thing?"

"Yep! I'm dating you for your title."

"And a character profile."

"Right. Both those reasons."

He laughed.

"Don't hate me," she said with less laughter in her voice.

"Why would I—"

"I have to bail on our date tomorrow."

He really hoped he wasn't hearing her right. He switched off the TV, not wanting the distraction.

"Seriously?"

"I have to fly to New York tonight. My agent pitched my latest book to my publisher and she wasn't happy with their first offer."

"So what does that mean?"

"She pitched it to three more publishers and now there's a frenzy building."

Walt knew nothing about publishing but somehow understood *a frenzy* in Dakota's world was better than in his. "This is a good thing?"

"Crazy good."

"Do you like your current publisher?"

"Love 'em. But in business, you try to get the most for less. Desi, that's my agent, suggested we push for more money, and everyone is outbidding the last. They call it an auction . . . it's never happened to me before. So I'm going to New York to meet with the different publishers. I want to know who I'm signing with and if I can work with them."

"Sounds exciting."

"It is. Sucks that I have to flake on you."

"Work comes first." Still sucked, though. "How about next weekend?"

"You'll be in Colorado."

He leaned back on his couch, scratched his head. "Join me."

She hesitated. "In Colorado?"

"Yeah." He'd probably kick himself for this later. "Fair warning . . . I'm using you so my mother doesn't set me up with unwanted women."

"As in plural? More than one?"

"So my sister tells me."

"So I use you for my current book, and you use me to get Mummy off your back?"

"That about sums it up." Should he mention his supply of condoms? *Nawh!*

"OK, Doc . . . you have yourself a weekend date. Oh, wait . . . saying that aloud brought up all kinds of images."

It certainly did.

"Separate rooms," he offered. "I don't expect—"

"Won't that raise a red flag on your plan?"

"I don't have a plan, Dakota. Come with me to Colorado and we'll figure it out when we get there. One thing for sure, my work won't get in the way."

"And I'll have this deal worked out before I get back to LA."

"So you can use me, and I can use you."

She busted out laughing. "I'm rubbing off on you, Doc. Your parents are going to hate me."

"I doubt that."

"Can you add me to your flight at this late of notice?"

Shit. He hadn't bothered booking a flight. "I-I'll figure it out."

"Walt?"

"Uhm . . ."

"You seriously haven't booked your flight yet, have you?"

He stood and started toward his office with the phone to his ear. "I was hoping for an outbreak of the pig flu."

"The pig what?"

"Inside joke. I'll take care of it."

"You need a personal keeper."

"You might be right about that."

New York was nothing like LA . . . nothing! Flip-flops and shorts ruled on the West Coast. In New York, few in the professional world would be caught in flipping shoes and shorts, which were reserved for weekends and days at the Shore. If there was one rule Dakota's mother taught her in life it was *if you don't know what you're doing or have no idea how you managed to get where you are . . . fake it.* Dakota lived by that on her first trip to The Big Apple . . . and now she had it down.

For reasons of neutrality, Dakota paid for her own upscale hotel room. Damn thing cost more per night than a month in her college dorm. She chose a Morrison to stay in. Might as well stay loyal to those she actually knew . . . or in her case, knew by proxy.

After her second meal with as many publishers the next day, Dakota's head spun.

"They're trying to make me fat."

Desi set her purse on the desk in the small suite. "They're trying to hand you four million. That's what they're trying to do."

Dakota sat on the edge of the bed, kicked off her shoes. "A hell of a lot of money."

Desi leaned against the desk, crossed her tiny arms over her chest. The woman was polished from head to toe. Her dress probably cost close to a grand, her shoes five hundred. Dakota knew she worked hard and deserved her eighty-dollar manicures but Dakota had only recently gotten used to handing out generous tips.

"Tell them it's a series and we'll double that amount."

"I don't know if it's going to be a series . . . not yet. I have to write the book first, Desi. You know that about me."

A light blinking from the phone caught Dakota's attention. She used the distraction and picked up the phone to check her calls. "Hold that thought."

The desk answered, but instead of patching her through to a message center, they took her call to the concierge.

"Ms. Laurens. We didn't anticipate your arrival. Please accept our apology."

"Excuse me?"

"Mrs. Morrison has asked that we meet your every need, Ms. Laurens. We have a bellhop coming to you now and your room is ready."

Dakota looked around her suite . . . which she had to admit was the smallest one she'd found available. But this was New York and everything here cost way too much per square inch.

"I'm in a room."

"Yes, ma'am . . . but we have another waiting for you. Please accept our apology."

Dakota couldn't be more confused.

Desi answered the door while Dakota tried to figure out what was going on.

"Ms. Laurens?" the bellhop asked.

Desi motioned toward Dakota, who decided to hang up the phone and deal with the person in front of her.

"I understand you're moving rooms." The bellhop stood rod straight, his hair gray at the sides. His uniform had straight lines and not one off-putting stain.

"This is the one I paid for," Dakota told him.

"Yes, ma'am. Please follow me. If the room doesn't meet your needs, you're more than welcome to stay here."

Dakota sent a puzzled look to Desi.

Her agent shrugged.

After grabbing her purse, Dakota let the employee lead her and Desi away.

They entered the elevator, where the bellhop swiped a card over a sensor before handing her the key. "In order to enter your room you must swipe this key here and press the floor within five seconds."

The elevator shot to the top floor.

"We have you in number two."

The bellhop opened the penthouse doors wide. The massive room spread out in front of her. Her suite faced west and the sun was setting. The view from this floor, the lights, the crystalline angles, the endless rows of buildings . . . New York lay sparkling in all her energetic glory below. "It's breathtaking."

The bellhop rocked back on his heels. "Mrs. Morrison asked that you call her sister if you have any concerns about the room. If it's all right with you, Ms. Laurens, we'd like to transfer your things here."

"I . . . ah, I can—"

"I assure you . . . nothing will be missed."

Dakota's head bobbed on her neck like a doll's.

When the bellhop left the suite, Desi moved to the center of the living room and turned in a full circle. The great room spread over eight hundred feet, a piano sat in one corner, a bar and kitchen in another. Floor-to-ceiling windows offered views of the city and a portion of Central Park. Fresh flowers sat on a table by the door, a basket of fruit graced the dining table.

"How do you know a Morrison?" Desi was already headed toward one of the doors on the far side of the suite.

"I don't."

The master bedroom was larger than the living room in her condo. King-size bed, massive TV . . . a balcony with French doors. The bathroom looked like a Tuscan spa.

"He said Mrs. Morrison arranged this."

"I know Monica, not her sister."

Desi hesitated in the doorway of one of the extra rooms off the main suite. "Who's Monica?"

"I met her at the conference." Distracted, Dakota moved to the massive windows and stared at the setting sun. "She used to work with Walt."

"Who's Walt?"

"The doctor I'm dating . . . holy shit, Desi. This view is amazing."

"Dakota!" Desi's voice actually rose above Dakota's thoughts. "Can you please connect the dots for me?"

"Monica is a sister-in-law to Mr. Morrison."

"As in the owner of the hotel?"

"As in owner to many hotels . . . or so I found out when looking them up. Monica is a nurse practitioner who once worked with Walt. I told you about Walt, right?"

Desi shook her head and sat on one of the two plush sofas. "No."

Dakota brought Desi up to date on her love life.

"So this is the guy who prompted your idea for the book."

"This is the guy I had to blow off for this visit to New York."

Before Desi could say anything else, the bellhop returned with her bags. She directed him to the room with her luggage and removed a tip from her purse.

He pocketed the cash quickly. Before he left the room, he said, "Again, we're sorry for the inconvenience. The room provisions are complimentary, as is any in-room dining you may need during your stay. Have a nice evening, Ms. Laurens."

"Room provisions?" Dakota asked the closed door.

Desi laughed and moved to the kitchen. "Open bar, doll . . . what do you want?"

"The flight home won't be as nice," Walt warned her when he pulled out of her driveway early Friday morning.

"I'm surprised you found a flight at all." Dakota wore large-rimmed sunglasses, her hair slicked back in a ponytail. She had a light sweater in her lap and a knit top that left her arms bare. Her slacks hugged her hips and moved to sensible two-inch heels. Walt's mouth watered a little more every time he saw her. "Do you always wait for the last minute?"

"Not always . . ." He turned off her street, merged into traffic.

"So what do you do on time?"

"Work."

"Outside of that." Walt caught Dakota shaking her head.

"Some of my bills."

"Automatic bill pay doesn't count. Do you remember birthdays?"

"I remember Mother's Day."

"All that last-minute shopping, or booking of flights, must cost you a small fortune."

He glanced at her, winked. "Online shopping is the bomb."

John Wayne Airport was much smaller than LAX. Walt found the VIP parking and told them his name.

When they were whisked through security with only a metal detector and a baggage X-ray, Dakota started asking questions. "When does our flight leave?"

"As soon as we board."

The man handling their luggage placed it on a dolly and walked away.

"Dr. Eddy?"

They both turned toward the man calling his name. He wore a pilot's uniform and a smile.

"Trent said someone would meet us. I assume that's you."

"Rendell," he said, extending his hand. "I'll be your pilot today. Sean is on board getting the aircraft ready."

Dakota removed her sunglasses and spun toward the massive windows that looked out on the tarmac.

"I just need to see a picture ID."

Walt pulled his wallet out of his back pocket.

"We're . . . you chartered a private plane?" Dakota's voice actually dropped an octave.

Walt took her by the elbow and led her toward their flight.

"Pulled a favor. Like I said . . . the flight home won't be as nice."

Walt took pride in the ability to silence Dakota. The woman had a lot to say . . . but she was quiet now.

They walked straight to the small jet and climbed the short stairway into the cabin.

The plane sat six passengers, but it was only the two of them, the two pilots, and one flight attendant.

Walt guided her into a middle seat and took the one across from her. The hatch was already being shut before they buckled. "This has Monica and Trent written all over it," Dakota finally said.

"They offer all the time but I don't often take them up on it."

Dakota ran her hands over the plush leather seats and crossed her legs. She completed the space and looked as if she'd ridden on a private plane many times. "I like your friends, Doc. Did I tell you Monica pushed me to the top floor of The Morisson while I was in New York?"

Walt buckled his belt, sat back. "You didn't."

"Penthouse with all the trimmings. When I called and told her she didn't have to, she brushed me off."

"Get used to it. The Morrisons and the Fairchilds are generous beyond belief."

"I can see that. But I barely know them."

The flight attendant wore black slacks and a white silk blouse. Her smile was genuine. "I'm Stacey. I'll be your attendant today. As soon as we're at cruising altitude, I'll prepare your meals. There's a small menu in the console. Welcome aboard Fairchild Charters. If there is anything you need, don't hesitate to ask."

Dakota's smile grew bigger. "Thank you."

Stacey moved to the back of the cabin and the pilot's voice sounded through the speakers. "Dr. Eddy, Miss Laurens, we'll be in the air within five minutes. Please remain seated with your seat belts in place until I tell Stacey it's safe to move about the cabin. Welcome aboard."

Dakota leaned forward and whispered. "I could get really used to this."

"Sometimes it pays to book things last-minute."

Dakota ordered eggs and toast and Walt asked for the works. When Stacey suggested mimosas, they both took her up on it.

"What are your parents going to think when you introduce me?"

Walt sipped his drink and dug into his eggs. "My mother's head will spin a little. She's not expecting you."

"You didn't tell her I'm coming?"

"No . . . and before you accuse me of forgetting, I didn't. I chose not to say a thing until we get there. Twenty questions without you there would be awkward."

The eggs were surprisingly good. *How did Stacey manage that on an airplane?*

"Are we sticking to the truth? We just started dating . . . or more to the point, we keep trying to date but haven't caught a break yet."

Walt pointed his fork in her direction. "If we say that, my mom will try and set me up with someone even with you there."

"So we lie."

"We omit."

Dakota sat back, the smile on her face drew to a soft line. "You really are using me."

He lowered his fork.

"Be honest with me, Doc."

He hated how much his back teeth hurt when his jaw tightened. "Truth is we haven't caught a break. Carving this weekend out of our lives might be the best thing."

"Or it might not."

He didn't like the squeeze in his chest her words created. "If we don't work out, duping my parents over the weekend will only affect me."

"It sounds like you're already calling us over." Dakota lost her smile altogether.

This conversation wasn't working out like he'd planned. Then again, he hadn't planned it.

"I already told you I like being single," he reminded her. "You said the same."

Her chest rose and fell with a slow deep breath. "You're right . . . I did . . . and I do. No woman likes to think they're being used. We're going to Colorado to sneak away from our lives . . . your parents are simply a distraction."

"Exactly." Maybe she did understand. Then again, it sounded as if she were relaying a plot in one of her books. That thought left him flat.

She looked out the window, her expression unreadable.

"You're upset," he told her.

Her gaze met and pierced his.

A thousand questions were asked in the moments that passed between them . . . none were spoken.

A smile . . . the Southern kind with teeth and a complete lack of sincerity followed. Dakota lifted her glass to his. "To duping your parents and having a wonderful weekend away from work."

He lifted his glass to hers but didn't feel anything close to wonderful.

Chapter Eight

She was a Southerner . . . born of grit and guts and she'd be damned if she'd be derailed by Walt's honesty, even if it cut. She'd make the most of this weekend, do it right or don't do it at all . . . in for the penny in for the pound . . . all the clichés she avoided in her writing sprang to her head.

Dakota had no idea if Walt was with her because he really wanted to be with her, or God forbid, needed her, to get through a weekend with his parents. Or, was she a convenience? It killed her not to ask. Honesty . . . the complete kind often scared off the right guys. A part of her wanted Walt to be the right kind of guy.

Stacey removed their plates and Dakota sucked back a second drink. She wasn't doing this weekend completely sober. Didn't think she had it in her to.

She thought of Mary's questions and started a short inquisition. "My parents are Baptist . . . loosely. Yours?"

"Protestant for major holidays."

"Close enough. Do you have any siblings?"

"A sister, Brenda. Married a couple of years now. Dakota—"

She kept talking, not letting him interrupt. "I have a sister, married her high school crush . . . two nephews. All of them live close to my parents."

"Why are you telling me all this?"

"If we're deceiving your parents, it might be best to have a little more information about each other."

"Dakota?" His gaze softened and he leaned over the space separating them and grasped her hand that rested on the arm of the plush chair.

The air in the cabin crushed in. She slid her hand from under his and stood. "I need to use the restroom before we land."

She felt his stare as she walked away. A practiced smile reached her lips as she passed Stacey, who sat reading a book in the galley.

The bathroom was larger than any in a commercial jet, but it was still confined. She locked the door out of habit and leaned her head against it when she was alone.

You're stupid, Dakota. Always falling before thinking.

Through all her hard exterior she never failed to leap into relationships . . . seeing romance where there was only attraction. Or falling for married men who posed as single and in love. Or wanting to find love and stumbling over sloppy kisses and weak intentions.

She wanted Walt to be different.

She had no right to be upset . . . Walt had told her he was using her to get his mother off his back, but she'd still hoped that he was joking with her. Lord knew she couldn't care less about his title of doctor or a character profile. She had been joking about that. The doctor in her book was a woman . . . and nothing like Walt.

She left the bathroom a few minutes later, a painted smile on her lips.

The Eddy estate—and there were no other words for the world in which Walt had grown up—was massive. The property alone took up over twenty acres. The sprawling two-story ranch home overlooked a private lake with tall pines and plenty of trails for the unknowing to get lost. According to Walt, there were two guesthouses, one doubled as a boathouse and the other was a comfortable two bedroom complete with kitchen and private drive. The groundskeeper had his own home, but Walt didn't include that as an actual living space since the same man had lived there since Walt was ten.

"A doctor's salary didn't pay for all this," Dakota said as they drove the rental car up the tree-lined drive.

He glanced out the window, unimpressed with the view. "Probably not."

"Your mother is from a rich family?"

Walt laughed. "My father came up with the design for the Eddy Clamp. It's a device used in open heart surgery. Diverts blood flow . . ." His words trailed off. "It made him a lot of money."

"I guess it made sense that you follow him in cardiology."

"It did to him."

Like the last half hour, Dakota observed more than she talked, and Walt kept glancing her way without words.

They parked behind several cars in the open driveway. Dakota pushed out of the car and moved to the trunk, where they'd placed their bags.

Walt pulled their luggage from the car and closed the trunk. When Dakota turned away, Walt caught her arm.

"Dakota."

Her playacting smile was in place.

He frowned. "I said something on the airplane that upset you."

She gave a swift shake of her head. "It's OK."

"It's not." There were more words on his lips but he didn't say them. Instead, he moved his hand to the back of her head and kissed her.

Her composure lasted for a few seconds and started to melt. As much as she'd like to be unaffected by his touch, she wasn't that strong. His lips were soft, searching . . . she sighed and pressed closer.

The sound of someone clearing their throat broke them apart.

To Walt's credit, he kept his arm around her when he turned and faced the woman standing on the landing. "Mom."

The woman's tolerant gaze moved over Dakota briefly, and then to her son. She wore a pantsuit, high-end . . . probably silk from what Dakota could tell. She wore heels that seemed like overkill for a woman lounging about the house. Walt's father's party wasn't until the next evening, so this was daywear for the Mrs.

Walt left the bags and urged Dakota forward. "She doesn't bite," he whispered in her ear.

Dakota doubted that.

The second they were in arm's reach, Walt moved to his mother and kissed her cheek. "It's good to see you."

Mrs. Eddy kept one eye on Dakota through the entire exchange. "Are you going to introduce me to your . . . friend?"

"Mom, this is Dakota, Dakota, this is my mother, JoAnne."

Dakota extended her hand and was offered a lukewarm handshake. "It's a pleasure, Mrs. Eddy. I've heard a lot about you."

JoAnne blinked several times and moved her sharp eyes to Walt. "That places me at a great disadvantage, Miss . . ."

"Laurens, but you can call me Dakota." She waited for Walt's mom to offer the same courtesy of using her first name, but the invitation never came.

"All right. My son was delinquent in telling me he was bringing a guest."

"It was a last-minute decision," Walt said. He moved to Dakota's side and placed an arm around her waist.

For a woman who wanted her son to settle down, she was mighty chilly.

"Are we going to stand on the porch and talk all day, or can we go inside?" Walt asked.

"Of course." JoAnne Eddy turned and started to move inside.

Walt hesitated, looked back at the bags sitting by the car.

Dakota grabbed his arm, pulled him close. "Don't you dare leave me alone with her."

He snapped tall, and grinned. With his free hand, he offered a mock salute.

"We prepared your old room, Walter." JoAnne glanced over her shoulder. "I will have to shuffle others to prepare another one for your . . . guest?"

Outside of her own parents' disapproval of how she earned money, Dakota liked to think she didn't have an insecure bone in her body . . . but JoAnne Eddy had a way of making her uneasy.

"We'll take the guesthouse," Walt told his mother.

"The guesthouse is already promised to your sister."

"The boathouse then."

JoAnne turned, glared. "That's hardly fitting, Walter."

"My apartment is smaller, Mom. We'll be fine."

The entire exchange was cold and intimidating, and Dakota wasn't happy with her reaction to it. Digging deep, she forced a smile to her lips and a slight accent to her voice. "Your home is lovely, Mrs. Eddy. Positively stunning." The open-beam ceiling and mountain cabin charm, albeit huge and nothing like a cozy cabin that Dakota would prefer . . . it was beautiful. Everything from hall tables to chandeliers were oversized, heavily ornate with ironwork and western charm.

Yet it wasn't country in any way. The mix of sophistication and culture spoke of money.

Lots of money.

Dakota hesitated at a painting in the hall. Early nineteenth century Impressionist. The piece barely fit the décor . . . yet it worked. She leaned toward Walt. "That must be one hell of a clamp."

Walt laughed and squeezed her arm.

"Thank you. It would be nice to see my son in a home instead of that silly apartment he insists on."

"I don't have time for a house." The argument sounded old.

JoAnne guided them into a great room with a massive fireplace filling one entire wall. Windows opened to a view of the lake that made Dakota's mouth water. She could sit on the outside veranda and write for hours. "Wow."

"Walter?" JoAnne said to the lone man sitting with glasses perched on his nose, a newspaper in his hands. "Look who's here."

Dr. Walter Eddy II had a full head of salt-and-pepper hair, a clean-shaven jaw, and a guarded smile. His eyes had the same quality of his son's that darkened when his gaze landed on the two of them.

"I was wondering if you'd make it."

Dakota was surprised there wasn't more affection than a handshake between father and son . . . but that was all that passed between them.

"I told you I would."

"That doesn't always mean you'll be here."

Walt didn't respond to his father's dig, and introduced her. "Dakota, this is my dad. Dad, Dakota."

"Dr. Eddy. A pleasure."

Handshakes said a lot about a person. Dr. Eddy's was born of confidence without an ounce of insecurity.

"Did we know you were coming?" Dr. Eddy glanced at his wife. "We did *not.*"

Dakota spoke up. "I hope I'm not an inconvenience."

Walt and his father both jumped on her concerns.

"Of course not," Walt said.

"We welcome all our son's friends."

Happy with the response she wanted, Dakota stood taller. "I was just telling your wife how lovely your home is." She moved out of Walt's reach and toward the windows with the view. "I can see why you chose this spot."

"Winter can be difficult, but the view is always worth it."

"I would imagine it is."

"How long are you planning on staying?" JoAnne asked.

"We're flying out Monday," Walt told them.

Walt moved to her side and the room grew quiet.

Dakota gave up. "Where is that boathouse, Walt? We might as well settle."

———

The boathouse had been a sanctuary when Walt was young. A place to escape his parents and be a kid.

With one bedroom, a living room, and a full bath, the boathouse was originally set up as living quarters for a groundskeeper. Over the years, a groundskeeper's house was built away from the water. The winter months made living on the water less desirable. Even with the cast-iron fireplace, the space was freezing when the lake froze over and snow reached several feet.

Walt brought their luggage with them as he walked Dakota down toward the lake.

"I find it interesting that neither you nor your sister want to stay in the house with your parents over the weekend."

He dropped their bags on the steps, and opened the door for her. "I'm shocked Brenda and Larry are staying here at all. I thought they'd just show up for the party and leave. If I came alone, I'd stay in the house."

Dakota stopped, turned, and stared at him.

"At night. To sleep anyway."

She laughed and followed him inside. "Oh!"

"Nice, huh?"

"Cozy . . . I like it."

"The guesthouse is even better. Has a full kitchen and not just a sink, microwave, and fridge."

Dakota moved to the window and opened the curtains wide. "It's so gorgeous. I have a friend in Lake Tahoe that I visit every year. Her place has a view of the lake, but nothing like this." She cracked the widow and sucked in a deep breath through her nose. "Love the smell of pine."

"We don't get a lot of that in California, do we?"

Her smile was contagious. Walt moved beside her and looked out over the lake. "I know it looks inviting, but that water is cold."

"I'm sure it feels great on a hot summer day."

"When you're twelve." Walt laughed.

"Well, if I get the urge to jump in, you better come with me."

He grasped her hand and pulled her toward the back door. A deck extended over the water to where the boats were pulled in and out of the water in the winter.

She hesitated when they reached the end of the dock. "You wouldn't push me in fully clothed, would you?"

His grip tightened and she attempted to pull away.

"Doc!"

He had no intention of pushing her in, but liked the playful smile that had replaced the fake one she'd been wearing since the airplane.

Instead of pulling her, he moved closer and swept her into his arms. She immediately started pounding on his chest and struggling against him.

He moved quickly to the edge and pretended he was going to toss her.

Her arms placed a death grip around his neck. "Don't you dare!" She was laughing.

"What's the matter, Dakota? It's just water."

He felt the bite of her nails on his neck. "I go . . . you go."

She squealed and closed her eyes when he lurched toward the water. "Walter!"

Instead of tossing her in, he lowered her legs to the pier, laughing.

No sooner did her feet hit wood than she swung on him, placed a hand to his chest, and shoved.

Shock registered in her eyes when he kept hold of her hand and they both lost their balance.

No matter how many times he'd willingly jumped into the lake, the shock was the same.

He came up sputtering. "Son of a bitch."

The first words from Dakota's mouth were, "Shit, that's cold."

Walt splashed her soaked face while he attempted to tread water with his clothes pulling against his efforts.

Dakota returned fire with a well-aimed splash, her teeth already chattering.

Walt swam over, pushed her head in.

She kicked away from him, came up from behind, and jumped on his back. His face was once again underwater; his lungs expanded, looking for air. This time when he surfaced, Dakota was swimming toward the shore. Once she had her footing, she turned his way, laughing. Clothes hung on her, dripping. She lifted a foot, wiggled bare toes. "I-I lost a shoe."

Walt thought about turning around to find it, abandoned the idea nearly as quickly as it entered his head. "I'll buy you a new pair."

His feet touched solid ground and he hauled himself out of the water.

Dakota delivered one final splash, and before he could retaliate, she was running toward the boathouse.

He caught her when she reached the door, grasped her around the waist. She was a stunning, drowned, shivering, giggling rat.

"I'm going to get you for that," he teased.

"You s-started it." Her lips quivered, her eyes finally held the laughter inside her.

As water dripped into a pool by the front door, Walt crushed his lips to hers. He loved her taste, the way her arms were playfully slapping him away one minute and pulling him closer the next.

Her lips opened and her tongue mingled with his.

Walt backed her into the door, fumbled behind her, and opened it.

They stumbled inside, Dakota's hands pulled at the shirt that stuck to his back.

He pushed her against the door. His hand ran down her waist and over her hips.

Dakota's lips were warm even if her body shivered. "We need to get you out of these," he said as she tugged his shirt over his head.

"One step ahead of you . . ." Her words trailed off as she kicked off her leftover shoe and ran her fingertips over his chest.

He started to harden, despite the chill left by the lake.

With cold hands, he unbuttoned her blouse and let it slide to the floor with his.

The flesh peeking from under her bra tasted divine, better than any meal, any wine. "You're beautiful," he murmured over her breast.

She arched into him. "When did cold water become a turn-on?" she asked.

He removed his shoes, reached to tug at his socks, which refused to let go of his feet. All the while, he kept kissing her chest, her neck.

When she wiggled out of her pants, Walt found himself staring.

She shivered. "Less looking, more doing."

He dripped through the small boathouse, pulling her into the bedroom. When he battled with his pants, which were just as stubborn coming off wet as his socks had been, Dakota was laughing and crawling to the middle of the bed.

Walt kicked free of his pants and grabbed at her firm ass, pulling her under him. They laughed, kissed, and laughed even more. Then he found a spot between her clavicle and her neck that stopped all laughter and made her moan.

Dakota made love with her whole body, her nails sent chills over his already sensitive skin, her leg draped over his, opening for him to settle between them.

Their wet bodies dried as they rolled on the comforter. Walt wasn't sure who removed her bra, but he lavished her breasts and ignored his rock-hard erection, which demanded attention. That was until Dakota took hold of him.

He felt the first rush as she stroked him, her thumb rolling over his tip.

She lifted her hips as he guided her panties down her thighs.

When he sought her with his hand, she lost her grip. "Don't make me wait," she pleaded.

Heat pushed against his hand, made him groan.

When he moved away, her leg clamped tight, her eyes found his and held.

"Condom," he managed.

She loosened her hold and he found his pants. One pocket held his ruined cell phone. He looked at it, looked at Dakota, and tossed it across the room.

While she laughed he retrieved his wallet, unearthed a condom.

She helped him roll it on, leaned back against the pillows, and guided him close.

He kissed away her laughter and took his time when he pushed inside of her.

"Yes," she said with a sigh, her hips welcomed him, her legs tangled with his. "Glad that cold water didn't stop this."

"You and me both." He started to move and let his body claim the woman in his bed.

Her unladylike moans kept a smile on his face, kept his hands and lips moving over her as he brought on her first climax. All the tension of the day melted from her face when she came. The way she called his name made him hold back his own release to give her more.

Before her tremors receded, he grasped her hands and held them above her head, and moved faster. They made love without words, her eyes telling him she loved what he was doing.

He kissed her when she came the second time, released her hands when he emptied and collapsed on top of her.

───

Walt slipped away, found the comforter at the end of the bed, and pulled it on top of them.

She'd never laughed so hard while making love, didn't know it could be so wonderful, sensual, and comical all at the same time.

With her head resting on Walt's chest, the sun streaming in from the windows in the room, she wondered if the warmth in her chest was simply endorphins or something much more powerful.

"I didn't plan that," Walt said against her hair.

She giggled. "Yet you had a condom in your wallet."

His chest moved with a quiet laugh. "OK. I hoped . . . wanted."

"We're both adults, attracted, and spending the weekend together. I think we both hoped and wanted."

"I like your honesty, Dakota. So many women play games, pretend they want something they don't or—"

"I don't like games." She looked into his eyes, noticed them darken, and his smile fell before he kissed her.

When they broke apart, she rested against him again. "For the record, I've been on the pill since high school. In case your supply of condoms ended up in the lake with my shoe."

He laughed. "My phone is toast."

"You started it."

"Doesn't work well up here anyway."

"Trying to convince yourself it's OK you killed your phone?"

"You killed it."

"Good excuse to get a new one."

He agreed with a sigh. "I hate to say this, but—"

"We should probably shower . . ." she finished his sentence.

He nodded. "Before someone comes looking for us."

"Your parents will come down here?"

"Probably not. But when my sister and her husband get here, Brenda will be dying to meet you."

Dakota glanced around the room, noticed their clothes everywhere. Probably not the best first impression to make.

Pushing back the blanket, she rolled out of bed, felt Walt's eyes on her as she moved to the bathroom.

Chapter Nine

Brenda showed up while Walt was in the shower.

When Dakota opened the door, she thought she was looking at JoAnne's younger sister. Both women had elegant lines in their faces with high cheekbones and bright eyes . . . only Brenda's eyes had one thing in spades that JoAnne's didn't. Kindness.

"You must be Brenda," Dakota said as she kicked the wet clothes from the front door, hoping Brenda didn't notice.

Brenda looked behind her, probably searching for her brother. "Uhm, yeah . . ."

"Walt is in the shower."

Brenda's eyes traveled to the floor where standing water tickled Dakota's bare toes.

"We, ah . . . *accidently* fell in the lake."

Walt's sister had dimples.

"I'm Dakota."

Brenda shook her hand, laughed. "Fell?"

"I *might* have pushed him."

They both laughed. "Knowing my brother, he probably deserved it."

"He did." Looked like Dakota had a friend among the Eddy family.

The sound of the water turning off caught both their attentions. "Larry suggested we wait until you both emerged, but I thought I'd catch you before you returned to the house."

"Oh?"

"Looks like Mom has invited a few people over tonight for a pre-party dinner. I wanted to warn Walt."

"You're staying in the guesthouse, right?"

"We are."

"Then why don't we join you there before going to the main house, and you can warn Walt then."

Brenda nodded. "Sounds good. It's nice meeting you, Dakota."

———

Walt held her hand as they walked to the guesthouse. The path along the lake was edged in stone, but clear of view from the main house.

"Brenda looks a lot like your mom."

"Don't hold that against her," Walt said.

"Your mom is beautiful. Cold . . . but beautiful."

Walt didn't seem convinced. "I warned you."

He had . . . many times.

They reached the guesthouse and the door opened before they could knock.

Unlike with his father, Walt gave a genuine hug to his brother-in-law and held his sister in an extended hug. "I've missed you."

Dakota watched the exchange and marveled at the contrast between the couple. Larry was nearly an inch shorter than Brenda, and at least twenty pounds overweight. The match was so unlikely Dakota thought she might be misreading things. That was until Walt introduced Larry as Brenda's husband.

The two of them stood by each other's side and Larry's hand fell to Brenda's hip.

"I brought an old friend," Larry said as he left his wife's side and moved to the kitchen.

Dakota watched as Larry removed a bottle of Crown Royal and pulled two glasses from the cupboard.

"Dear God, don't leave me out of that!" Dakota called from the living room.

Larry lifted a brow, and grabbed an extra glass.

"Wine, hon?" Larry asked.

"Is the pope Catholic?"

Dakota laughed and Brenda cringed. "Oh, shit, you're not Catholic . . . I mean, it's OK if you are . . ."

"I'm not. It's OK . . . funny."

"Our parents have that effect on both of us." Walt took one of the glasses filled with two fingers of whiskey and handed it to Dakota. His eyes caught hers and he winked.

Her body heated even before she tipped back the glass and let the liquor warm her throat.

"Not that I'm ungrateful," Walt started, "but why are we having predinner drinks here?"

Brenda wore a summer dress, casual and elegant, her sandy blonde hair shoved up in a messy bun that looked sloppy but Dakota knew better.

Brenda tucked her feet under her when she sat on a sofa and sipped her wine. "Mom invited the Phelps . . . all of them, for dinner."

From Walt's long gulp, she knew the information wasn't what he wanted to hear. "Lily?"

Brenda squeezed both eyes together with a nod.

"Who's Lily?" Dakota asked.

"I took her to junior formal," Walt told her. "As in high school."

"Mom's trying to help rekindle an old flame," Brenda said with a laugh.

"Formal was a favor . . . not a flame," Walt said. He sat on the arm of the chair beside Dakota.

"Does Lily have a thing for you?"

"God, I hope not!"

Brenda laughed. Her husband chuckled alongside her. "Lily still lives at home with her parents, moved back after college."

Walt leaned back, played with Dakota's hair. "Anyone else coming that I need to know about?"

"I know a few people who said they'd come, but I don't know everyone who RSVP'd."

Dakota listened while Brenda spouted off several names, some of which resulted in groans from Walt's lips. "It's so much easier in California where I don't know anyone."

Brenda gave him a playful shove. "You know me."

"Not what I meant. I can't believe Mom invited the Vanderkamps. I never even liked Jean."

"Doesn't mean she didn't have a thing for you." Brenda glanced Dakota's way. "I hope you know what you're getting into."

"I've been warned. Walt told me his mother was trying to set him up before we boarded the plane."

"Oh, good."

Dakota turned to Walt, placed her hand on his thigh. "Shall I tell all these women how wonderful you are about pulling poor defenseless women into frigid water?"

His genuine smile melted inside of her. "You pushed me."

"You pulled me . . . and you were going to toss me in."

"I pretended to toss you in."

She caught her lip between her teeth. "Then I'll tell them about your tastes in dive bars."

His scowl had an ounce of mischief. "Guilty. But some of the women Brenda just mentioned would be turned on by the dive bar idea."

Dakota doubted that. "Perhaps I need to loan them my stun gun."

Walt rubbed his arm, the mischief in his scowl moved south.

Dakota laughed. "Serves you right for sneaking up on me."

"Stun gun?" Larry asked.

"Dakota zapped me with a stun gun."

Brenda gasped.

Dakota waved her off, finished her drink. "Oh, he lived. Besides, he snuck up on me in the dark parking lot of said dive bar. A place I don't think I'll be returning to, by the way."

"She hit you with a stun gun and you're still dating her?" Larry lifted his glass. "I think you'll fit right in, Dakota. Welcome to the family."

———

Lily was stunning. Porcelain skin so smooth Dakota wondered if she spent any time in the sun. The dinner was slated for casual, but Lily Phelps wore a skintight strapless black number that went to midcalf. The woman had curves . . . and if Dakota hadn't just sampled the talents of Walt in the boathouse bedroom, she might be concerned.

But no, Walt was by her side, supplying her with drinks and whispering in her ear.

"Was she a cheerleader in high school?"

"Buckteeth and glasses."

Dakota sipped her drink. "Looks like she cleared those issues up."

Walt's grip on her waist confirmed he was with her. Then he kissed her temple. "Thanks again for being here."

"You thank me by tossing me in the lake."

Walt wiggled his eyebrows and Dakota's cheeks warmed. "We're even for the stun gun."

She was laughing when JoAnne interrupted them. "We're about to sit for dinner." She placed a hand on Dakota's arm. "I hope you don't mind. I placed you next to Brenda this evening." JoAnne lifted her eyes. "I had no idea our son was bringing a guest."

Dakota was about to tell her hostess that was perfectly fine when

Walt pulled her closer. "I'm sure whoever you have sitting beside me won't mind moving."

JoAnne blew out a long-suffering sigh and gave him an insincere smile. "You know how I feel about table arrangements, Walter."

Dakota lifted up on her toes and kissed Walt's cheek. "It's OK, honey," she said, pouring on the sugar and her normally buried Southern accent.

"It's not OK."

"Walter—"

"I brought a guest, Mom. Work with it or we can leave."

Dakota stood back.

JoAnne lifted her chin, turned on her heel, and left.

Dakota turned in to Walt so only he could see her face and hear her words. "Nice going, Ace. Your mom is bound to hate me now."

Walt pulled her back, away from the room full of Phelps and Eddys.

Once they were out of sight of his family, he pushed her against the wall. His tongue was pushing past her lips and claiming her before she could gasp.

God, he felt like heaven.

Her body heated instantly, her hips moved against him without any permission.

She wasn't sure what brought on this sudden urge for intimacy, but Dakota didn't want to stop it. The drink in her hand tilted and she felt liquid drip over her hand.

She placed a palm against his chest, moaned when his hips met hers and said hello, and forced him away. "Walt?"

His eyes carried a smoky quality, one that made her want to be at the boathouse and not a dinner party. "You have the most seductive voice," he told her.

Dakota placed her free hand on his cheek and he leaned into it. "You have me all weekend, Doc."

"Best decision ever. Don't let my mom get to you."

So that's what prompted this sudden urge for intimacy. "Mom who?"
He kissed her again, soft, smooth.

A bell . . . a freakin' bell was ringing from the other room. "Dinner."

Dakota broke away, ran a thumb under his lower lip, wanting to
see if her makeup was smeared as much as she assumed it was.

"You look fine," Walt whispered in her ear.

They stepped around the corner and caught the attention of a
scowling JoAnne and a giggling Brenda.

The Phelps were family friends. Lily was the second oldest to a
brother who was already married with a kid on the way . . . then there
were the twins. The boys were just past their seventeenth birthday and
they certainly had a better idea of how to spend their Friday night than
with a bunch of adults celebrating some *old guy's* birthday. They huddled together and practically ignored everyone else in the room.

Tonight they were blessed with the twins, and not the pregnant
mama and her hubby. They apparently lived in Texas.

Dakota sat on Walt's left while Lily was on his right. Across from
them sat Brenda and Larry, the twins on opposite sides of the table
from each other, Dr. and Mrs. Eddy on each end with Mr. Phelps
next to Dakota and Mrs. Phelps next to Mrs. Eddy.

The arrangement spoke volumes. The women separated by the
men . . . the kids across from each other as to not place a gap in the
conversation . . . and Lily by Walt's side. A part of Dakota wanted to
grab a pen and take notes. Family dynamics always lent to great plots.

The first course was served by a staff brought in for the weekend.
According to Walt, there was a full-time housekeeper, but meals were
often of the heat-up variety brought in once a week from a caterer.

Lily sat stiff-backed beside Walt, her attention on whatever
Brenda was saying when the soup was served.

"Are you enjoying our state?" Mr. Phelps asked Dakota.

"It's amazing. The wide-open space, the fresh air. Outside of the
airport, I can't say I've seen much of Colorado."

Dr. Eddy placed a napkin on his lap and tilted his head. "Do you travel a lot?"

"I do."

Walt was commenting on something Lily said.

"You must work with Walt's traveling staff," Mr. Phelps said.

She laughed. "I'm not a doctor or a nurse."

One of the caterers set a bowl of tomato bisque in front of her. Dakota turned to the opposite side of the table. "This looks lovely," she said to JoAnne.

Walt's mother smiled, but it didn't reach her eyes.

She hates me.

Brenda offered a sympathetic look from across the table and lifted her wine to her lips. Dakota mimicked her.

"So what is it you do that has you traveling through Colorado?" The question came from Larry.

For the first time in a long time, Dakota actually debated omitting her profession. She wasn't ashamed of what she did for a living, but the subsequent conversation with this conservative crowd might push the Eddys past the point of comfort about her presence.

Dakota waited a beat, and Walt answered for her. "Dakota is an author."

A hush went around the table.

"Published?" Brenda asked.

Dakota found her pride, sat tall as she picked up her spoon. "Yes."

"What do you write? Maybe one of us has read your book." JoAnne's words might have held little malice, but her tone minimized the accomplishment. Every book was full of blood, sweat, and tears . . . not to mention weeks if not months of neglect of her personal life.

"I doubt that," Dakota managed.

The entire table was now staring.

JoAnne moved her attention to her soup. "Well, don't be discouraged. Many authors write books that aren't read."

Dakota clasped her left hand in her lap and bit her tongue.

"You might want to back up that boat, Mom," Walt said.

Dakota glanced at him, saw the devious grin on his lips. She shook her head and left her spoon in her soup before placing her hand on his thigh.

"I'm just saying that authors are often like any other artist . . . they work for years and never really find their audience."

"Mom."

"I'm trying to be encouraging, Walt."

"Dakota doesn't need your encouragement. Trust me."

Walt's hand now caressed her thigh and they were both smiling and sharing a private thought.

"What have you written?" Brenda asked.

Speaking to no one other than Walt's sister, Dakota leaned forward. "I write romance novels."

JoAnne laughed out loud.

Walt scowled.

"Brenda loves those."

Dakota waited . . .

The reaction came from Lily . . . "Wait! You're Dakota Laurens?"

Lily's stiff exterior shifted and her smile became genuine for the first time that night.

Brenda dropped her spoon with a loud clank. "You're *that* Dakota?"

———

After-dinner drinks at the boathouse were just as entertaining as before-dinner drinks at the guesthouse. Dakota wondered if Dr. Eddy and his wife knew how much fun their children were having outside of their home.

"I thought Mom was going to keel over right there."

Larry's cheeks were flushed, just as Dakota thought hers were.

Lord knew she'd drunk more that night than she had in many months.

"I'm not sure who was more shocked, Phelps or Dad, when Lily kept asking for details about your ability to research your characters' sexual habits. Tell me that doesn't happen all the time?" Brenda asked.

"The research question comes up in nearly every interview. I'm used to it." Dakota was tucked beside Walt, his hand rested intimately on her thigh. The comfort in his touch kept a smile on her lips the entire night. Once it became apparent that Lily, as gorgeous as she was, was more interested in Dakota than in Walt, she relaxed and enjoyed the rest of the evening. It helped that Walt's father didn't have a stick as firmly up his backside as JoAnne did.

Brenda picked up a pillow and lobbed it at her brother. "Why didn't you tell me your girlfriend was famous?"

After deflecting the pillow, Walt's eyes met Dakota's. He offered a half smile and didn't correct his sister about her girlfriend status.

"I'm not dating her for her fame."

Dakota dropped her gaze, and before tilting back her drink, said, "He's dating me for the sexual research."

Larry choked on his drink and Brenda roared with laughter.

An hour later, Dakota was removing her makeup in the boathouse and talking to Walt, who was stretched out on the bed.

"Can I be honest with you?" she asked.

"I don't like lies."

"Your mom hates me. I'm not sure if it's on principle or if it's me."

"I never understood what 'on principle' meant."

Dakota leaned closer to the mirror, caught some leftover mascara that didn't want to let go of her lashes.

"She didn't invite me and you didn't tell her I was coming. She'll feel like an idiot with all the young, single women she invited with the sole interest in setting you up. JoAnne hates me, but I don't really care."

"She's not that bad."

Dakota paused, looked behind her, but knew Walt couldn't see her from the angle of the door. Perhaps a white lie would prove best to save his concerns. "Maybe she just needs to get to know me."

The springs on the bed let loose a squeak and Dakota continued. "Your dad was quiet most of the night. Is that normal?"

"It's . . . no, actually, he's usually more like my mom."

Was that concern in Walt's voice?

She leaned back, caught a glimpse of Walt sitting beside the bed, his head in his hand. "Do you think everything is OK with him?"

"I don't know. We haven't really talked in years. Not since . . ."

She waited, turned on the water, and started brushing her teeth. "Since?"

"Since I told him I wasn't taking over his practice." He paused. "We've talked, just not in the way we did before I told him what I really wanted to do with my life."

Dakota watched the foamy water wash down the drain, rinsed and wiped her face. "That's a hard conversation." She moved to the doorway and leaned against the frame. "It's hard letting your parents down. Doesn't matter how old you are or why you're doing it. There's something inside us that always wants to please them."

Walt turned with a smile. "Did you minor in psychology?"

She shook her head. "Psych 101 was as far as I went in college. The school of life and studying people is something I've done since birth. Every character I create in a book is real in my head. They have a family, a history, and something that drives them to do the things they do within the pages of fiction. Pleasing our parents is taught since birth. From ER Dr. Eddy to Dr. Eddy, master of all things cardiology." She pushed off the doorway and moved to the opposite side of the bed from where Walt sat. "Most of our needs and wants are the same; we simply have different ways of meeting them."

Walt reached across the bed and captured her hand. "Every time I think I'm smart, I meet someone like you."

The compliment made her smile. "I study people, Doc . . . you fix their issues. I have the easier job."

He lifted her hand and kissed the tips of her fingers before moving into the bathroom.

While Walt moved about the bathroom, Dakota dimmed the lights and stripped.

"I don't think my mom hates you," she heard Walt say from behind the bathroom door.

"Oh?"

"No . . ." He opened the door. "She—"

Dakota liked to think she knew a thing or two about men. Nudity wasn't something they expected. Ever. She had some sexy lingerie in her overnight case, but she really didn't have any desire to put it on.

From the dropped jaw and wide eyes of the man standing over her, she knew she chose the right outfit for the evening.

"I think we should stop talking about your—"

"Don't!"

She laughed and placed a hand on her bare hip.

Even from several feet across the room, she noticed his eyes darken.

When he covered her body with his, there wasn't any room for conversation.

———

He wasn't sure if it was the sexual high from the day before, or the actual hours of restful sleep he'd managed in bed with Dakota, but

Walt rose ready to take on the free world. Or his parents . . . which in his case was the same thing.

Dakota liked to sleep in . . . or maybe it was a little bit of the alcohol from the night before. Either way, Walt woke with the sun and started a pot of coffee.

The evening before played in his head while he watched a thin layer of fog lift from the lake. He missed this . . . the quiet time at the lake. Only the birds to keep him company or the occasional interruption of his sister.

He thought of Brenda and smiled. How had the two of them turned out to be so together? Seemed both their parents were hellbent to break them of their free will, and yet they both forged their own paths.

Who were Dakota's people? Did they get her? Did they give her crap at every turn? Would they accept her and all her adult decisions or would they fight them every step of the way?

Walt wanted to know. For the first time in a long time, he really wanted to know.

"Hey!"

Brenda walked along the shore of the lake and waved.

Walt looked behind him, thought Dakota would sleep a little longer, and met his sister.

"I see you're still an early riser," he told her.

"Larry still sleeps until eight. The day's half over."

Walt laughed, draped an arm over his sister's shoulders. "Married life agrees with you."

Brenda hip-bumped him. "Dating life agrees with you."

He smiled.

"I like Dakota."

"I like her, too."

"Have you guys been dating long?"

Walt glanced over the lake, wondering how much he should say. "Define long."

Brenda laughed and tried not to stare.

"Truth is we're so busy at home we haven't spent much time together until this weekend."

His sister snuggled into her jacket, warding off the morning chill. "I would have thought you've known each other for months."

Yeah, Walt thought the same thing.

"I'm glad you're moving on," Brenda told him.

Is that what I'm doing?

Chapter Ten

Dakota brought more than one formal outfit, not sure if the Eddys would keep the party going all weekend.

She wore silver without sequins and a modest neckline. The glitz of the gown spoke wealth and class, and JoAnne couldn't suggest for a moment it was inappropriate in any way.

"Avoid Vanderbilt," Walt warned her as they walked through the crowd. "He's sick."

"He's not the only one sniffling here, Doc. Must be quite the occasion to come to a doctor's party ill."

Guests were still arriving and the main living room was already filled. There were waiters in black bow ties holding trays of appetizers while others carried champagne.

The evening before killed Dakota's appetite for copious amounts of alcohol. The glass in her hand had been there for over an hour with hardly an inch removed from it.

"Damn it, Walt. Doesn't your mother know not to let sick people in here?" Walt's grandfather, the original Dr. Walter Eddy, was as vibrant as he was old. At nearly eighty-three, his eyes were sharp and his hands were fast.

"I guess not."

"You must be immune after all those strange places you go off to. Does he make you ill?" he asked Dakota with a wink.

"I haven't . . . no."

The man kept talking. "Give him time. ER medicine makes everyone sick from time to time. Great thing about the heart. Not contagious."

Looked like Dr. Walter Eddy I wasn't done preaching about the youngest Dr. Eddy joining the family practice.

"Damn boring after a while, though," said Dr. Eddy Senior.

Or maybe not.

"I hear you write sexy books."

Dakota didn't have time to comment.

"That ought to get the heart pumping."

Dakota turned to Walt, jumped when she felt a hand on her ass. When she turned, Dr. Eddy Senior was walking away.

Walt was laughing at his grandfather when Dakota whispered, "He just grabbed my butt."

Walt's laughter ebbed. "He didn't."

She tilted her head. "Would I lie?" Then she laughed.

Dr. Eddy Senior was already accosting another young woman.

"I'll deck him later."

"I can't believe he is the great patriarch of this family."

Walt shrugged. "My grandmother was his stability. When she passed, my dad took over the practice."

"How long ago was that?"

"Sixteen years . . . I think. A long time."

"Walter?" Someone called from behind them.

Dakota pasted on the smile that had been on her face all evening. Only Walt's expression paled.

He turned and his words sounded dry. "Mrs. Adams."

There wasn't a hug, or even a handshake.

Mrs. Adams took a great interest in Dakota. The woman's gaze moved over her slowly and left her bare. Without realizing she did so, Dakota moved closer to Walt. Only he held himself away just enough to wiggle a sense of insecurity in her veins.

"We really didn't think you'd be here," Mrs. Adams said.

Dakota waited for an introduction that didn't seem to be coming.

Walt set his drink down on the table beside them, stood back.

Tension started to build as the seconds ticked by.

Dakota sought a pleasant face in the crowd, found Brenda nearby, and pleaded that she join them with a look.

A man approached Mrs. Adams's side, his expression less than friendly.

When Walt's hands started to clench, Dakota set her drink aside and placed a hand on his back.

He flinched, and she dropped her hand and stood back.

Mrs. Adams gaze stuck with Dakota. "She looks nothing like our Vivian."

Brenda reached their side, offered a smile. "Hello, Harriett."

The woman scowled.

Dakota wasn't sure what was going on, but she hadn't yet seen Walt this tense. Not even his parents placed as much stiffness in his spine as the couple in front of him did.

Mrs. Adams sucked in a deep breath and turned to the man at her side. "We should make our excuses."

They started to walk away and Walt called out. "Lee?"

The man escorting Mrs. Adams away sneered. "We have nothing to say to you."

Something inside Walt deflated, his shoulders slumped, his smile long gone from his lips.

For a brief moment, no one said anything. Walt stood motionless, and Brenda stared at her brother.

Dakota waited.

"That was ugly," Brenda finally managed. "I don't know why Mom invited them."

"It's OK, Brenda."

"It's not. They should have realized how that would play out."

Dakota moved in, not willing to be left unaware of what had just happened, and why it had affected Walt so deeply. "Who were they?"

Brenda glanced at her briefly before returning her attention to her brother. "Vivian's parents."

Dakota's practiced grin slid. A rock in her stomach started to grow. "Who's Vivian?"

"Walt's late wife."

Late . . . what?

It took Dakota's mind a moment to catch up with Brenda's words. When Walt's eyes found hers and a layer of ice closed over them, she understood.

Walt was a widower.

It's strange how the head buzzes in times of stress. Lee's retreating back parted old friends, those who knew the truth, and those who simply assumed. Most of those watching had no real idea what had happened and why.

Walt's head started to pound.

"Walt?" He felt Dakota's hand on his arm. A huge question sat behind her eyes but this wasn't the time, or place, to tell her about Vivian. He'd hoped to avoid the conversation altogether.

"I'm . . . sorry you saw that," he told Dakota.

She tilted her head. "What's a little family drama?"

"There you are." His mother approached from behind and Brenda jumped on her.

"How could you, Mom?"

JoAnne pushed closer, lowered her voice. "Harriett and Lee just excused themselves. What did you say to make them leave?"

Walt's back teeth met up and threatened to break. "Your loyalty is astounding."

Dakota squeezed his arm and stared at his mother. "I could use some fresh air. If you'll excuse us, JoAnne."

It was probably a good thing Dakota led him outside.

The image of a caged animal caught him when they stepped out in the cooling air while Brenda and his mom stared each other off. He broke away from Dakota the moment they were alone on the back porch overlooking the lake. The moon glistened on the lake like diamonds . . . a sight he would enjoy if his insides weren't twisting on themselves.

Dakota leaned against the large wooden pillar, her eyes following him.

"She was in her last year of medical school," he told her.

Dakota lifted a hand. "You don't have to explain."

He liked that about her, he decided. If he'd just learned that Dakota was a widow he'd have a million questions. Besides, this wasn't something he ever talked about, yet confronting Vivian's parents made the details surface.

"I was a first-year resident. We grew up in the same town but didn't really notice each other until med school. She was smart . . . funny." He glanced at Dakota and noticed that practiced smile start to surface. "You don't want to hear this."

Her gaze softened. "No. I do . . . please."

He pushed away from the rail, stared at the lake while he talked. "We saw each other off and on. It wasn't serious . . . more like when we had moments of homesickness, or were in need of a familiar face, we took each other up on the other's company."

"So what changed to make you two marry?"

He saw Vivian's foggy image deep in his memory. "I was four months into my first-year residency. God, I was tired . . . so tired. I didn't want to date, didn't have the time. Vivian was just as exhausted. Struggling to finish her final year in med school. I didn't get it. She'd always been so full of energy." He rubbed his temple. Feeling the fatigue all over again like it was yesterday. "She ignored her symptoms . . . didn't tell me." He ran his hand through his hair. "She had an advanced form of pancreatic cancer. One trip to the ER . . . one trip and we both knew."

"Oh, Walt. I'm so sorry."

"She opted for surgery . . . was going to follow up with chemo. There were new drugs available. But she was scared. It's like she knew." *She knew she was going to die.*

"What happened?" Dakota's voice was soft, concerned.

"Lee and Harriett aren't doctors. They don't know when it's time to let someone go. Vivian was an only child. Only Viv didn't want to prolong her life and make everyone else around her suffer. As her husband, I could make decisions on her behalf if she wasn't able to make them. So before she went in for surgery, we eloped." He remembered the justice of the peace, the two of them trying to laugh with the fake bouquet of flowers he'd grabbed from the hospital lobby.

"The surgery went well, or so they thought. An incredibly small percentage of patients don't recover from anesthesia. Viv had a massive stroke. Maybe she gave up. Problem was she kept breathing and I had to deny feeding tubes, anything that would keep her artificially alive. She'd written all that down before going under, but Lee and Harriett . . . they didn't want to let go."

Walt looked up and saw tears falling down Dakota's cheeks.

As much as the story burned, telling it was easier than it had been in years. Then again, there weren't many he'd told.

Dakota approached him, slowly, and placed her hand on the side of his face. "Vivian was a lucky woman."

He laughed. "She died before her twenty-seventh birthday."

"Which would have happened with or without you."

He sucked in a breath, blew it out slowly. Noise from inside the house grew, caught their attention.

Dakota dropped her hand to his arm, nodded toward the lake. "Let's blow this off. Larry left a perfectly good bottle of whiskey at the boathouse."

For a second, he thought of his dad . . . then remembered that his mother knew the history between him and Viv's parents and still asked the Adams over for the party.

"A bottle of Crown just might do the trick."

———

The sun blinded him as it spread over the lake. He closed his eyes nearly as quickly as he opened them. The pasty film in his mouth, coupled with the pounding in his head, reminded him why he didn't drink very often.

"Dakota?" he groaned. She wasn't in the bed. He could tell by the way he was stretched out over it.

He rolled away from the window and cracked one eye. He croaked out her name a second time, this time a little louder.

"I was wondering if I needed to start an IV on you." His father's voice surprised him.

Walt closed his eyes again.

When he opened them, his dad filled the doorway to the bedroom. "You look like shit, son."

"Good to know I look how I feel."

His dad moved into the room and set something green, thick, and liquid next to the bed. "Still the best cure for the morning after."

Walt pushed his feet over the bed and cursed as his head kept moving long after all the motion in his body had stopped.

His dad laughed.

Walt lifted the glass and gave it a sniff. "You're trying to kill me."

"It's been years since I needed this, but it works."

Green really wasn't a drinkable color, and this one was grainy with chalky bits of God knew what, and a splash of whiskey. The whiskey was the only thing Walt identified before emptying the glass. He wiped his lips with the back of his hand and forced himself to keep the liquid down.

"Next time I want the IV," he told his dad.

The bed dipped under his father's weight. "Brenda told me what happened last night."

Walt tried not to moan. Such an undignified sound from son to father.

"We've invited the Adams many times in the past few years. They've never shown up."

"They think I'm responsible for Vivian's death."

"That's preposterous. They lost their child, needed to blame the universe."

The light from the window wasn't as blinding when Walt turned his eyes on his dad. He'd gathered a couple more wrinkles in the past year. A few more gray strands in his hair. The civility in his father's tone was new. "You're usually riding my ass, Dad. Reminding me of my place. What's up?"

Walter huffed, placed both palms on his knees. "I'm not getting younger."

Walt waited for the riding to begin.

It didn't.

"I don't see you nearly enough. Don't even know where you are half the time."

"I live in California."

"I'm talking about the trips out of the country."

"A lot of parents don't know where their adult children are. You're not unique there."

His dad moved from the bed, opened the blinds all the way. Surprisingly, the sun didn't burn and Walt noted that his head no longer spun. He glanced into the empty glass, still felt the nasty taste on his tongue.

"What father doesn't want their child to live close?"

"It's hard to be close when all we do is argue over my choices when I'm here."

"I-I know. I'm trying." His dad met his gaze and held it.

This was good. The timing was strange, but the result was decent. "Where is Dakota?"

The grin that spread over his father's face was more genuine that he'd seen in years. "She and your sister went to town to pick up a prescription."

"Is she sick?"

Walter glanced at the ceiling. "Let me see if I can remember her words. 'Dr. Eddy,' she said, 'since your son is sleeping off last night's bender, and I can't ask him, you're going to have to write me a script.'" His dad was laughing.

"A script for what?"

"Seems your girlfriend woke with cystitis."

Walt felt his shoulders drop. Urinary tract infections were common, and nothing to worry about. Still, blame rested on his shoulders. The term *honeymoon cystitis* was coined from patients who were overly sexually active. Considering how many times he and Dakota managed to get naked over the past couple of days, he wasn't shocked.

"I like her."

"We're just dating, Dad."

"Still like her. Did you help her buy the gift?"

Walt rubbed a hand over the stubble on his chin. "Gift?"

"I'll take that as a no." He moved toward the door. "She gave me a stethoscope dating back to the Civil War. Thoughtful."

Walt found himself smiling. "Dad?"

"Yeah?"

"What the hell was in that?" He nodded toward the empty green glass.

"I'll e-mail you the ingredients. Nice to know it still works."

Chapter Eleven

Dakota reached over her keyboard and picked up the phone. She tucked the receiver between her shoulder and her chin. "Hey."

"Do you always answer the phone that way?"

She finished the sentence she'd been writing and leaned back in her chair. "Doctor . . . so nice of you to call."

He'd called her twice since their return from Colorado and it had only been three days. "Are you feeling better?"

"Much. Lots of water, antibiotics. I'm good."

"Perfect." He sounded rested, more than when he'd called after his shift the night before. "Can I convince you to take a break?"

Dakota glanced at the blinking cursor on her screen. The word count was already over ten thousand. The opening scene of her new book had played in her head like a tape, and now it was crafted on the page and flowing like river water after a storm.

"I'm talking food, not the microwaveable kind," Walt suggested. "Do you cook?"

"No. Well, pasta, but that's not what I had in mind."

She lowered her voice. "What do you have in mind, Doc?"

"I'll be there in thirty minutes."

"Wait . . . you live farther away than that."

"I wasn't going to take no for an answer."

She clicked a few keys, saved her file, and turned off her computer. "So forceful. I think that's sexy."

He laughed. "You know, if this book gig doesn't work out you'd be a shoo-in for a phone sex operator."

"I would, would I? What do you know about phone sex?"

There was a pause and Dakota offered a throaty laugh.

"Thirty minutes."

She showered, dusted enough makeup on to be presentable, and blew her hair dry. When she opened the door to Walt twenty-five minutes later, she wore a teddy and a smile.

The smell of food in bags caught her attention right before Walt moved into the house, slammed the door behind him, and devoured her. They were lips and arms, removing clothes and reaching for the other as she dragged him to her bedroom.

Later, they were eating out of box containers sprawled over her bed. "How did you know I liked Chinese?"

"Everyone likes Chinese," Walt said as he dug his fork into a tub of fried rice.

"It's sinful. All the salt, the oil."

"Which is why everyone enjoys it." He leaned forward and licked a grain of rice off her bare breast. "Naked eating. I like." He ran a sticky finger over her nipple and pulled a moan from her as it puckered.

"If I didn't know better," she said while Walt pulled away and filled his mouth with more orange chicken, "This was a thinly-veiled booty call."

He lifted his brows and made a show out of chewing. After he swallowed, he filled his fork again. "You're the one who answered the door in lingerie."

"I could say that you showed up five minutes early and that I wasn't yet dressed."

"You could. But you'd be lying."

She reached into his box, pulled out a chunk of chicken with her bare fingers, and popped it into her mouth.

Dakota returned the nipple favor and dipped her fingers in the sauce. She ran her fingers down his chest, low on his hips. Before she reached for his responding erection, she caught his eyes. "I'd be lying."

The slow descent of her tongue down his chest was tangy sweet. Food sex . . . she'd written about it, had fun with whipped cream at least twice, but Chinese food?

"Holy . . ."

She hesitated at his hip, licked off the sauce she'd placed where his thigh met his torso.

"Looks like I missed a spot," she said, finding the sauce with her lips and tracing the trail up his length.

He was sweet on her tongue, the length of him filling her mouth, which pulled a gasp from his lips. Walt's hand caressed the side of her face as she took him. When she looked, he was watching her.

Her heart leapt, his intense stare looked through her. He guided her away and swept the boxes of food to the bedside table.

When his lips took hers, the taste of ginger and spice mixed between them, Dakota leaned back and welcomed him. Unlike how they'd made love when he first arrived, this was slow, calculated, and a little heartbreaking.

Dakota felt her heart slipping a little further into Walt's world. A dangerous one . . . one filled with crazy hours and the need to be single. Only as he called her name and plunged into her more times than she could count, Dakota couldn't picture him without her by his side. More, she was having a hard time seeing her world without him.

Her release was like a slow, spreading fire that started at her toes and burned through her center.

He collapsed on top of her, his breath just as rapid as hers.

"Chinese food will never look the same."

She laughed, felt him slip from her as his own mirth caught in his chest.

The bed was empty when his eyes opened. Dakota's side of the bed was cool and it was still dark outside.

Walt found his boxers and pulled them on when he left her room.

He found her in her library office with a dim light and her radio playing from her computer on a low volume. She was laughing, and typing faster than anyone he'd ever seen. "You're such a bitch. Love it." Dakota kept typing, stopped long enough to reach for a water bottle on her desk, sip it, and then returned her fingers to the keyboard. He'd never seen her work and wasn't sure what he'd expected. Typing, yeah, but excitement as the thoughts streamed from her head and onto the page . . . no, he hadn't expected that. Somehow he thought she'd type in silence, all focus on the page . . . then again, she was animated in every other aspect of her life. He shouldn't be surprised, yet he still was.

She finished whatever thought she had on her mind and leaned back. That's when she noticed him.

"Oh . . . did I wake you?"

"No. I think it might have been the rice."

She yawned and rubbed her eyes. Her eyes traveled to the clock on the wall and that's when Walt noticed the time. Three in the morning. "I'm not sure if you're the earliest riser ever, or if it's a late night."

"I woke about an hour ago and couldn't go back to sleep. Then I had this brilliant idea."

He moved closer to her desk, looked at the bright screen. "Can I read it?"

Dakota grabbed the mouse and clicked her word program to the sidebar. "Not until it's done."

He laughed. "So that's how it is?"

"Yep. This is raw, sloppy. You can read it when it's polished."

Walt pulled his fingers through her dark hair and combed it behind her back.

She tilted her head back and closed her eyes.

"Come back to bed?"

He didn't have to coax. Whatever thought she'd had must have been hammered out in the hour she was typing away. After tucking her in his arm, he heard her breathing even out as she fell back to sleep.

It was his turn to lie awake and watch the shadows on the wall. He'd missed this. A hookup, an occasional lover didn't often result in overnight stays and weekends. Dakota was different. If Walt was honest with himself, that scared him. Her no-nonsense approach to life, her humor, her independence. Her ability to make Chinese takeout erotic . . . good Lord, he hadn't expected that. His eyes drifted close and his mind started to clear. He smiled, on the inside, in a place that hadn't felt this good in years.

Mary huddled over her coffee, her eyes wide open and ready for gossip. "I've seen his car here twice this week, and you were gone at least once."

"You're stalking me?" Dakota poured more java into her cup and sat down.

"Living vicariously through you. I'm jealous so give the details, baby."

Details . . . were there details? "He's nothing like I thought a doctor would be. I bet he can be serious when he wants to be, but most of his stories are just hysterical."

"I can't imagine his daily life at work. That has to be hard."

"If it is, he doesn't show it. Some of the things he talks about churn my stomach, but he talks about them as if he's describing a walk through the supermarket."

"Any more talk about his late wife?"

Dakota had shared that with Mary when she'd returned from Colorado. "Nothing. Every once in a while he stares at me and I want to ask what he's thinking about. You know . . . what did she look like, how was it after she died. But I can't. I want to know, but I don't."

"Do you think he loved her?"

"I think he did. He might not have been *in love* with her, but he cared enough to make sure she was taken care of in death. That couldn't have been easy."

Mary traced her fingers along the writing on the coffee cup. "So where do you think things are going with you guys?"

"Please, Mary. We've only been dating for what, two months?" Not that she hadn't asked herself that very question. They led different lives, and yet when they were in the same room it felt as if they shared the same one.

"You're right. Two months is too soon to think about forever. But after three we need to bring this up again."

"What's so magical about three months?"

"Three months is the honeymoon phase of dating. You show your best face, don't let your annoying habits show. Chances are you haven't fought . . . you haven't, have you?"

"Does the stun gun count?"

Mary smiled. "No."

"Pushing him into the lake?"

"That was foreplay. I'm talking a major disagreement."

Dakota shook her head. "Nope. Not even his witchy mom could wiggle between us."

"Any annoying habits that you can't stand?"

Were there any? "He procrastinates."

"That can be annoying. And we know how type A you are."

"I'm not type A."

Mary stood, moved to Dakota's pantry, and opened the door. Inside there were supplies of food that would take care of her for at least six months. All the cans were lined up, the dry goods rotated with every purchase. The powdered milk was replaced every couple of months . . . and the water bottles . . . "Oh, damn. I am type A."

"I bet Walt doesn't know about this habit."

"He knows I'm a closet prepper."

"He probably thinks it's cute. Now."

Dakota felt the smile on her face fall. "You mean he's going to hate it after three months?"

The thought of messing up her pantry just to make Walt happy waved a thin veil of anxiety over her.

"He might not hate it, but he won't say a negative thing about it until next month," Mary concluded. "And his procrastination isn't a problem until he procrastinates with something important to you. That is when the fight will happen."

"Geez, Mary. Sounds like we should just break up now and avoid any issues."

"Don't jump. How you fight will tell you how well you actually work together. It's easy to work when the sex is hot and you're both discovering each other. Adversity," Mary said, pointing a finger at Dakota, "that's when you see the guts of a relationship."

What will our first fight be over? Why was she sitting here sipping coffee and spending any time worrying about an argument that hadn't yet happened? "I feel like you just psychoanalyzed me."

Mary grinned, spoke over the rim of her cup. "I did. The bill's already in the mail."

Walt stood in the trauma room with gloves already on, a full gown covering his scrubs. He heard one of the techs announce that the ambulance was pulling in with the patient. He knew she was in her early thirties, thrown from the car she rode in on the freeway. She was unconscious and in severe respiratory distress. The paramedics had already intubated her en route to the ER.

"How soon before Dr. Meeks is down here?" Chuck Meeks was the trauma surgeon. The two of them would work together to stabilize the patient as quickly as possible before Chuck took the patient to surgery to fix what he could.

"Five minutes, maybe less."

Fair enough.

He heard the familiar shuffle of firefighter boots as the medics wheeled the gurney into the room. There was one medic on the Ambu bag, breathing for the patient. Two more helped push the gurney. They lined up to the ER gurney and started to coordinate the transfer, all the while one of them spouting off the patient report. Only Walt had a hard time hearing the man once he caught a look at the woman on the bed. Dark hair was matted with blood, her face stone white with high, cut-up cheeks and full lips that circled around the tube.

She looked like Dakota. It wasn't the woman he was spending his off hours with, but this woman could be her sister.

"She was unconscious on scene with bystander CPR. She had a pulse when we arrived. Blood pressure is dropping 80 over 42 with a pulse of 135, occasional PVCs."

Walt moved in once the patient was on the gurney. He listened to her lungs, didn't like the gurgling he heard on the right. Was equally unhappy with the sound on the left. "We need X-ray to jump in. I need to see what's going on inside her chest. John," he called to the nurse. "Pull two chest tube trays." Walt methodically moved down her body, her pulses were thready, her body looked like she was run over by a car and not just thrown. The laceration on her scalp went from ear to ear, exposing more of her skull than he cared to see. "Do we know how this happened?" he asked the medic.

"We found her on the other side of a barbwire fence."

"Second line is in, Dr. Eddy," Valerie said while she attached an IV bag of Lactated Ringers. "Labs are on their way. We have four bags of O negative on standby."

The radiology techs pushed in and shoved a plate under the patient as gently as they could.

"Her temp is 96.5, Walt."

"We need to warm her up, but not too fast." Her head wound had lost a lot of blood, but was only a trickle at this point.

Before radiology could snap a picture, the monitors started alarming. Everyone turned, saw the rhythm of the patient's heart. V-tach.

The woman who was not Dakota, but looked so much like her Walt had to stop glancing at her face, had just lost a functioning heartbeat.

Four units of blood, one chest tube, three rounds of CPR, and one hour later, his patient lost her battle. They never managed to get her to the OR.

He pulled off his gloves, his soaked gown, and slippers, dropping them in the contaminated waste container by the door. After washing his hands, he went through the department to take a moment in the doctors' room.

"Walt," one of the nurses who wasn't in the trauma room called out.

He turned, knew what to expect. "Smith's CT is back, labs are on his chart. The child on eighteen has finished his Albuterol treatments and his fever is down—"

He lifted a hand, stopped her. "Five minutes, Deb."

The ER was packed, patients in the halls, ten deep in the lobby. Some moaned, some coughed, some bled. But all of them were breathing, except one.

He never made it to the doctors' room.

"Dr. Eddy?"

He didn't want to respond, but the hospital chaplain wasn't someone he could ignore.

"Mrs. Comer's family is in the chapel. John is ready to go with you."

Mrs. Comer's husband couldn't be any older than Walt. He jumped when the three of them walked into the room. Fear, anguish, and dare Walt say, hope, filled the man's eyes.

The chaplain introduced them and Walt delivered the news no one ever wants to hear.

Chapter Twelve

He lurched from his bed, his heart pounding too fast. "Fuck!" he swore to the empty room. The images of Dakota mixed with the fading memory of Vivian . . . and Mrs. Comer. Damn it, he hadn't brought his work home with him in years. Now, two days after the trauma, his head kept going there.

He kept seeing Dakota dead, felt the heartache of another doctor telling him she was gone.

The clock by his bed said two thirty. The hotel shades he'd placed over his bedroom window blocked out the daylight after a graveyard shift, but his body knew it was sleeping at the wrong time.

Giving up on sleep, he pushed out of bed and slid into a pair of pajama pants. His refrigerator was pathetically bare. Dakota scolded him the first time she saw it. "One week supply minimum, Doc. The only thing you're prepared for is a ball game."

"Don't underestimate the game," he'd told her.

He finished the milk with the tail end of a box of butter crunch cereal.

He couldn't stop thinking about her.

Yet he hadn't called her in three days. He was being a coward, he knew . . . but life was so fragile and he didn't think he could handle losing Dakota. Not to death.

He'd cared for Viv . . . but the growing pressure in his chest every time he thought of Dakota was so much larger, and that scared him.

The threat of loss kept his dates with other women to only a few and then it was time to move on. So why had he broken his own rules with Dakota?

"Back off, Walt," he told himself. "Slow down."

What he needed was a distraction. Space and time away from the woman who had forced her way into his thoughts every damn day.

He moved to his small office and removed his new cell phone from the charger. Sure enough, Dakota had sent a text. I'm told that sexting always ends up on the Internet, so just imagine the picture I want to send. Call me when you wake up.

His palms itched with the desire to hear her voice, take her up on her obvious invitation. Instead, he listened to the voice message blinking on phone.

"Eddy! It's Klein." Dr. Klein was one of his colleagues with Borderless Doctors. "BD is looking for a full-time doctor to coordinate staff, train, and be first on scene. I thought of you. Call me."

Instead of calling Dakota, Walt made a detour.

The same blinking cursor had mocked her on chapter fifteen for a full day. *What comes next? What comes next?*

Dakota checked her phone for the fifth time that hour.

She gave in and let a call go through.

Walt's voice told her to leave a message. "Hey, Doc," she attempted to sound unaffected by his sudden absence in her life. "I'm calling to see if you're still breathing." Which wasn't a lie. A part of her worried something awful had happened. A bigger part of her worried that he wasn't calling her, texting her, for an actual reason. She didn't add anything else to her message before hanging up.

Her eyes started to blur and her head started to pound so she gave up on *what comes next* and turned off her computer.

It was after six when her phone buzzed. She jumped, like a teenage girl with a one-way crush. And that pissed her off. When had she become so needy for a man's attention?

Still, she smiled when she saw Walt's face appear on her screen. "You're alive," she said when she answered.

"Yeah. Sorry. I've either been working or sleeping." His voice was flat and the background was filled with noise.

Was it too demanding of her to suggest a text, a quick call? Was admitting she worried about him too big a step? Channeling her latest heroine, Dakota found her backbone. "You know, Ace, a text between shifts so I know you're alive isn't a time-intensive activity."

He paused. "I know. My bad."

My bad? What are we, sixteen?

"I'm at work. Picked up a shift," he told her. "I'm going out of town for a few days. Didn't want you to worry."

There was a definite chill in his voice as he rattled off his incomplete sentences. "Is everything OK? Any natural disasters I haven't noticed happening in the world?"

"Nothing like that—"

Dr. Eddy? Dakota heard his name called over the phone.

"I've got to go. I'll let you know when I get back." Not *I'll call you*, not *we'll get together* . . . just a *let you know*.

The back of her throat tightened. "Fine. Be safe, Doc."

"Yeah . . . you, too." Then he hung up.

What the hell just happened?

———

"Did he tell you where he's going?" Mary asked from across the table.

The pizza between them was getting cold. The go-to food for a breaking heart would normally work wonders. Tonight, the thought of eating mushrooms and pepperoni wasn't sitting well with her. "No. Just that he was going."

"Maybe he'll call you later with details."

"He won't. I've heard this before, Mary. He was cold."

"Hmm . . ." Mary hummed over the bite of pizza. "How does that make you feel?"

"Like shit. Like I'm being dumped." Dakota picked up her whiskey and downed the glass. Even that tasted like crap. "Don't turn that psych shit on me. I need my friend, not the therapist."

Mary dropped the pizza on her plate. "I know. I'm sorry. With me, you get both. I don't know how to turn it off."

"You're supposed to tell me I'm overthinking this, or call him a dumbass. His loss. Anything." Damn the moisture gathering in her eyes.

"You're not overthinking this and you have the right to feel hurt." Mary placed a hand over hers and squeezed. "If Walt is dumping you, then he is a dumbass. A dickless asshat who can't even tell you. And if I see him again I'll tell him that."

"Yeah." She hated tears. Hated them. But her friend was finally getting it. "Dickless asshat." Dakota tried to laugh but failed.

"He might have a reason—"

Dakota snapped her hand away. "No psych shit. Stick with dumbass, counselor."

"Fine . . . but—"

"Mary! I'm warning you. I'm wallowing and need you to wallow with me." Dakota moved to Mary's fridge, opened the freezer. She grabbed the ice cream that Mary never did without before pulling a spoon from the utensil drawer.

"Wow, you really are wallowing. There's lots of refined sugar in that, Dakota."

"Yeah, well . . . tonight I don't care. A proper sulk needs ice cream." She ripped off the top of the carton and dug straight into the mix. It hit her tongue and the smooth texture melted in her mouth. "God, this is good."

Mary was staring at her.

Dakota shoveled in another spoonful. "I need to stock up on this."

Mary's hand stopped Dakota's from devouring another bite. "Dakota, you're scaring me."

"It's this or whiskey."

Mary let her hand go.

"I thought so."

———

San Antonio was hot, humid, and just this side of a smoldering death. But Donald Klein had arranged this meeting at the central headquarters. A place where the weather, albeit sucky in the summer, seldom had issues the rest of the year.

Walt was 1,200-plus miles away from California . . . from Dakota.

He thought of texting her, calling her, daily. He didn't.

He listened to Donald's proposal, met with different members of Borderless Doctors, and went through a lengthy interview process.

Juggling an ER job full-time while taking on this charge wouldn't be possible. Yeah, he could moonlight, but anything other than a temporary fill-in for his current job wouldn't work.

When Walt had first started with Borderless Doctors, he knew he wanted more. He loved the ER, loved the autonomy of walking away from his patients at the end of a shift, learning from them, and moving on.

What Donald was suggesting sounded perfect.

He could live anywhere so long as an airport was nearby. And with the Fairchilds on board with emergency flight plans, Walt could take his pick of locations.

So why am I hedging?

Because being a nomad, someone without any roots, shook him. Running off to the next disaster always had an end. Taking this job without a home base would feel a lot like being on a constant rotating coaster . . . chaos.

"Can I be honest with you?" Donald asked over the dinner they were both enjoying on Walt's last night in Texas.

"I would hope you know to be honest by now."

"I thought you'd already be signing the contract."

Walt placed his fork down. "I'm seriously considering it."

"What's keeping you back?"

"Nothing," he lied. "I want to consider everything. Now, tomorrow . . . ten years from now."

Donald ran a hand over his bald head. "Really, Walt? Do you have a crystal ball? Who the hell knows where any of us will be in ten years?"

Walt released a short sigh. "You're married, right?"

"Yeah."

"How does what we do interfere with your family life?"

Instead of answering, Donald sat back and regarded Walt. "There's a woman?"

"Maybe."

Donald laughed, picked up his knife and fork before continuing to eat the prime rib on his plate. "We both know what it means to be away during a disaster. We focus on what has to happen, what we need to do during the time we're knee-deep in crap so deep we can't see. Finding a woman to share your life who understands that, and doesn't hold it against you, is key." Donald plunked a chunk of beef between his lips and started to chew. After a few seconds he continued. "You and I were born of the same cloth, Walt. We don't do normal. As much as you tell yourself you hate graveyard shift, you show up night after night and suck it up. If you didn't have to go in, there would be nights you'd be staring at the walls."

Walt shook his head. "Three a.m. sucks if you don't have a drink or a woman under you."

"You're not that shallow."

His memory moved to Dakota . . . three a.m. with her was worth everything.

Damn it! Why couldn't he shake her?

Walt dug into his food. "How long before Borderless Doctors wants an answer?"

Chapter Thirteen

Chapter fifteen sucked. Dakota had written three different twists in her story and none of them manifested into an easy chapter sixteen. She tried running to clear her head, but that wasn't working. Running sucked. Who willingly put on shorts, a sports bra, and jogged around the block?

She hadn't heard from Walt in three days.

On her phone was a missed call from him, but she refused to pick up the phone. She was stronger than that, damn it!

Dakota tapped a well-manicured nail against the desk and stared at her phone.

She grabbed it off the receiver as if it had insulted her by its mere existence.

With a forced smile on her face, Dakota lifted her voice and smothered it with Southern charm.

"Emergency Room, this is Rick?"

"Hello Rick. Can you be a dear and tell me if Doctor Eddy is on today?"

"We don't give out the doctors' schedules."

"Oh, I don't want his schedule. You see, he was so wonderful with my stepdaughter last week. I just wanted to send him a little something. It would be a shame if I sent it on a night he wasn't working." Dakota crossed her fingers and closed her eyes . . . as if those motions could change the outcome of this call.

"Oh . . . well . . ."

"I just need to know if I'm sending pizza or doughnuts. I have a feeling Doctor Eddy has a sweet tooth but doughnuts in the evening simply aren't the same . . . wouldn't you agree?" *C'mon, Rick.*

One of the tidbits Walt had given her about the ER staff was their desire for food.

"In that case. He'll be in tonight at seven."

Gotcha! "Bless your heart. I'll be sure and send enough for everyone. Everyone was so kind. Thank y'all for being here for us."

"No problem."

Walt was back in town and yet a call hadn't happened.

There were things she could forgive, but going back on your word wasn't one of them.

Before turning off her computer, she found a local pizza joint that delivered and ordered six pizzas for the staff of the ER. She *was* a woman of her word.

Then she went to her bedroom and put on an extra layer of polish and a change of clothes.

Never go into any breakup looking your worst. Make 'em wish they had made a different choice.

Sometimes her Southern upbringing came in handy.

Before she left the house, she managed a couple of aspirin to help with the headache that seemed to be with her daily since Walt brushed her off.

The tears didn't help.

After today, she wouldn't shed another one. If Walt wanted her out of his life, fine. But he was going to offer some kind of explanation for the sudden departure.

———

He pulled into the doctors' parking lot, found a spot on the second level, and locked his car before finding the back stairs close to the ER.

He hesitated at the bottom of the stairs.

She wore black stiletto boots and a mini with a tight-knit white turtleneck without sleeves. Her dark-rimmed sunglasses hid her eyes but the lack of smile on her face said everything.

Walt didn't like the twist in his gut. The desire to reach for her, tell her he was being an ass, try and make her understand his worries even when he didn't quite know them, was a physical ache. It didn't help that she looked hotter than he'd ever seen. "Dakota," he whispered her name.

"Oh, shucks, Doc. You remembered my name. I'm flattered."

He deserved that.

"We should talk."

She placed her fingertips on her forehead and squeezed her temple. "You know, Walt. I thought we were doing fine. I'm only here to find out what the hell I did that made you run."

"You didn't do anything." And standing by her side made him kick his own ass for not calling her.

"If you tell me it's not me, it's you, I won't be responsible for my reaction." She pushed the heel of her hand to her head. "This was a mistake."

When she started to walk past him, he reached out. "Please."

She shook out of his hold and removed her sunglasses with a swipe of her hand. The fatigue he saw in the mirror every day sat behind her eyes. The words *I fucked up* sat on the tip of his tongue. He opened his mouth to tell her he was an ass, a scared ass, and then she wiped the back of her hand under her nose and looked down.

Blood.

"Damn it," she muttered.

She leaned forward and dug into the purse, retrieved a tiny tissue, and blotted her nose.

"Are you OK?"

"It's a bloody nose, Doctor. I'm fine."

Only the blood was overfilling her tissue and running down her arm.

His forearms throbbed as he fisted his hands to keep from reaching for her. It was obvious she didn't want his touch.

That gutted him.

A drop of blood hit her white shirt, and she blew out a string of obscenities that would make a sailor take note.

"The ER is ten feet away with plenty of gauze to help you with that."

She glared before twisting on her heel and walking toward the back entry.

He walked beside her, not touching, and punched in the access code. The double doors of the bay opened to the activity and noise of the department. A few heads swung their way.

"Hey, Walt."

He smiled at Valerie before reaching into a supply cart just past the nurse's station. He found a pack of four-by-four gauze and pulled a stack. He brushed her hand away as he pinched her nose and kept pressure.

"I got it." She tried pulling away, but he reached around her to keep her put.

"Hold still!"

She growled and glared.

That he could deal with, then he saw a tear fall down her cheek. "Damn it, Dakota. We were moving too fast. I care too much."

Now the tears were rolling. Thankfully, Valerie moved in and stopped all conversation. "You should sit down," she told Dakota. "B-nine is empty. I'll put her there."

Valerie placed a gloved hand over his and led Dakota away.

<hr/>

Her head was pounding and her brand-new angora sweater was ruined.

Damn him!

Valerie moved her behind a curtain and pulled more gauze. Without taking away any pressure, she switched the cloth and forced Dakota's head down.

The taste of blood rolled down her throat with a gag.

"Thanks, Valerie."

"No problem." Valerie took Dakota's free hand and placed it over hers. "Hold this . . . tight."

They made the switch and Valerie stepped away to pull more supplies from a cart at her side. "Does this happen a lot?"

Dakota shook her head. "No. Well, a couple times this past week."

"This bad?"

Is this bad?

She swallowed again, hated the taste.

"No."

"The humidity is down. Nosebleeds increase with the dry air."

"I live closer to the beach," Dakota told her.

Instead of asking more questions, Valerie pulled the blood pressure cuff from the overhead monitor and turned it on. "I'm just going to check your blood pressure."

Dakota looked up only to have Valerie place a hand to her head and push it back down. "Humor me."

Dakota rolled her eyes and lifted her left arm. What blood pressure and nosebleeds had in common was beyond her.

The cuff on her arm pumped up, started to loosen, then pumped up again. "Ouch."

"Hold still."

The death grip of the cuff finally gave way with an error message on the monitor.

Valerie moved away, saying she'd be back.

If not for the feeling of her nosebleed continuing, Dakota would have slithered out of the department. So long as she didn't need to see Walt, she'd stay put.

Valerie returned with a manual blood pressure pump and replaced the automatic one.

After encouraging Dakota to spread out on the gurney, with her head down, Valerie took her pressure again. On the second attempt, Dakota started to worry. "Is there a problem?"

Valerie removed the stethoscope from her ears and attempted a smile. "Do you have high blood pressure?"

Dakota shrugged. "No. Not that I know of . . . why?"

"You're pressure is high, which might be why your nose sprung a leak."

"What does blood pressure and nosebleeds have in common?"

"Quite a bit, actually."

Not convinced, Dakota swung her feet off the gurney. With the movement, the bleeding worsened. "Make it stop, Valerie."

"Keep the pressure and your head down. I'll be right back."

She disappeared again, when she returned Walt was with her, his face stone white.

Here she'd taken so much time to make herself sex in high heels and now she was lying on a gurney with perfectly brilliant sweater ruined and ready for burial, dried blood down her arm. So much for her plan.

"Hey, hon."

"Don't!"

He took her warning and passed a look to Valerie, who looked away.

"Your blood pressure is probably driving this nosebleed. We bring one down, the other will slow. In the meantime we need to stop up this bleed."

As much as she wanted to tell Walt to go to hell, she couldn't. "What do we need to do?"

"I'm more than willing to take care of you without paperwork, but the hospital needs to start a chart."

Dakota closed her eyes, not willing to look at him any longer. She forced a slow, deep breath between her lips and blew it out. "Fine."

Blood pressure was about emotions . . . right? She was young, not a chance it was about her crazy diet . . . which if anyone asked was damn good.

Valerie rolled over a portable computer and typed in a few facts while Walt rolled in a cart. Another nurse Dakota didn't know stepped in and started hooking her up to the cardiac monitor.

"Isn't this overkill?" she asked.

Walt pulled on a pair of gloves. "Your blood pressure is 210 over 120."

She zeroed her gaze on him. "I've been a little stressed, Doctor."

He swallowed, sat in a rolling stool, and pushed close. "Try and relax."

Valerie interrupted them and sent a menacing look to Walt. "Dakota, are you allergic to anything . . . medications?"

"No."

"Health problems? High blood pressure in the family?"

"I'm fine. As for my family, we're from the South. We don't know a damn thing about our parents until they reach seventy and then we know everything. Hard to tell what's truth and what's contrived." While Dakota was talking, she lifted her head and more bleeding made itself known.

Walt stood, pushed his hand over hers, and pressed hard.

"That hurts."

"Direct pressure stops bleeding."

"I've been adding direct pressure for a while, Doc. It's not stopping!"

Instead of commenting, Walt looked at the second nurse in the room. "Pull out a nasal tampon."

"A what?" Dakota pulled away.

"Damn it, Dakota. Hold still."

Valerie placed a hand on her arm and directed her attention away. "Do you take any medication?"

She started to shake her head, and then said, "Birth control."

"Last period?"

Last what? Walt was pinching so hard she couldn't concentrate on what Valerie was asking her. "Three weeks, give or take. Ouch!"

"Hold this," the second nurse handed her a blush-colored bowl and placed it under her chin. "Spit out any blood going down the back of your throat."

"Spit?"

"Yes."

"Southern women don't spit."

Walt wasn't amused. "Blood in your stomach will make you vomit. Do Southern women puke, Dakota?"

Curse him! He was really starting to piss her off.

If she wasn't already feeling the overkill of unwelcome fluid in her stomach, she'd argue. Instead, when the need came over her, she lifted a hand to help shield the need to spit.

Disgusting!

"I need to pack your nose."

"What?"

Didn't matter what Walt said, Dakota didn't hear him. Valerie caught her attention, explained what they needed to do.

Instead of arguing, Dakota sat back and closed her eyes.

The pressure and pain of the packing made her want to fight. She didn't. When they were done, the blood flowing down her throat stopped and she was able to relax. As undignified as it was sitting with her nose stuffed full and a sweater full of blood, she at least felt a little better.

Dakota opened her eyes to find the second nurse gone and Valerie walking out of the room.

Walt sat beside her. "How long have you had the nosebleeds, Dakota?"

"A week, two. I've been a little on edge."

She blew out a sigh.

"A little stress doesn't do this." He was pale, not a hint of a smile on his face.

She wasn't sure what this was, but she knew her blood pressure wasn't going down with him by her side. "I'm not her, Walt. I'm not dying. It's a nosebleed."

His jaw visibly tightened.

Instead of commenting on his emotions, she asked, "How long does this need to stay in?"

"We'll give it a while, bring your blood pressure down, and see if we can cauterize the bleed."

"Burn it?"

"Kind of."

"Great!"

He laid a hand to her side and she pulled away. "I'm trying real hard to calm down here, Doc. The timing of this couldn't suck more. So give a girl a break and back off."

"Damn it, Dakota . . . I'm sorry."

She felt tears and closed her eyes. "Me, too."

———·———

Dakota didn't sleep that night. Walt left her bedside for nearly an hour before he returned to remove the stupid thing in her nose. He found something to burn, did so, and left again. When she'd left the ER it was just after ten. Boxes of leftover pizza were on the nurse's desk and the staff was running. She didn't know where Walt was, and didn't ask to talk to him. Dakota was just thankful the bleeding had stopped and her head wasn't as thick as it had been when she walked in.

She held a cold glass of milk and watched the sunrise hours later. The need to get away tugged at her. The last thing she wanted was a guilty doctor showing up at her doorstep making excuses.

He'd walked out of her life.

With her big-girl panties in place, she was willing to move on.

Dakota's personal physician pushed her into an early appointment. Dr. Chin took care of any ache or pain Dakota could come up with since her move to California. That had been since college.

"Your blood pressure is better today, 146 over 86, but that isn't great. The last time you were in it was 118 over 62."

"I've never had a problem. I don't understand what's happening."

"Any other symptoms?"

"Headaches. I'm not sleeping . . . but I've had a recent breakup."

Dr. Chin wrote a note in his chart. "Stress was something we called a reason back in the eighties. Now we look for other causes. Any recent illness?"

She shook her head. "I had a urinary tract infection a month and a half ago."

Dr. Chin flipped through the chart. "Did you go to a clinic?"

"No. I did talk to a doctor. I've had them before. A little Bactrim and I was good."

"Did you finish the prescription?"

"Of course."

He closed his chart. "I'm going to run a few tests, probably refer you to a cardiologist."

She couldn't help but think of Walt's dad. Pushed the thought aside.

Three vials of blood, one urine sample, several blood pressure retakes later, Dr. Chin returned.

"We did a few tests but will send out the bulk of the blood work. We did find something." Dr. Chin tapped the chart in his hands and lifted an eyebrow.

A chill ran over her.

"Nothing bad. At least at this point," he offered.

She wasn't sure how to respond so she kept silent.

He sighed and finally finished his explanation. "I believe your high blood pressure is a temporary thing. Gestational hypertension isn't completely uncommon."

Her head went blank. "Gestational what?"

Dr. Chin met her gaze. "I need you to follow up with an obstetric doctor and not a cardiologist, Dakota. You're pregnant."

He kept talking, but she didn't hear him.

"But I'm on the pill."

"Which does have a fail rate. Plus you were taking Bactrim. There are plenty of Bactrim babies out there. The drug has been known to decrease the effectiveness of birth control. Says so right on the warning label."

She dropped her head in her hands.

Holy hell.

Chapter Fourteen

"You're running!" Mary stated the obvious.

"I need to get my head back on."

Dakota continued to move around Mary and pack two oversized bags and a carry-on. She told Mary about confronting Walt. Told her about the nosebleed and the three hours she spent in the ER. But that was all.

"It's still running. Who are you and what have you done with my friend?"

Dakota stopped packing long enough to catch her breath. Controlling her blood pressure until she could find the right doctor would be a combination of diet and stress relief. She'd already downloaded several books on high blood pressure in pregnancy. She'd deal with the blood pressure, and skim over the reason she was dealing with it for now.

She hadn't wrapped her head around a *bun in the oven*.

Damn clichés were running in her head like an old movie reel.

"Your strong, self-sufficient friend needs to get away. Walt's called twice since I left the ER." Dakota didn't even listen to his messages. She deleted them unheard.

"That's a good thing, isn't it?"

"He just wants to play hero. Probably feels guilty for my stress level." If he knew he'd impregnated her and *that* caused the blood pressure, his hero complex would soar. "I don't want a pity date. I don't want him."

"Bullshit on that. If you didn't want him or didn't care, you'd stay right here and tell him to blow."

Dakota blinked a few times, her lips a thin line. "I hate you sometimes." She twisted away, continued to pack.

"Because I'm right."

"Fine. Now be my friend and help me pack."

Mary started with her shoes, lifting two pairs at a time and packing the ones Dakota agreed to. "Where are you going anyway?"

"You have to promise not to tell Walt if he comes asking."

"I'll tell Walt he's a douche bag. He broke Dakota's number one rule."

Dakota laughed for the first time in what felt like a week. "'Don't be a douche bag.' Followed closely by 'don't be a fucking douche bag.'"

"Sensible or sexy?" Mary lifted two sets of black heels, one with a four-inch lift, the others with two.

"Sensible. I won't be hitting any clubs back home."

Mary dropped the shoes in the case and popped her head up. "You're going home?"

Dakota tucked the shoes in place, grabbed another pair. "My family's annoying, catty, snarky, but . . ."

"They're family. God, Dakota, you really love him."

Dakota snapped the case together and started to zip it up. Hearing her best friend, who accompanied her to conventions because she loved the idea of love as much as Dakota preached it, shook her. "Don't be ridiculous. I've known him for three months."

"There isn't a timeline for falling and you know it."

"I don't know what I am. I need to find out and I can't do that here where I see him in my bed, in my kitchen. Damn, I see now why people sell their houses after a divorce. The shadows a breakup leaves behind are dark."

The drive to LAX was full of instructions. "I set the timers on the lights to come off and on. I'll call you to remind you to change the times every so often. Put your garbage in front of my place once in a while so people don't realize I'm gone."

"You make it sound like you'll be gone for a long time."

The traffic rolling by distracted her. There were plenty of cars on the freeways at home, but nothing like this.

"Dakota?"

"Yeah?"

"I asked when you thought you'd be back?"

They turned into the departing terminal ramp.

"I-I don't know." She offered a humorous laugh. "Seven and a half months."

"You're kidding."

Mary snagged a spot against the curb and pulled in. They both moved behind the car and removed her luggage.

Dakota embraced her friend. "Thank you for keeping my secrets."

Mary pulled away, narrowed her eyes. "Not telling Walt where you are will be a pleasure. The jerk."

Dakota hugged her again and whispered in her ear, "I'm pregnant."

Mary sucked in a breath, drew away.

Lifting a finger to her lips, Dakota said, "Shh!"

"Oh, hon."

Car horns started to honk and airport security started walking their way. "Better go. Don't want a ticket."

Mary moved around the car. "I'm calling you tomorrow. We're going to talk about this."

Yeah, but Dakota could actually avoid that call from thousands of miles away.

Lost in her thoughts, Dakota stood at the curb until another car skidded into the spot.

She half expected to see Walt jumping from the town car. When a family of four emerged from the back with one toddler and another preteen, Dakota dragged her luggage behind her.

———

If Walt didn't calm down, *his* blood pressure was going to go ape-shit crazy or he'd crash his car from a lack of paying attention.

She hadn't answered her phone, didn't return his calls.

He couldn't blame her. He'd been an ass.

Although he wasn't sure what to do about the rampant emotions inside him, he knew that distance and time away from Dakota only made him feel worse.

If she wanted to ignore him, she'd have to do it with him on her doorstep.

She'd shown up at his place of work, he justified. So he'd just show up at hers.

It was past six and the wind was blowing in off the ocean, making the air chill as he pushed out of his car and jogged up the path to her front door. He ran both hands through his hair and rang the bell.

He rang it a second time and looked over the peekaboo window into the house. No movement. He knocked and called her name.

Nothing.

There were windows lighting up the garage, he moved to them and looked inside. Her car sat dormant.

So she wants to ignore me.

A light went on in the window above the garage.

He smiled, returned to the door.

After a quick rap, he leaned close. "I know you're home, Dakota. We need to talk."

Nothing.

"I'm not going to leave."

Still nothing.

"I fucked up."

When all he heard was silence, he leaned his forehead against the door.

"You sure as hell did."

He jumped and turned.

Mary.

"Can you talk to her?" he asked, motioning toward the door.

"Why should I talk when avoiding is so much more effective?" Mary tucked a long string of her wavy blonde hair behind her ear.

"What I need to say I need to say to Dakota."

Mary crossed her arms over her chest and grinned.

Giving up on her, he pounded on the door again. "Dakota?"

Mary started to laugh. "Where is my cell phone when I need it?"

He knocked again.

"She's not home, Walter."

"I saw a light go on."

Mary lowered her voice. "Automatic lighting."

Walt gave Mary his full attention.

"I dropped her off at the airport at noon."

He frowned and his heart dropped. *She's gone?* "Conference?"

"Wouldn't you like to know?"

"Her publisher?"

"Might be."

"Her agent?"

"Desi *is* demanding."

"Damn it, Mary."

Mary snarled. "Damn it, Walt."

He stepped close to Dakota's best friend. "High altitude and high blood pressure aren't a great combination."

The smirk on Mary's face fell.

"Sparks nosebleeds."

Mary throat contracted. "Why do you care? You dumped her."

"I didn't dump her."

"Ignored her. Same thing."

At that very moment, Walt hated that women were so open with each other.

"Tell me where she went."

Mary offered a full-throat laugh. "Give me one good reason."

He hesitated and lost his chance.

"Well, Walt, Chinese water torture won't bring forth where Dakota flew off to. You might as well go home." Mary turned to leave.

"She won't answer my calls."

"Smart woman. Talking to a douche bag is a waste of her time."

He jogged in front of Mary, stopped her in the middle of the residential street. The reality that he might not be able to contact Dakota left him breathless. Scared. Wait! Mary was a psychologist, or some such thing . . .

"I was scared."

She moved around him, kept walking. "Come back when you have more than that, Walt."

"Tell her I was here," he called out after her.

"And prolong her misery? I don't think so. I love her too much for that."

Mary walked through her front door and slammed it.

———•———

Dakota spent the entire flight coaxing her headache into submission, drinking milk—because somewhere in her head she thought that might help—and listening to piano drifts on her phone.

What she really thought would help was a whiskey . . . but she couldn't bring herself to ignore her pregnancy that far.

Lucky for her, the first-class seat beside her was empty and she didn't have to pretend happiness with pleasant conversation. She counted the silent miles that drifted between her and Walt and finally fell asleep somewhere over Texas.

The need to pee woke and annoyed her.

When she made her way back to her seat, she checked her phone. Luckily, the plane closed in on landing.

Even though she sat in first class, she didn't jump to leave the plane.

When she did, the pilot was watching her from the door to the cockpit with a crooked smile.

"Visiting family," she managed as an explanation before exiting the plane.

It was dark in Savannah, and she still had a drive to get home, which was closer to the coast. She obtained a rental car with an indefinite return date, loaded her luggage, and headed home.

Her parents didn't know she was coming. On the off chance they weren't home, she had her key. The same damn key she left on her ring when she went off to college.

The closer to home she got, the harder it was to hold back tears.

Familiar houses, and driveways, dotted the landscape. Beyond the houses, she could hear the sea. She loved the ocean. The waves.

The humidity of summer was passing and the night was chilling enough to know that fall was in the air. She had memories of holidays past and missed her people.

Since when did she become homesick? Damn hormones were getting the best of her.

The gateway was as it had always been. Same rock, same lights . . . same plants. Though the plants had grown and were barely tamed.

She moved into the circular drive and killed the engine.

Lights were on in the back of the house and the occasional flip of the television set flickered.

She stepped out of the car, stood between the open door and the seat, and looked around. The willows were starting to drop their summer growth and the air around her made her shiver. It wasn't exactly cold, but it wasn't California in late September. The air was scented with magnolia, fading jasmine, and salt air.

Home.

The light on the porch lit and the front door opened.

She caught her breath. Held it.

"Dakota?" Her mother's voice was soft, and full of Southern song.

Without words, Dakota moved from the car—tears running down her cheeks—and into her mother's arms.

Chapter Fifteen

Guest room appropriate artwork had long since replaced the teenage heartthrob posters. The closet no longer held her clothes, and the dresser was empty except for the bottom drawers where her mother stored extra towels.

The walls, however, were the same. The view from the back of the house and the lush landscape that only the South had to offer welcomed her home.

Dakota lingered in bed longer than she ever would have been allowed when she actually lived with her parents. She'd been a wreck when she walked into the house. Never in her life had tears been so close to the surface. Her mom had shuffled her into the house while telling Dennis, her dad, to gather her things.

Her mother handed her a tissue and put a kettle on for tea before offering to listen. Thankfully, her mother hadn't probed when Dakota shook her head.

If there was one thing she knew without any doubt, Elaine Laurens wouldn't last long without an explanation of Dakota's unexpected appearance.

Dakota looked across the room to the flowery wall clock. It was already after eight, which meant that half the town would already know of her visit. In the absence of truth, the wagging tongues would make up their own minds why she was there. Half of them would be right.

After a long shower and an extra twenty minutes of time in front of the mirror to repair the damage of too many nights of missed sleep, Dakota descended the stairs. Voices carried from the back of the house where the kitchen and den made up the great room.

"She didn't say a thing, Carol Ann."

Dakota slowed her steps and listened to her sister's response. "Well, that just isn't like her. Something awful must have happened. I'll bet it's a man."

"Of course it's a man. Remember when you packed up a bag and came home not four months after you and Dale were married? I didn't think you'd ever leave."

At least Dakota knew she wasn't alone in her need to flee home because of a guy.

She forced a smile and walked around the corner. Both her mother and sister promptly closed their lips and painted on fake smiles. Carol Ann jumped up from the kitchen stool and walked around the counter. "Oh, Dakota . . . you look positively awful."

Dakota accepted her sister's hug. "Thanks for the vote of confidence, sis."

Carol Ann was a mini version of their mother. They both had blonde hair that was groomed by the same beautician. Not a hair was out of place with the use of a half a can of spray. Elaine's hair was just above her shoulders. A cut she said had to happen on her fiftieth birthday "because long hair on old women isn't right." Carol Ann had her hair up in a controlled bun with enough of the edges surrounding her face so she didn't appear uptight. Her sister inherited her mother's blue eyes and thin lips. They all had the same nose and body shape. Except that Dakota didn't mind having a few extra pounds on her hips as opposed to her sister. Carol Ann had always been the thin sister, the bashful blonde with impeccable manners. Dakota on the other hand took her father's hair and dark eyes. She tanned easier than her sister, and always had an independence Carol Ann never managed.

They were opposites on many things, but they were sisters. Having grown up only a bathroom away, they shared many confidences that would go to the grave.

"Well, you do. Sit down, let me pour you some coffee."

The second after her sister shoved a cup of coffee under her nose, the two of them stared without words.

She sipped her coffee, waited for one of them to speak.

They didn't.

Dakota sat taller, circled her cup with her hands. "There's a guy."

"I knew it!" Carol Ann acted as if she'd won the big stuffed animal at the county fair.

Her mom watched her with a half smile.

"I thought we were doing great."

"So what happened?"

Dakota looked down at the black coffee and watched the ripples of movement from her hands shaking the cup. "I can't tell you. One day he just stopped calling."

"He didn't tell you why?" Carol Ann asked.

"In the beginning, no. Nothing. Only after I confronted him did he offer his crappy *we're moving too fast* excuse."

"That's rude. He should have flat-out told you his concerns instead of leaving you guessing. You're better off without a rude and inconsiderate man in your life."

Yeah, maybe.

Carol Ann moved closer and offered another hug. "We'll take your mind off Mr. Rude and have you smiling in no time."

"Thanks. I just need a little time to get my mind off of him."

"This is just the place, isn't it, Mama?"

Elaine kept a watchful eye on her as she moved around the kitchen. "What's family for if not to come home and sulk with?"

"I'm around during the holidays."

"Not last year," her mom reminded her.

"I was in Europe."

Elaine opened the massive refrigerator and pulled out eggs, orange juice, and bread. "You could have flown home."

"The airport was snowed in. No one went anywhere." Spending Christmas in a hotel wasn't ideal, but she and her fellow stranded travelers had made the most of it.

"Do you still like them scrambled?" Her mom was heating a pan and cracking eggs into a bowl.

"You don't have to do that, Mom."

"You're right, I don't. And after a few days you're no longer a guest, so enjoy my attention while you have it." Elaine winked over her shoulder.

"Scrambled is fine."

Carol Ann leaned over the counter. "So how long are you staying?"

That was the zillion-dollar question. "I don't really know."

"You don't have a return plane ticket?"

Dakota caught her mother glancing over her shoulder.

"I didn't buy one."

Her sister patted her hand. "Oh, darlin', you must have really loved this one."

It took three days for Dakota to leave the house. The driving need was the headache that had started in the middle of the night and didn't let go by noon the next day. The last thing she wanted was to have her blood pressure shoot up and end up back in the hospital. Explaining that to her parents wasn't how she wanted to tell them she was pregnant.

Her mother's weekly gossip session disguised as a bridge party took her mom away from the house.

"Dad?" She walked onto the back porch and caught him with his eyes closed.

"Hey, sugarplum." He patted the seat beside him.

She moved to his side and tucked into him. "I was just coming to tell you I'm going into town for a little while."

He patted her shoulder, didn't comment. "Are you getting your head back on?"

She grinned. "Little bit at a time."

"That's good. Seems your visit is without a lot of yelling this time 'round. Not that I want my daughter's heart broken, but you and your mom seem to be getting along."

"That's because she hasn't asked about my work."

He snorted. "Let's not remind her. I like the quiet."

"You haven't asked either." And her father used to be an echo of her mother's disdain in her career choice.

"That's because the doctor told me I needed to decrease my stress level. Bad for my heart."

Dakota pulled back. "What's wrong with your heart?"

"Nothing that shouldn't be for a man my age. Had to cut back on some of the pie, and fried cooking."

"Are you seeing a cardiologist?"

He narrowed his eyes. "What would you know about cardiologists?"

"I did go to college."

"I play poker with Dr. Olsen the last day of the month."

"Dr. Olsen is a general. Not a cardiologist. If you have any pain, high blood pressure, you need to see a specialist." Olsen had been the family doctor since Dakota was ten. The man had to be seventy by now.

"Don't worry your pretty head about my heart. Mine isn't all broken like yours. I'm fine."

Dakota massaged her forehead. "My heart isn't broken . . . fractured maybe, a little."

"Lot you know," her father huffed. "Broken and fractured are the same thing. Learned that when you broke your leg in the third grade."

"I cried when I couldn't have a black cast."

Dennis started laughing and Dakota felt a smile on her lips. "Your mama was livid. Made them wrap you in baby pink."

"Then I found a black marker and fixed that right up."

They were both laughing now.

"I thought she was going to break the other one when she saw what you'd done."

Dakota glanced at her watch, realized she was going to be late for her own doctor's appointment if she didn't end this trip down memory lane.

She stood and kissed the top of his head. "I needed that laugh. Thanks, Daddy."

"We're always here for you, sugarplum."

"I know. That's why I'm here."

———

"She isn't answering my calls or texts."

Walt stood on Mary's doorstep, hands on his hips.

"Welcome to the club. She's not saying much to me either, and for that, I blame you." Mary knew that Dakota had made it home and that she'd yet to tell her parents about the baby. Sadly, Mary managed this information through a few scattered text messages. Dakota had yet to answer her call. The last time Mary sent a text, she threatened to call her parents' home if she didn't make an attempt to speak with her.

Dakota had a few hours to call or she'd make good on her threat.

Walt looked like crap, and that made Mary smile. "Tell me she's OK."

"She's not in the hospital or anything." At least Mary thought that was the case. Surely Dakota would call her if something dramatic happened, right?

"Is she getting my messages?"

"I don't know."

He turned away, pounded a fist against the side of her garage. "Hey, respect the plaster, Doc."

He pulled his wallet from his back pocket, removed a card, and handed it to her. "All my numbers are there. Day or night."

"I'm not—"

"I'm worried about her, Mary. I care too much to let this go."

Mary released a sigh. He sure sounded sincere. The cell phone in her back pocket buzzed. She jumped when Dakota's face popped up on the screen. She answered. "Hey, Mom."

"Mom?" Dakota's voice spelled relief.

"Hold on," Mary told her.

Mary glared at Walt and hoped her face didn't give anything away. "I'll call if anything dramatic happens," she told him.

He shook his head and walked away.

Mary cradled the phone and slammed her front door. "Holy cow, girl. I've been worried sick."

"I know. I'm sorry. I'm in a really strange place right now."

"I know you are. Are you taking care of yourself?"

"I'm actually sitting outside a doctor's office with a list of instructions a mile long."

Mary flopped on her couch. "I can't believe you're pregnant."

"You and me both. I've been on the pill since the day I told Mom I needed Midol."

"So how did it happen?" Mary couldn't believe she asked such a stupid question.

Dakota must not have realized how crazy the question was. She launched right into answering it. "Get this, the antibiotic I was on last month countered the effect of the pill. Can you believe it? Walt's dad prescribed a pill that is going to make him a grandfather."

"Wow."

"Tell me about it. If I thought the man liked me at that point, I would swear he did it on purpose."

"You don't think—"

"Please, Mary. My life is nutty, but it's not a soap opera."

That was a relief. "Does anyone else know?"

"No. Not yet."

Mary squeezed her eyes shut. "I hate to ask this . . . but . . ."

"What?"

"Are you going to keep the baby?"

Dakota sighed. "I never really thought it was an option. I'm not a kid. I have money."

"You don't sound happy about it."

"I can't even think of what's happening as anything but a pregnancy. The thought of a baby scares the crap out of me."

The psychologist in her was on high alert. "We really need to work on this, Dakota."

"I-I know."

Mary glanced at her closed front door. "Are you going to tell Walt?"

"Eventually. He has a right to know."

"Good. Good. Has he, ah, has he called you?" Mary was fishing for information, hoped her friend was off her game and didn't catch on.

"He's left a dozen messages. I just delete them."

"Without listening to them?"

"I can't get over him if I hear his voice."

Well, that answered that. "He's been by your house twice."

Dakota was silent.

"I told him you left, but didn't tell him where."

"Oh."

"He seemed a little desperate."

"Probably feeling guilty."

"I don't know, Dakota, seemed to be more than that. I think he knows he screwed up."

"Yeah, well, he did. And if there is one thing all this taught me is that I need to depend on only one person. Me."

The fight in her friend's voice was better than the sorrow that had been there a second ago.

"You can depend on me, too."

"You know what I mean."

Mary did, but changed the subject. "If you're going to keep the baby, you'll need to tell your parents."

"The doctor seems to think I should hold off until the second trimester. My blood pressure is still high. We won't know if I'm at risk of staying that way throughout the pregnancy until next month."

"I didn't even think about that."

"A part of my mind is working. I need to stay here for a while. If this pregnancy is high risk, I'm going to need my family."

"I didn't think you got along with them."

"So far everything is fine. I'm sure all hell will break out when they realize why I'm really here. But they're family. They have to put up with me."

Mary laughed. "If they hurt more than they help, I'm here. Use and abuse me, babe."

"I appreciate that, Mary. More than you know. I'll do better with calling."

"You better."

"Love ya."

"Love you, too."

Walt had managed more sleep as a resident than he did since Dakota left. He'd pushed away from her because he worried about losing her. Where the hell was the logic in that? He ended up losing anyway and the pain cut deep.

Problem was, he didn't know where to look or what key words to tell Mary so she would reveal her whereabouts.

He slammed into his apartment and checked his messages. He sifted through his mail and noticed a shutoff notice for his water bill.

"Ah, crap."

He paid two bills before he thought of Monica. Maybe his friend knew something about his girlfriend. Women talked, after all.

She answered on the third ring.

"Hey, Walt. I hear you're being groomed for the exec position at Borderless."

"They've offered. I haven't accepted yet."

Monica was oblivious to the anxiety in his voice. "Really, why? I thought you'd jump."

"I'll probably take it. I just need to . . ." How was he going to play this? "Ah, damn, Monica. Dakota and I had a disagreement. She's not taking my calls."

"Really?"

"Yeah, I was wondering if you've heard from her. You two seem to be hitting it off."

"Can't say I have. Have you gone to her house?"

He ran a hand through his hair. "She left town. Mary won't say where."

Monica actually laughed. "Must have been one hell of a disagreement. Is that what you called it?"

He wanted to growl. "I was an ass, Monica. I've told Mary the same thing and she still doesn't budge."

"If Dakota left mad at you, Mary won't say a thing."

"That's what I thought." Frustration boiled his blood. "Thing is, right before she left she had a bout of high blood pressure that gave her a nosebleed that needed treatment to stop."

Monica sighed. "Is she OK?"

"I don't know. She won't take my calls."

"Chances are she won't take mine either. Tell you what, why don't you give me Mary's number. I'll see if Dakota's healthy."

For the first time in days, relief filled Walt's heart. "Thanks, Monica. I owe you."

Monica offered a little laugh. "You know, Walt, it does my heart good to hear you so flustered over a girl. I didn't think you had it in you."

"It's my fault we fought. I just want a chance to talk to her."

"I'll see what I can do."

Monica hung up laughing.

———

Mary was packing her briefcase with patient files for the few she had who needed to talk in the evenings when the phone rang.

"This is Mary," she answered, assuming a patient was calling.

"Uh, hi Mary. This is Monica Fairchild."

"Oh, hi Monica. How are you?" *And why are you calling me?*

"I'm good, thanks. How are you?"

Mary set her case down, noted the time. "Good. Running out the door at the second."

"Oh, sorry. This won't take long. I got a call from Walt—"

"Stop. I'm not going to tell anyone where she is."

"I would think not."

"Then why are you calling me?"

Monica paused. "I want to know if she's healthy? It's one thing to keep Walt wondering where she is, but to think she's sick somewhere is . . . cruel."

"Is that as cruel as, let's say . . . stopping any and all phone calls and brushing off your lover for no good reason?"

"He did that?" Monica asked.

"Communication went to zilch overnight."

"That doesn't sound like Walt. Why would he do that?"

Mary sat on the edge of her sofa, glanced at her watch. Two minutes and she'd have to cut this conversation off. "My guess is it has something to do with his late wife. Struggling with his growing feelings—"

"What? His late what?"

"Wife. You didn't know he was married before?"

Monica squealed her answer. "No! Are you serious?"

"I hate gossip. I thought you knew."

"I did not. Walt was married?"

"Yes." Lord, how much of his story should she tell? Then again, Monica was Walt's friend and calling for recon on Dakota. "Medical school, or sometime in there. She had colon cancer . . . no wait, pancreatic cancer. Sounded like he married her to keep her parents from hooking her up to a bunch of tubes or something."

"Oh, damn. I didn't know. No wonder he's stressed about Dakota's health."

"I'm sorry for his loss. I am. But Dakota needs someone who's going to stick around and not run off. Now more than ever."

Monica moaned. "She's sick, isn't she?"

"Not sick . . . just . . ." Oh, shit. "She'll be fine . . . I think." Only Mary wasn't so sure. Maybe the best thing for Dakota was to make up with Walt. Even if they decided to go their separate ways, she could put him out of her mind.

"That answer will make him crazy."

"That answer was for you, not him."

"Fine, that answer is making *me* crazy."

"I hate the position I'm in. I'd do anything for Dakota. I'm not sure Walt is the best thing for her right now," Mary said.

"He's a doctor. He can help with whatever she's going through. He's a damn good doctor, Mary."

"Yeah, but he kinda sucked as her boyfriend. And she needs the man who put her in this position to man up." Mary wanted to suck the words back in her mouth as soon as they spewed. "Forget I said that."

Mary knew Monica was a bright woman the night they met.

"You're kidding!"

"I've got to go."

"Mary, wait!"

They were both silent.

"Please tell me she's with someone who knows. This kind of secret, the kind that drives blood pressure high and makes women do irrational things, can have disastrous consequences. She needs to be watched."

"She's seeing a doctor."

"I'm talking about more than a monthly visit, Mary. Her blood pressure was high enough to cause a stroke."

"Don't tell me that. She said she's fine. Needed another month to make any decisions."

"Her hormones are crazy. Add a heartbreak and high blood pressure and who knows what she's dealing with. Was she acting herself when she left?"

Mary hated how sound Monica's words were. "No."

"Has she acted herself since she left?"

"No, damn it."

Monica released a long breath. "Listen. I get that you want to protect her. I do, too. We can play this a couple different ways. Either you or I can show up at her door and refuse to leave until we know she's OK . . ."

"Or?"

"We piss off our friend and tell Walt."

"No!"

"He's not *that* guy, Mary. He can't man up if he doesn't know what's going on. And he doesn't. If he did, he'd be camped out on your doorstep."

Mary's throat tightened. "She's my best friend, Monica. I can't betray her."

"And Walt saved my life once. I can't betray him."

"You're pissing me off, Monica."

She grumbled. "I stick a needle into everyone I'm trying to help. Piss them off, too. You have a lot of company."

"Damn."

"Listen. If you don't tell me, you're just going to delay the inevitable. Because you see, I'm going to hang up this phone and call my friend Katie. She knows this crazy awesome private investigator who can find anyone. My guess is we would only have to tap into Dakota's cell phone to find where she is."

"That's illegal."

"Medical emergency."

A string of unladylike words passed through Mary's lips.

"He has the right to know about the baby."

"She's going to tell him."

"It might be too late."

"I hate that you know more about this than I do."

Monica's voice was stern and cold. "Great, hate me. Where is she?"

"She's going to hate me."

"For a day . . . maybe a week. She'll get over it."

Mary's back teeth bit her tongue. "If I find out you've played me . . ."

"You can sue. I don't care. Dakota needs friends making rational decisions since she's not making them."

Mary hit her briefcase. "South Carolina. She went home like any pregnant, unwed woman would."

Chapter Sixteen

Walt noticed the number calling and pounced on the phone when it rang.

"Tell me you know something, Monica." During his days at work he could drag Dakota from his mind for short stints of time. Sitting at home, debating his life . . . that didn't happen.

Instead of saying anything, Monica sighed over the line. "I know where she is."

His entire body tingled. *Finally!* "Where?"

"I know why she fled."

The tingling cut short. "I told you I screwed up."

"It's not that, Walt. Though I think you must have messed up really bad. Her fleeing to get over you isn't the half of it."

He stared at the pen he'd broken, closed his eyes.

"I shouldn't be the one telling you where she is or why she's there. For the record, if I wasn't worried about her health I would follow the girl code and make you guess."

Her health? "You're killing me here, Monica. Is she dying?" He surged to his feet and started to pace. Could he do this a second time? *Not Dakota. Please, God, not Dakota.*

"No—"

"Her high blood pressure?"

"Is temporary."

He paused, a thought tickled his brain. He stopped pacing, grasped the back of his desk chair.

"Her high blood pressure is temporary, Walt. A few months down the road . . ."

"Oh, hell." Sudden onset high blood pressure, young woman of childbearing age . . . recent infection. "Bactrim. My dad put her on Bactrim." She hadn't been on it a week and he had . . . "I'm going to be a father."

Monica was silent.

And he'd walked away before Dakota could tell him. Did she know when she'd cornered him in the ER? He couldn't be sure, but even if she did, why would she have told him then? He swiveled his desk chair around and fell into it. "Where is she, Monica?"

"Home. She went to South Carolina."

His head started rearranging his schedule, plugging favors, switching others, thinking about a position with Borderless Doctors that would make this easier. "I need a flight."

"We can help with that, Walt. But before you pack a bag you need to know something else."

There's more?

"I'm listening."

"Dakota hasn't told anyone anything. She's with her family nursing a broken heart. The only reason I'm telling you about the baby is because of the possibility of preeclampsia. I don't think she understand the risks."

"Has she seen an OB?"

"According to Mary she has. Either the doctor wasn't clear, or Dakota downplayed her condition to Mary. I know she's an adult. I know she has money . . . but she's still a single pregnant woman. I've watched that happen in full living color. It's scary, it's lonely, and it's completely irrational at times."

His breathing came in short spurts. "Do you have an address?"

Monica came through. He would arrive on the East Coast just after midnight on yet another private jet. His favors to Monica and Trent were adding up fast. He would stay at the Savannah Morrison, which put him within spitting distance of Dakota. With a plan in motion, Walt paid his bills in advance for two months and closed his front door.

Thank God he didn't have live plants. They wouldn't survive.

He'd make this right.

All of it.

Dakota should have known the first day she wanted to join the world of the living she would wake up heaving. She'd escaped the nauseous part of pregnancy until the end of the second month. It hit fast and obnoxious the moment she opened her eyes. After tossing the nothing that was in her stomach, she crawled back into bed and buried her head only to be awakened by her sister an hour later.

Carol Ann bounced in the room, oblivious to Dakota's condition. "You can't mope around here another day. I won't hear of it."

"I'm not moping."

Carol Ann sat on the edge of the bed. "Then what would you call it?"

Puking?

She couldn't let on to her sister how she was feeling physically. Everyone would guess her condition in a nanosecond. She didn't need that. Not yet.

"Fine." Feeling green, and not at all ready to leave her bed, Dakota tossed off the covers and headed to the shower.

Carol Ann watched her with a smug look.

A shower, soda water, and a few dry crackers later, Dakota was ready to go. The weather had turned as much as it was going to in South Carolina. There was a slight nip in the air and a woman needed to shop. Or so the excuse was for getting together with some old high school friends while she was in town.

Louise was five foot nothing and still the tiny twig she'd always been. Then there was Sis. The three of them had always called her Sis even though her name was June. Maybe it was because Sis was an only child and always wanted sisters . . . or maybe she just hated her given name. Either way, they called her Sis and treated her thus.

"If it isn't the elusive Dakota Laurens." Louise opened her arms and placed a practiced smile on her lips.

"Hello Louise, long time."

"Not because I moved away."

Dakota would have laughed if she could do so without bringing up the crackers. Louise was destined to stay in their hometown until her parents died and left her their home. They all came from money . . . old Southern money that survived generations and wars. And it would be years before Louise lost her parents. Louise wasn't going anywhere.

"California is great, thanks for asking."

Louise offered a playful, but slightly hard slap to Dakota's forearm. "You tease. You look . . . good."

She looked like crap with makeup. She'd checked before leaving the house. Much as she tried to disguise her current level of pale and general yuckiness . . . it wasn't working. Physically she was feeling worse, not better, since coming home.

Dakota placed her Southern smile firmly in place and did what she'd always done. "You never were a good liar, Louise."

"I'm just trying to be polite."

Yes . . . now Dakota was reminded why she left the South.

Sis rushed in from the parking lot and stood outside their rendezvous spot at the mouth of the shopping strip. "Sorry I'm late. I couldn't get Junior down for his nap without a shot of whiskey."

Carol Ann gasped.

"For me, not him!" Sis was a little less polished than Louise and Carol Ann, married the high school bad boy to spite her parents, and seemed to be happy.

"Dakota!" They hugged. "You look tired."

Strange how refreshing honesty was. "There was a guy, he sucked, I'm here getting over him."

Sis's smile fell. "It's always a man. Half the time I want to shoot Billy and the other . . . well, you write all *those* novels. You know what I want to do."

Those novels. The reference to her day-in and day-out life reminded Dakota of why she'd left home. It had always been difficult to determine who truly supported her life, or if they smiled to her face only to talk behind her back. Carol Ann and Sis she could trust . . . Louise, not so much.

Sis wrapped a hand over Dakota's shoulders. "I missed you. When Carol Ann told me you were back in town I nearly ran to your house. Then I realized there must have been something really wrong for you to come home. I know how much you wanted out of here growing up. I figured you'd let us know when you were ready to play."

Dakota took in her sister, Louise, and Sis and grinned. "I'm ready. So long as no one asks about *him*. I'm not ready to talk about *him*." They referred to the guy who shall remain nameless, as *him*. *Him* was the man they all collectively hated on principle. If *himself* did bad by one of them, he did bad by all of them.

Sis wove her arm through Dakota's and offered a side hug. "Are we back to the *hims*? Who was the first *him*?"

Louise raised her hand. "That would be my Tommy."

"Of course," Dakota said. "Tommy became *him* when he did Daphne Mayson."

Louise dropped her fake smile. "That was a long time ago."

Dakota laughed. "You showed him by doing half the football team."

"I did not."

"That's right," Sis corrected. "You only did three of them . . . all within two months."

Why Louise had to scold them with a look at her age was yet another reason why Dakota left home. There were more Louises in her circle of friends than Sisses. "She's right."

"Doesn't matter. Tommy and I are very happy."

Dakota doubted that. Tommy had always been a player. Louise had served a purpose and was discarded. Then her football team debacle nearly ruined her reputation. Dakota always thought Sally was conceived on purpose. Tommy really didn't have much of a choice but to stand up and do the right thing. His parents . . . her parents . . . wouldn't have tolerated anything else. And since his parents held his trust fund, he wasn't going to disappoint them.

Carol Ann chimed in. "Kevin was the second *him*."

"Barely."

"Yeah, like for three seconds. Standing you up because he was grounded and not able to call you only made him a *him* for one night," Sis reminded them.

Carol Ann offered a smile. "Well, when Dakota is ready to tell us about *him*, we'll be here to listen."

Louise grinned. "That doesn't mean we won't pry."

"I would think you were ill if you didn't. Unlike you, I know how to keep my lips shut. My *him* shall remain nameless, faceless, and enemy number one."

Sis laughed. "Well c'mon. I never have time to shop so let's get to it."

Shopping actually involved some shopping . . . but it also involved manicures, pedicures, sometimes a trip to the salon or day spa. There was usually lunch included with mimosas, sangrias, or something equally sickeningly sweet that a *good Southern woman* could drink in the middle of the day and not be considered a lush. If one of them was on a mission to buy a new dress, then the four of them would concentrate on that one purchase and be happy with the outcome.

By the time the lunch portion of their day had passed, Dakota was feeling ten times better than when she woke that morning.

Sis pulled them all into a toddler clothing store for a special out-fit for Junior.

Dakota pasted on a smile and walked through racks of pink, yellow, green, and blue. Tiny sweaters, tiny jammies, socks so little they wouldn't serve as thumb warmers.

She ran the tips of her fingers over a mini white angora sweater that reminded her of the one she'd ruined.

"Dakota? Dakota?"

She forced a smile and glanced up.

Sis held a little dress jacket. "What do you think?"

"I think your husband would rather it be in leather."

The three of them laughed and Dakota's focus centered on the sweater once again.

I'm pregnant.

Without words, she swiveled around and left the store. She found a bench outside and sat. The cool slap of wind helped push her thoughts away.

One at a time, her friends found her.

"You're thinking about *him*, aren't you?" Louise asked.

Actually, she'd been thinking about what *him* left her. "I guess. And here I thought I was doing so well today."

Carol Ann draped an arm over her shoulders. "You've smiled more today than I've seen all week. It's perfectly normal to have a small setback."

"So long as it doesn't linger."

Sis jumped up, gathered her bag in her arms. "I know exactly what will cheer you up."

Please don't let it involved alcohol. As it was, she'd poured most of her mimosa into Carol Ann's glass when she wasn't looking. "It's a terrible idea when Sis has *just the thing*," Louise said.

Unaffected, Sis rolled her eyes and pulled Dakota to her feet. "C'mon. Follow me."

They walked around the far side of the shopping mall and over to the independent bookstore. "What are we doing here?"

Sis grinned, opened the door. "You'll see."

Dakota hovered in the doorway. The smell of leather and books met her nose and the quiet that always accompanied a bookstore or a library kept her from raising her voice. Her first love of books came from reading. She'd spent hours in bookstores like this one long before she wrote her first novel.

Dakota looked up when she heard Sis squealing like a teenager being asked out to prom. She hovered at the register and two sets of eyes swung Dakota's way. The woman at the cash register hustled around the counter and beelined to her side. "It *is* you. Sis promised to drag you in here one day. I'm such a fan."

"Thanks." Even though Dakota wasn't ready to face the public, she felt a genuine smile on her face. "Is this your bookstore?"

"It is. Been in business for three years. I'm not afraid to tell you, your books sell well here. Seems there are a lot of people who knew you when."

Dakota had a hard time imagining that. Polite society referred to her as the woman who wrote smut. Then again, they had the most hidden *Playboy* magazines, which she'd always found when she did the babysitting circuit.

Sis kept her Cheshire Cat grin.

"I did grow up here."

"Would you mind signing the books I have in stock? It won't take but a few minutes."

"Oh, well, I'm with my friends—"

"We don't mind . . . do we?" Carol Ann asked the others.

"Of course not," Sis chimed in.

Louise painted on a smile. "Don't be silly."

Within seconds, Lillianna, the owner of the store, found a table, tucked it and Dakota beside a row of romance novels, and started bringing over armloads of books.

"You absolutely must sign one of each for me. My personal collection. I can't wait for the next Surrender book to come out. That Mathew is one hot man."

While Lillianna sat beside Dakota asking about her characters, about her books, Sis and Carol Ann were on their cell phones. Before Dakota could say *the South will rise again* a group of people were walking into the bookstore and heading straight toward her.

After Dakota signed her fifth book, she waved Sis over to the table. "You planned this."

Sis smiled at the woman in line and said, "Last-minute change in plans. I knew this would cheer you up."

In the twenty minutes they'd been in the bookstore, Dakota hadn't thought of Walt, or her pregnancy. Here she was simply Dakota Laurens, Romance Author, with a few books sold under her belt.

Lillianna brought out a box, inside was a stockpile of Dakota's titles.

OK, maybe more like a few million copies.

Sis started to walk away and Dakota tugged her into the chair Lillianna had vacated to man the cash register.

"Not sure where you're headed, Sis. I need an assistant and I dub you."

Sis rubbed her hands together and wiggled her ass in the chair. "Tell me what to do."

Dakota greeted the next lady in line with a smile and showed Sis where to open each book up to and scoot them over to make sure they kept the line moving. When someone asked to take a picture, Dakota brushed on more makeup and lipstick and painted on a smile.

A few familiar faces dotted the line, making Dakota smile a little larger and add a snarky line to the signature page.

"It's not for me, of course." A woman in her late sixties informed her.

"Naturally. Who shall I make it out to?"

The woman stared, blinked, and stared some more.

"No worries, I'll just sign it and skip the name."

"Bless your heart."

Oh, the South. Who couldn't fall a little in love with the slow living and facade of polite tolerance of blatant lies?

"Dakota!"

"Missy?"

Missy had been a close friend up until their junior year. Dakota couldn't remember what catfight made them pull apart, but they had one. Missy held the hand of a toddler in pink and an infant in blue bundled in a car seat. "Look at you."

"When I heard you were here, I had to run. No time for a sitter."

"It's OK."

Dakota looked at the pigtailed toddler, her curly brown hair and big blue eyes were the spitting image of her mother. How often had their own mothers placed them in similar dresses? Dakota smiled. "And what's your name?"

"Dana."

Dakota offered a wink and glanced at the car seat and the tiny bundle within. She swallowed, felt her smile slide. "And what's your brother's name?"

"His name is Nicholas. He cries a lot."

"Is that right?" Nicholas had a tuft of light brown hair on his head, his eyes the same color of blue as his sister's.

Dakota found herself reaching for the baby and stopped herself. "Your children are beautiful."

"Thank you, darlin'. They are my pride. Do you have pictures of yours?"

Dakota dropped a hand in her lap. "I'm . . . I don't . . ."

Sis kicked in. "Dakota doesn't have children, Missy."

"Oh." Missy's sympathy was palpable. "I'm so sorry. I'm sure the right man will come around." Then, as if she knew she was bringing up a harsh subject, she launched into a diversion. "Just look at you. I've followed your books ever since Carol Ann brought yours to our book club."

They caught up for a short time until Sis helped Missy along so the next woman in line could have her book signed.

Dakota agreed they should see each other before she left, but knew they probably would meet up again when Dana was in high school.

When the line died down, Dakota signed the last of Lillianna's supply and made her excuses.

Carol Ann and Sis walked with her out into the parking lot. "That was fun."

Carol Ann wove her arm through Dakota's. "I'm proud of you. My famous sister."

"I'm not famous."

Sis laughed. "No one was asking for our autographs."

"Write a hot book and that might change," Dakota said.

Once Carol Ann and Dakota were on their way home, Dakota asked, "What happen to Louise?"

"Oh, she left after Missy showed up. Those two—"

"That's right. I remember now. I hope they grow out of the *gossip and scandal* stage of life."

Carol Ann rolled her eyes. "Seems the older they get the more covert they become, but honestly, they spread more bunk than they did in school."

"That's too bad." Gossip was the favorite pastime of a small town. Although their town wasn't all that short on people, everyone knew everyone. "Is Tommy still a two-timing prick?"

Carol Ann gasped. "Dakota!"

"Well . . . is he?"

It took her sister half a breath to confirm. "I've heard rumors."

"I thought so. I'd rather be single than put up with that."

"Is that what happen between you and *him*?"

She shook her head. "No. It wasn't like that." For the first time since she'd arrived in South Carolina, Dakota opened up to her sister. "I thought everything was great. We would juggle our schedules, meet at each other's place . . . then he just stopped calling."

"No argument?"

"Nothing. I liked him, Carol Ann. I hurt when he left."

"I'm sure there have been others that hurt."

"Not like *him*." Walt left a gaping hole and a whole lot more.

Dakota's childhood home screamed the South much like Walt's echoed the West. The tall columns and plantation shutters were just the start of his observations. The two-story house sat on at least an acre of manicured land. The front porch had a bench with plush pillows. He would bet money the back of the house would have rocking chairs and a vast expanse of grass where children would run around at Easter collecting colorful eggs.

Walt couldn't help but wonder if his child would have memories of his or her grandparents' home.

He walked past the rental car in the circular drive. Was she inside? Would she answer the door?

Walt looked at the bench with renewed interest. He might be sleeping on that bench. A light rain started to fall as he jogged up the steps, when he laid his knuckles to the back of the door and stood back.

Walt didn't imagine Dakota's mother would have blonde hair and a touch of Botox around her eyes. Mrs. Laurens stood tall, a questioning smile on her face. "Can I help you?" Her Southern accent reminded him of Dakota.

"Mrs. Laurens?"

She hesitated. "Do I know you?"

"No, ma'am. I'm Walt."

Not one muscle on her face so much as twitched.

"I'm here to see Dakota."

If Walt wasn't looking, he would have missed the rise and fall of Mrs. Laurens's smile. "I'm not sure she wants to see you."

"Can you tell her I'm here?"

"She's not home."

Walt wasn't sure he believed her. Was he really going to be told he couldn't see her?

"Elaine? Who's here?" a voice called from the rear of the house.

Elaine stepped back, started to close the door. "You really should go. I'll tell Dakota you were here when she returns."

Walt placed his foot in front of the door. "Please, Mrs. Laurens. I've flown twenty-five hundred miles just to talk to her. I know she's upset. It's important that I see her."

Elaine glared at his foot as if she'd never seen one in a door and then turned that glare on him.

"Elaine?" A man Walt could only assume was Dakota's father moved behind Mrs. Laurens and looked directly his way. "Who are you?"

"This is the man our Dakota fled from when she returned home."

Could she sound more dramatic? Probably.

Mr. Laurens opened the door wider. "Dakota's not here."

So that is true. "Then I'll wait." Walt removed his foot, stepped back.

"We don't know when she'll return."

He wasn't sure if Mr. Laurens was more receptive to his presence than his wife or not.

Walt shrugged. "Doesn't matter." He glanced at the bench. "I'll just sit here if you don't mind."

"I most certainly *do* mind," Elaine said. "What will the neighbors say?"

Mr. Laurens opened the door wide. "Seems we have a choice, let the man inside, or have a scene that will be relived repeatedly over the next decade."

Walt smiled and detoured into the house. He extended a hand the moment he stepped inside. "Thank you. I'm Walter Eddy."

Mr. Laurens shook with strength. "Dennis Laurens, my wife, Elaine."

Elaine closed the door behind them.

"Well, Mr. Eddy . . . you've breached the walls. But when our daughter returns, if she wants you to leave, you must respect her request, is that clear?" Who knew Dakota's mom would be so fiercely protective?

"Yes, ma'am. I just need to talk to her."

Elaine started to walk away. "If I know our Dakota, one conversation will not fix what drove her here."

Mr. Laurens shrugged. "She always was our stubborn one. Hard to sway her when she has her mind on something."

Stubborn or not, Dakota would just have to get used to him. Now that he'd found her, he wasn't going anywhere.

Chapter Seventeen

Walt realized two things during the time he waited for Dakota to return. First, from his name to his profession, Mr. and Mrs. Laurens knew nothing about him. Second, talking to strangers and doing his best to avoid revealing anything personal was impossible.

"So, Mr. Eddy, what is it you do for a living?" Mr. Laurens asked.

"Dakota hasn't told you?"

Pursed lips and scowl intact, Mrs. Laurens offered a half a smile, half a scowl that might prove to be a lethal weapon in this country. "You don't have a job." It wasn't a question.

"I'm employed, Mrs. Laurens."

They both turned . . . said nothing.

"I'm a doctor."

Mrs. Laurens turned away with a huff. "If you're going to lie, at least make it believable."

Walt glanced at his frame. He wore jeans . . . a short-sleeved shirt. He hadn't shaved, which probably threw Dakota's parents off. He hadn't slept much in the days since he'd last seen Dakota.

"We drink sweet tea in the South." Mrs. Laurens set a glass of iced tea in front of him, and turned away.

"Thank you." He took a sip, did his best not to show the effect of the sugar as it hit his palate. "Refreshing."

A snort from across the table came from Mr. Laurens.

"Have you ever been to South Carolina, Mr. Eddy?"

"No. This is my first time."

"First time? You plan on returning?"

Walt held his tongue, then said, "If I can convince your daughter to give me a second chance, then yes."

Mr. Laurens swept him with his eyes. "While I find it admirable that you've managed to fly here to see our Dakota, I certainly hope it's not to disappoint her twice."

"That's not my plan."

Mrs. Laurens huffed, turned on her heel, and moved into the kitchen.

Walt ran a tired hand through his hair.

Mr. Laurens laughed. As in actually laughed and Walt looked at him through spread fingers.

He heard the front door open and jumped to his feet.

Mrs. Laurens walked in front of him, lifted an index finger in warning that kept Walt from moving.

He gave her two seconds and then rounded the corner.

His gaze started low . . . she wore flat shoes, slacks, and a soft sweater that reminded him of the blood-soaked one from the ER. Her hair was caught halfway up in a clip, her cheeks pale . . . beautiful. Her eyes found his and she sucked a large breath into her nose.

"Is that *him*?" he heard the woman with her ask.

Then Dakota turned to bolt.

Walt ran, jumped over a cat that came from nowhere, and pushed in front her.

"Dakota, please."

Her hand was already on the door, her breath came fast. "Go home, Walt."

"I can't. Not until you listen to me."

"I-I'm . . ."

He took a chance, placed both hands on the sides of her face so she wouldn't look anywhere but at him. "I messed up, Dakota."

She wasn't pushing away so Walt continued to pour out his thoughts. "There was this woman . . ."

He heard someone in the room gasp.

"She looked exactly like you. She was thrown from a car. I tried. We all tried but she didn't make it. I can't tell you how often I look into the eyes of a patient or a family member and cringe. I kept asking myself if I could handle if it was you? Could I handle losing you?"

Dakota started to tremble. "So you let go?"

"I couldn't function, Dakota. I thought if maybe we slowed down I could deal better."

She shook out of his hold. "You stopped retuning my calls. That isn't slowing down."

Behind Dakota, he noticed her parents watching, the woman she came in with stood close by.

"I screwed up."

She met his eyes. "You more than screwed up, Doc."

"I know."

She placed a hand to her head, reminding him instantly of her high blood pressure . . . of their baby. "You should sit down."

Her hand fell, her eyes snapped to his. "Don't . . ." she started one sentence, stopped, and glared. "You should leave." She moved to the door, grasped it.

He shoved a hand in front of it.

"I think you should leave, Mr. Eddy." Mr. Laurens moved to his daughter's side.

Walt never played the doctor card . . . but he did now. "That's Dr. Eddy, Mr. Laurens." Walt placed his gaze squarely on Dakota. "I care too much for your daughter to walk away when she's *this* upset." He let his eyes move from hers down her frame to her flat stomach.

Her hand fell from the door, her face went stone white. "Who told you?"

Her family lurked over her. Who knew eye-shooting daggers could wound him? "Talk to me, Dakota . . . without an audience."

———

Even though the door to the study was closed, Dakota knew someone, somewhere, was listening. She forced several deep breaths and slowed her speeding pulse. Walt found her, and he knew.

He knows.

Walt knows about the pregnancy.

"What did you tell Mary to have her betray me? I'm sure she didn't do it willingly."

Walt stood behind her. She moved to the floor-to-ceiling window and stared out. "Mary refused to tell me anything."

"Then how—"

"I asked Monica to talk with Mary."

That made a little more sense, but still, Mary wouldn't have volunteered much without need.

"When Monica realized that you were—"

"Shh!" She uncrossed her arms and turned. "No one knows and I don't want them to . . . not yet."

"What about me, Dakota? Were you going to tell me?" Was that hurt in his voice?

"Of course. When I was ready." She moved from the window, sat in her mother's overstuffed chair, and kicked off her shoes. "I wasn't ready . . . not that it matters now."

Walt crossed the room and sat on the edge of the coffee table, close to her. "How are you feeling? Have you seen a doctor?" He spoke softly.

"Let's see . . . outside of having my heart stepped on by a man I thought I had a connection with, and finding out I have a temporary medical condition that is going to stay with me for eighteen years . . . I'm just fine. And yes, of course I've seen a doctor."

"We do have a connection, Dakota." He moved his hand to rest on her knee and she pulled away. "I was an idiot. I should have told you what I was feeling."

"Did you realize this before or after you knew I was . . ." Her words drifted off.

"Before. Didn't you listen to my messages?"

"No." Telling him his voice drove her to tears gave him too much power. "I didn't want to hear you then any more than I do now."

"Give me a chance to make it up to you."

"I don't know if I can."

"Don't say that."

"Why? It's the truth. I have a lot to figure out and only six and a half months to do it. Juggling a boyfriend isn't on my *to do* list."

He had something to say, she saw it in the way he held himself back. "I'm not letting you do this alone."

"I don't see as you have a choice in the matter, Walt. The last thing I need is to wonder if you're beside me for your baby or for me."

Walt grasped both her hands in his. "Look at me, Dakota."

She did, found the warm depth of his eyes and wanted to sink into them.

"If you lost the baby tomorrow I will still be here the next day. If there wasn't a baby at all, I'd still be here trying to convince you to come back to me."

"I'm not the one who walked away, Walt."

He kissed her knuckles, held her hands close to his lips. "I'll just have to work harder to get you back."

She shook her head. "Doc—"

"Shh. I'm not giving you up. You can try and convince yourself this is a bad idea, but you're doing that solo." He motioned between the two of them. "This . . . this is going to work."

"Walt—" How could he be so caring now? Where was the man who ignored her calls?

He leaned forward, placed a finger over her lips. "I know you're not ready to tell anyone . . . about . . ." he paused, looked at her stomach.

"Not yet."

His thumb traced her jaw, his voice softened. "How are you feeling . . . physically?"

This was the doctor asking. "I was sick this morning for the first time. I'm watching my blood pressure with one of those wrist monitors. The headaches remind me to lay down."

"Nosebleeds?"

"Not since California."

He smiled, dropped his hand into her lap. "Did the doctor want you on medication?"

She shook her head. "No. I'm going back next week. He said the high blood pressure could stop nearly as quickly as it started. Is that true?"

He seemed pleased she asked. "Second trimester will tell us what to look forward to."

"Me . . . it will tell me."

"Us, Dakota. I told you . . . I'm not going anywhere. The sooner you come to terms with that the better."

She wanted to believe him but the saying *fool me once, shame on you, fool me twice, shame on me* kept running in her head. "Well, you'll have to excuse my skepticism."

"You have every reason to doubt me. But outside of the last month I'm a pretty stand-up guy." He lifted one corner of his mouth.

Was she really going to give him a chance?

Do I really want to do this alone?

She met his gaze, lifted her chin. "Prove it."

He smiled now, squeezed her hands. "I plan on it." He removed a card from his back pocket. "I'm staying at The Morrison in Savannah."

She palmed the card.

"I didn't know there was a Savannah in South Carolina."

"Georgia doesn't own the name."

He tried to get her to smile, she didn't. "Call anytime."

A nod was the only commitment she offered him.

"I won't press today, but I'm very concerned that no one in this house knows about your condition," he said.

"I don't think you need to worry about that for long. Morning sickness isn't something I can hide."

"I can be here when you tell them."

"Maybe. I don't know." She needed some time alone, time to digest the changes that had happened with Walt's presence. "I need to think."

Walt stood, bringing her with him. As Dakota expected, her family stood outside the door, their expectant faces eager for any information.

"I'm going to see Walt out."

Walt attempted a smile. "It was a pleasure to meet you."

Dakota's mom huffed.

Carol Ann stared, mouth open.

Her dad narrowed his eyes.

When they reached the front door, Walt turned and kissed her temple. "I'll see you tomorrow," he said before walking away.

She watched him from the open door until he pulled out of the drive.

Someone behind her cleared their throat, and she turned around. Elaine now had her arms crossed firmly over her chest and Carol Ann wouldn't look at her.

The tick in her father's left eye was the only thing on him moving.

"You're pregnant . . . aren't you?" Her mother practically spit the question out.

She was an adult, damn it, and yet shame spread over her in a dark wave.

Elaine shook her head, uncrossed her arms. "I knew it. I told you,

Dennis. I knew you ran here for more than a broken heart. Oh, Dakota, how could you?"

"Like I planned it, Mom."

"Oh, Dakota. No wonder you've been so sad." At least Carol Ann understood.

"Isn't it enough that you write that smut? Now you're going to be . . . going to be . . ." Dakota wondered when her mother was going to come out and play. She'd been too quiet and too calm for days.

"Is he the father?" her dad asked.

"Of course."

"What are we going to tell our friends?"

"Mom!" Carol Ann yelled. "This isn't about you and your friends."

"I'm not a teenager, Mom."

"What's the difference? You're not married."

Dakota pushed her feet forward and walked past her parents into the kitchen. "You don't have to be married to have a baby."

Her mother followed behind, her quick steps a testament to her anger. "Don't take that tone with me. I knew this would happen. The longer you went without getting married, the more I just knew one day you'd show up here pregnant."

Carol Ann turned away. "I'll call Kevin, tell him to feed the boys."

Dakota waved her off. "No. Go home, Carol Ann. I appreciate your support but I can take care of myself."

"Is he really a doctor?"

"Yes, Dad. He works in emergency medicine."

"Then he should have done a better job of protecting you."

"I'm half the blame. It does take two."

"I can't deal with this right now." Elaine started toward the stairs. Before long, they heard the door to the master bedroom slam shut.

"Well, that was fun." Dakota set her hands on each side of the sink, looked out the window.

"Where is this doctor of yours staying?" her dad asked.

"The Morrison . . . why?"

Dennis grabbed his car keys from the hook by the garage door.

"Daddy?"

He turned on her. "That's right. I'm your daddy. Now you just stay put and let me do what I have to do."

She moved in front of her father. "We're adults."

He kissed the top of her head, smiled. "Which is why I'm leaving the shotgun at home."

Chapter Eighteen

Somewhere between the Laurens residence and the hotel Walt found his smile. *She didn't kick me out.* He wasn't sure if her hesitation to tell him to screw off with a set of instructions paving the way was because of hormones or fright. But she didn't tell him to blow. Now all he had to do was help her find her smile and remind her of how good they were together.

Prove it.

If that wasn't her to a *T.*

He'd prove it . . . *Operation Prove It* was about to begin.

He had no freaking idea how he was going to prove it, but he'd figure it out or call every woman he knew to find out what he needed to do to *prove it.*

Brenda could help . . . and Monica.

He'd even bug the crap out of Mary even though she wasn't on Team Walt. Still, he'd do what he had to.

He pulled the rental car to the valet and handed them the keys. "Good evening, Dr. Eddy."

He hesitated, looked at the twentysomething that was about to drive his car away. "How is it you know my name?"

The kid smiled. "It's my business to know who you are, Dr. Eddy."

The kid winked, jumped in the car, and drove away. Dumbfounded, Walt walked into the lobby, started toward the elevators, and detoured to the concierge desk.

"Good evening, Dr. Eddy. What can I do for you?"

The woman at the desk must have been in her fifties and Walt was positive he hadn't yet spoken with her. He glanced at the name tag. "Alice?"

"Yes, Doctor?"

He thought about asking how she knew who he was and shook his head. "This is my first trip to South Carolina."

"Is it?" Her smile was huge. "How are you liking our part of the country?"

"I haven't seen much of it, actually. I was hoping you might be able to help me."

Alice placed a hand on her chest and sighed. "That's why I'm here. Tell me what you have in mind."

"I'm going to be here for a while. There's a girl . . ."

"That's sweet."

He grinned. Women just ate this stuff up. "I need to know where the best restaurants are . . . the best places to spend the day. Getaways."

"We're talking romance?"

More than you know. "Exactly."

"You have come to the right woman. I will have a complete list of the right . . . and maybe more importantly the wrong things to avoid in our city to woo your girl. Would you like a suggestion for tonight?"

He shook his head. "I'm fine for tonight."

"I will have this ready for the morning." She was already clicking into her computer.

"Alice?"

"Yes, Doctor?"

"How is it you knew my name?"

A Southern practiced smile met her lips. "It's my business to know who you are, Dr. Eddy."

His next stop was the reception desk. "Good evening, Dr. Eddy."

He paused, shook off the strange *Twilight Zone* moment, and went on with business. "I'm going to be here for a while. If a reservation for my room is in place, please let me know so I can move. I know the Morrisons have cleared me to stay, but I really wouldn't feel right about bumping anyone."

"That's so kind of you, Doctor. I'll be sure and make a note. We do have more than one penthouse suite so there shouldn't be a problem."

"But if there is . . ."

"I'll be sure and let you know."

"Thank you," he said. "And another thing. Can I make sure that Dakota Laurens or any of her family are let up to my room without delay . . . day or night."

"Absolutely."

Operation Prove It was now under way.

Walt rode the elevator to the top floor more confident than when he'd left.

He stepped out and swiped his key in his door. He stopped cold. "I'm going to be a dad."

Laughter . . . he heard someone laughing and he wondered for a nanosecond if he was listening to his own thoughts.

"Not the greeting I expected."

"Trent!" Walt walked into the suite and closed the door. He shook his friend's hand, took the man-hug that followed. "I'm going to be a dad."

Trent kept laughing. "So I hear."

A tiny person was going to look up to him, depend on him to be there day, night, school, first dates . . .

The room spun.

His ass hit the side of a chair before he slid into it.

"I'm going to be a dad."

Laughter filled his ears. "You have no idea how much I wish my cell phone was on and recording this. Yes, Walt, you're going to be a dad."

Walt saw his friend but didn't really see him. "That's huge."

"As life's moments go. Yeah . . . huge."

Walt shook off his moment of insanity and smiled. "Not that I'm not happy you're here, but . . . why are you here?"

"My wife thought you might need a friend."

He might not ever stop smiling. "Monica's an amazing person. You're one lucky bastard, Trent."

"Damn right." Trent walked to the en suite kitchen, opened the fridge. "What's your poison, *Dad*?"

"Whiskey," he said with a laugh.

"I take it your conversation with Dakota went well."

Walt rubbed his hands over his face. "How much did Monica tell you?"

Trent laughed. "We're married. I doubt she skipped any details. Had she talked with Dakota, I couldn't say that . . . but that isn't the case."

"Dakota didn't kick me out. We came to some agreement."

"That's a start."

"I don't think her parents liked me."

Trent paused while he opened tiny bottles of liquor. "You impregnated their daughter. Probably puts you on their shit list."

"They don't know she's pregnant."

Trent poured drinks and brought them to the sofa. "Then all they have to go on is, she left LA because of you. Still won't make you top on their list."

Walt accepted the drink and let the liquid hit the back of his throat. "I'm going to have to change that."

"Change what?"

"The fact her parents don't like me. They're going to like me a hell of a lot less when they find out she's pregnant. What parent wants their baby pregnant and unwed?" He wasn't even a dad yet and Walt felt a severe case of hives coming on.

They sat in silence for a small space of time, then Trent asked, "Can I ask you something personal?"

"Seems we passed that."

Trent sipped his drink. "Do you love her?"

Walt sucked in a breath. "How the hell do you know when you're in love?"

"Aw, hell. I remember that. You don't know . . . you think of her all the time, wonder what she's doing. Something inside you dies a little when you know she's not going to take your call. I think the biggest deciding factor is just in knowing that moving on without her is so fucking dark you can't see straight."

"Damn." Trent just described the last week of his life. "I'm in."

Trent placed a finger under Walt's glass, helped him tip it to his lips. "Drink up, buddy . . . and welcome to the club."

Walt finished his drink only to have Trent fill it again.

The bell at the door rang and Trent answered it laughing.

———

"Mr. Laurens." Walt jumped, felt his heart in his chest.

The man's glare said everything.

"Come in."

Trent offered a sympathetic look over Mr. Laurens's head. Walt introduced the two of them, watched a friendly handshake. "I think I'll give you some privacy," Trent said. "You can find me downstairs in the lounge when you're done."

Walt offered a thanks and turned to face Dakota's father once they were alone. "Can I offer you a drink?"

"I'm not staying long." Mr. Laurens walked deeper into the room, looked around. "It certainly appears as if you have the means to take care of my daughter."

"I do."

"Yet you didn't."

Walt opened his mouth only to have Dakota's father stop him with a look.

"I have only been the father of daughters, Walt. When they were teenagers and first started dating, I put the fear of God into the boys picking them up. Elaine and I always worried. As I've grown older and my daughters have turned into women, the worry of one of them coming home unwed and pregnant didn't enter my mind. Until tonight."

Walt studied his shoes. "I will take care of your daughter."

"You're off to a booming start there."

"I know you're upset—"

"I passed upset before I got in my car. I'm pissed and I'm here to hear what you plan on doing. Raising children is a full-time job for two parents. Two!"

"I know that. I'm not going anywhere, Mr. Laurens. I am going to be here for your daughter and our child. I'm not sure what else you want me to say."

Mr. Laurens stepped closer, lowered his voice. "What do you think I want to hear? What will *you* say to the man, who is not your son-in-law, when you learn your child is pregnant?"

Even though Dakota's father was several inches shorter than him, Walt was happy the man wasn't in his twenties.

"Marriage doesn't scare me . . . but divorce does. I won't do that to your daughter or our child. So when we decide it's time for that step, you'll be one of the first to know."

Mr. Laurens rocked back on his heels, shoved his hands in his pockets. "I think I'll take that drink now."

"Not now, Mom." Morning sickness and her mother. Dakota groaned as she sat on the edge of the bathtub, her head in her hands.

What was I thinking running home?

Three seconds of compassion filled her mother's face before she crossed to the sink and ran cold water over a washcloth. "Guess who I just got off the phone with?"

"I couldn't tell you." *And right now I don't care.*

"Mrs. Pinkerton."

"Louise's mother?"

"Yes, Louise. Why did you feel it necessary to tell your friends about your indiscretion before you bothered to tell us?"

My indiscretion? She let her mother's words go . . . for the moment, and focused on the question. "I didn't. Other than Walt and Mary, you guys are the only ones who know."

Elaine squeezed water out of the washcloth and held it over Dakota's forehead. The cool relief helped pull her focus off her grumbling stomach. "Teri Pinkerton knows plenty. And if I know her mouth, half of this town will know by noon."

Dakota regarded her mother with one eye, the other remained under the cloth in silent darkness. "Louise knows nothing."

"Then she guessed. Oh, Dakota, this is awful."

She hid her other eye, found a quiet place in her brain, and tried like hell to stay there.

"I'm not the first pregnant twenty-eight-year-old, Mom."

"You're not married!"

"Thanks for your support."

"I'm serious, Dakota. I live in this town, shop here, go to church with Teri Pinkerton and all her friends."

"Why do you care a rat's ass what those women think?"

Elaine started to pace the small footprint of the bathroom.

"Holding your head high is hard when people are talking behind your back."

The motion in her stomach let up and drove Dakota from the bathroom. She found her bed and pulled the covers over her crossed legs. Once again, she'd lied to herself, made herself believe her mom would be less judgmental about the situation simply because she wasn't a kid. How short-sighted of her. "Let it go."

"I can't. You know that's not the way it works here. What am I going to tell my friends when they start calling?"

"Tell them I'm a slut." *Just go away.*

"Dakota!"

"Tell them whatever you want." Dakota met her mom's eyes. "And while you're telling them whatever you want them to hear, make sure to keep your chin high. Just make sure it's a chin and not a nose, Mom. Every woman in your friendship pool has had sex and I sincerely doubt they hit their marital bed a virgin."

With pinched lips, Elaine shot daggers with her eyes. "I didn't think you were a virgin. But you could have been more careful."

The room shot up ten degrees, or maybe it was her. Dakota tossed off the covers. "I think I overestimated you. I didn't expect you to be happy about this, but I didn't see you chastising me like I'm sixteen."

"What *did* you expect? Did you think your father and I would be pleased to find you entering parenthood single and struggling?"

"I'm not struggling," Dakota all but yelled.

"You ran home."

"My mistake. I thought I could turn to my parents to offer some emotional support. I'm supposed to lower my stress level, have people around me." She pushed off the bed, moved back into the bathroom, and mumbled, "I should have just hired a live-in nurse."

Elaine blinked several times, followed her. "Live-in nurse? What are you talking about? Pregnancy doesn't require professional care day and night."

"My blood pressure is too high."

"A lot of people have high blood pressure."

"This isn't about me, it's about being pregnant."

Elaine tilted her head. "I don't understand."

"When Walt comes over today, I'll have him tell you all about it. Right now I need to empty my already empty stomach." She pushed her mom out of the bathroom with an index finger and closed the door.

Chapter Nineteen

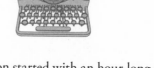

Walt's road to redemption started with an hour-long discussion with Dakota's parents about her health. He'd shown up at just after ten to hear that Dakota wasn't up to seeing him yet, but would he please explain her medical condition to her parents.

By the time he and Dakota left the Laurens' home, Elaine and Dennis were a little less worried about how their daughter's pregnancy looked to the outside world, and more concerned with their daughter's health.

Walt tucked her into the passenger seat and cracked the window to fill the car with crisp air.

"Morning sickness bites."

"I'm sorry. I can be here every morning to hold your hair back."

Dakota looked at him like he was crazy. "Yuck."

"I mean it."

"I don't think so."

He glanced over his sunglasses, smiled. "Offer still stands."

Walt handed her the key card sitting in the cup holder of the car. "Here. My room key."

"Why?"

"Because I want you to have it. I want you to think of me whenever you need anything."

"Do I get a drawer to put my things in your room, too?" she teased.

"You can have the other side of the bed . . . or the other room. Then you'll have to put up with me holding your hair back. Fair warning."

She played with the key but hadn't handed it back. Walt considered that progress. "Does this have anything to do with your talk with my dad last night?"

"No. Not directly."

"Not directly?"

He shrugged, followed the guidance of the navigation of the rental car. "I don't want your parents to hate me. I'd like them to know I mean it when I say I'm going to be here for you and our baby. More importantly, I want *you* to know I'm here."

"I want to believe that."

He hated that she didn't.

"What did my dad say last night? Wait . . . on second thought, I don't want to know."

Walt smiled. "Your dad is just looking out for you."

"Unlike my mom. Lord, what was I thinking? You'd think I was thirteen and you were a high school dropout strung out on crack."

Walt turned down a narrow road, following the signs to the first stop on his path to redemption. "You don't think she's just worried about you?"

"My mother worries about herself. About her image." Dakota blew out a breath. "I know she cares but she has a hell of a time showing it. I really hope I won't be like her."

Cars pulled alongside a dirt lot with families jumping from them. Walt pulled into a spot, turned off the engine.

"In some ways I think we are destined to be a little like our parents. I think the parts we despise the most will be the ones we know to avoid. I won't manipulate our child to go into medicine, and you won't chastise them for writing."

The warmth he'd grown used to seeing in her eyes started to return. "Is it that easy? We just make a decision not to parent a certain way and that's it?"

"I don't know if it will be easy, but yeah . . . why not? What possible profession can our child pick that we wouldn't approve of?"

Dakota blinked a few times. "Porn star."

He laughed. "Prostitution and all things sex trade we both agree to deter Junior from. We can add hired assassin or thief to the list."

"Those things are easy to agree on. What if our child wanted to be a nude model or a nun?"

Walt lost his smile. "Neither one of us are Catholic. Chances are that won't happen."

"Still could. Could we handle our son or daughter posing in the buff for others to get off on?"

For the first time in his adult life, Walt thought about the skin magazines he'd picked up in his youth and actually considered that all those women had parents. "I don't know how I'd handle that."

Dakota stared out the window. "I don't know either. What if we suck at being parents and we screw up our kid?"

He reached over and took her hand.

Her eyes met his. "We're going to be awesome . . . and we're going to screw up. I've delivered a few babies in my line of work and none of them come with an instruction manual."

The smile on her face warmed him.

"I'm scared, Walt."

"Thank God I'm not alone in that. We're going to make mistakes, Dakota. As long as we love and take care of our child, they're going to be amazing."

"I hope you're right." She looked out the window again, stared up at the big orange balloon. "So, why are we in front of a pumpkin patch?"

"Halloween is only two weeks away. Pumpkin carving and costumes are important."

He pushed out of the car and moved around as she opened the door. Walt took her hand after closing the door and didn't let it go.

———

The pumpkin patch was also a petting zoo, a farmers' market, and a craft zone for little kids. Walt pulled her to the first patch of jumbo pumpkins and spread his arms wide. "Now this is a pumpkin."

"It would take a chainsaw to carve it."

"But think of all the seeds."

The thought of salty food made her mouth water. "I do like roasted pumpkin seeds."

"Just salt, nothing fancy."

She licked her lips. "Do you know how to roast them?"

"No. Do you?"

"I'm sure we can figure it out." Dakota moved to a patch of smaller pumpkins. "Tall and skinny or short and fat?"

Walt rubbed his chin. "One of each." He walked over to a parking lot of red wagons and pulled one next to the pumpkins. They debated size and girth, moved to the extra-large monster pumpkins, and hauled one into the mix. They rolled the wagon around, found mini pumpkins and gourds that Dakota knew her mother would like to have as an addition to her fall centerpiece.

Dakota found a bale of straw to perch on while Walt stood in line at a popcorn stand.

A little girl, probably around three years old, walked behind her mother with a pumpkin half her size in her arms. Dad was close by, clicking pictures.

A tiny towhead with chubby cheeks sat in overalls as he tried to stack the small pumpkins on each other. He didn't look old enough to walk without help.

Walt sat beside her, offered the hot popcorn, and followed her gaze.

After a couple of bites, she interrupted their silence. "Did you ever think about having kids?"

"I didn't dwell on it. I figured it would happen someday." He grabbed a handful of popcorn and asked, "What about you?"

"When I was younger, I worried about having a baby. I'd stress about not taking the pill within an hour of the one the day before. I'd worry about a condom breaking. Then somewhere after twenty-five I just didn't think about it. The more my mother asked when I was going to settle down, get married, and have babies, the less appealing the idea became."

"Yet you write about happy endings as a day job."

The chubby-cheeked toddler pulled himself up onto a pumpkin only to fall back on his padded butt. He pursed his lips and tried again.

"The ultimate contradiction. I believe in happily-ever-after. But I know it's a lot harder to find than how I fictionalize it in a book." Dakota looked up to see Walt watching the little boy with a smile.

A shadow passed over his face.

"Finding the right person to spend forever with shouldn't be easy. When things come easily, the relationship ends up being temporary."

"Like with you and Vivian?"

He didn't stop watching the child when he reached for her hand. "I knew Viv was going to die. I loved her, but not the way a husband should love his wife. We both knew that if she made it out alive, a divorce was inevitable." He turned and smiled at her. "There's a difference between forever and not quite forever. Viv was the latter. When I get married again, it will be forever."

Walt let go of her hand long enough to place his on the side of her face. She leaned in and accepted his lips on hers. Her fractured heart started to fuse together as his tender kiss reminded her how complete she felt in his arms. How empty she was when he wasn't there.

When Walt pulled away, he ran a thumb under her right eye to collect the moisture that dropped from her lashes.

The sound of clapping broke their brief moment. When she turned, she saw the toddler standing on his own with arms opened wide while Mom crouched and encouraged her child to walk. The baby took one step, giggled, and plopped on his butt.

Dakota leaned her head on Walt's shoulder and watched the entire routine repeat. "We're going to have a baby."

His arm pulled her close. "We are."

"Wow." She thought of the graphics all over the social media platforms where she chatted with her readers, her fans. The phrase *shit just got real* came to mind. Dakota realized her free hand rested on her stomach. "Wow."

Walt smiled and pulled her to her feet. "C'mon, Baby Mama. We need to get you two fed. Do you feel like eating?"

The popcorn sat on the ground, the bag tipped over. "I'm famished. Such a crazy cycle. Sick all morning, hungry all day."

"Pickles and ice cream?" he joked.

She cringed. "No, but I have a crazy desire for cotton candy."

Walt shook his head. "Now I *know* you're knocked up. My Dakota eating refined sugar. I'll be watching for the zombie apocalypse next."

As they walked to the checkout, Dakota wondered if maybe things could work out.

"We need a tiny bit of advice," Walt told the helpful cook that had the misfortune of answering the phone.

"Anything to be of service, Dr. Eddy."

Of course! He hid a smile behind his hand and turned away from Dakota, who was checking out the suite. "We're roasting pumpkin seeds and would like to avoid burning down the hotel."

"I'd be happy to—"

"No, no! We need to figure this out. Just a small tutorial would be great. Roasting means top heat at a high temperature, right?"

"Doctor Eddy . . ." The man's voice hitched up a notch . . . or three. "I have at least twenty minutes before the dinner orders start coming en masse. Might I come up to your suite and help you?"

Walt placed a hand over the phone to ask Dakota. "The cook is asking to come up and help. What do you think?"

"I think you're going to make the Morrisons rue the day they met you."

He laughed, turned back to the phone. "We're college educated and catch on fast. Won't take but ten minutes of your time."

"I'll be right up."

Walt placed the phone back on the receiver and moved to Dakota's side. Her hands were stuck in the inner muck of her small, fat pumpkin. "This will never last until Halloween."

"Practice," Walt insisted. "When was the last time you carved a pumpkin?"

"I think I was twelve."

He picked up a scalpel, one he kept in his kit that he traveled with, and etched into his soon-to-be masterpiece. "We need practice if we're going to show Junior that his parents aren't completely lame."

"And if we have a girl?"

It didn't go unnoticed that Dakota stopped talking about a *pregnancy* and started referring to their child as a person. "I like the name JD. Junior Dakota works for me."

Dakota stopped midpull of stringy pumpkin crap. "No Junior. I will have to veto anything Junior."

Walt did his best to appear offended. "You don't like Walter Junior the Forth?"

Dakota had the good sense to offer a blank stare.

A grin started at his chin . . . he felt it inching up to his lips, his cheeks, and finally his eyes.

"I'll get you for that."

He couldn't stop the laugh that erupted. "I can't tell you how many times I was cornered in the hall because of my name. I thank God every day my grandfather wasn't named Horance."

Dakota raised two orange hands and laughed. "Never tempt worse." She paused, looked at him. "Not that I don't like your name. I do."

"My name is Walter. How many men under the age of seventy do you know who have that name?"

Dakota plopped an especially large portion of muck onto the counter and started squeezing the seeds from the guts. "Walter Cronkite?"

"I'm pretty sure he's dead."

"What about the old Vice President?"

"Over eighty-five . . . or is he gone, too?"

"I couldn't tell you." She drew in a quick breath and stopped mid–seed expunge, then dropped her hands.

"What?"

With a quick shake of the head she said, "Never mind."

"C'mon . . . who?"

"No one."

He moved around her and picked up the slime that sat on the counter and lifted a handful in her direction. "I hear this stains."

"Walt!"

"Who?" he moved closer.

She backed away, dripping pumpkin guts over the marble counter. "Disney. Walt Disney. But he's dead, too."

He backed away even though he would have liked to see Dakota covered in pumpkin guts. "So we agree . . . no Walter Junior if it's a boy."

"Fine!"

"Good."

"Strong names are a must for a boy. For the record, I think Walt is a strong name."

He laughed . . . couldn't help it.

"I'm not kidding."

When he looked again she actually appeared as if she meant it. He stepped into her personal space, covered her mucky hands with his, and kissed her. "Thank you," he said when he pulled away.

The doorbell of the suite rang. Only the penthouse would actually have a bell, he thought as he wiped his hands on a dish towel and met the chef.

"Dr. Eddy." The chef moved into the room with purpose, met with the kitchen, and removed ingredients from the small case he brought with him. "Miss?"

"Laurens," Dakota answered, her hands still in the muck.

"Perfect pumpkin seeds," he began and took the lot of seeds they'd managed to extract from the pumpkins and moved to the sink. "Start with a good cleaning, a little butter, and a dash of salt."

"I like a lot of salt," Dakota told him.

Walt shook his head. "A dash. Sodium increases blood pressure."

Dakota scowled.

The chef went through the motions of showing them the finer parts of roasting pumpkin seeds before taking the bits of carved pumpkin and placing them on another sheet and covering it with cinnamon, sugar, and spices Walt would never be able to identify. "Twenty minutes in the oven after the other is finished and you will understand why this time of year makes for the most amazing flavor."

After offering dinner suggestions, the chef blew out nearly as quickly as he flew in.

The seeds were roasting in the oven and Dakota was sitting at the kitchen table drawing on the pumpkin she deemed hers.

"I've been wondering," she started.

He found his own perch and started in on the design swimming in his head. "Wondering what?"

"How is it," she pushed the knife into the side of her pumpkin and stood for what he assumed was leverage, "you are sitting here with me in South Carolina and not saving lives in California?"

"Didn't I tell you?"

"Tell me what?"

He waited until the knife was deep into the skin of the pumpkin before he said, "I quit."

The knife went still and she stopped to stare. "You what?"

"I . . . quit. I needed to find you . . . needed—"

Dakota dropped her hands, her jaw hit the floor. "How can you quit? You're a doctor. Doctors can't quit."

"Fine, I took a leave of absence with no guarantee I'll return." He kept carving, knowing she was going to ask a dozen questions.

"Quitting your job to find me is crazy. Not to mention irresponsible."

"Not when my dream job was offered to me only a couple of weeks ago."

Her face softened. "Dream job?"

"With Borderless Doctors. It's managerial a lot of the year with periods of instruction and of course long stints in the field during disasters. True emergency medicine."

"That's fantastic. When do you start?"

"I have to tell them I'm taking the job first."

"Wait. You quit your job in Pomona and haven't taken the next gig yet? Isn't that risky? What if they hire someone else?" She'd pulled the knife from her pumpkin and was waving it in the air.

Walt risked losing a finger as he placed his hand over hers. "I was given until November to make my decision."

"Oh, that's . . . that's good."

She went back to carving and mumbled, "Where is this new job?"

"Europe," he said, deadpan.

"Oh . . ."

She was trying so hard to hide her emotions Walt almost felt guilty for leading her on. "Or Florida . . . or Canada."

"I don't understand."

He grinned. "I can do the job from anywhere, including South Carolina or California. The conferences and training take place all over the place, a lot in Florida. And the disasters . . . well, those can't be determined until Mother Nature strikes."

She pulled her knife and started waving again. "You did that on purpose."

"Did what?"

"Had me wondering if you were leaving again."

His smile faded. "Never. I'm not going anywhere. If you decided you wanted to move back here, then I'll find an apartment. If you want to go back to California, then I'll book a flight." It was his turn to wave a knife. "You're not raising our child alone. I promise you that."

The sparkle in her eye said she believed him.

Chapter Twenty

"My mother is seething. The gossip mill hasn't stopped chattering since I arrived and now that Walt is at the house daily to pick me up and drop me off, there is little doubt that the rumors are true."

Mary managed a snort over the phone. "The rumors are true. Why doesn't your mother just tell everyone to go to hell?"

"I've been trying to get her to say those exact words for weeks." Dakota sat on the back porch, a blanket tucked around her legs and a sweater warding off the fall chill. Not that it was overly cold, but fall had officially arrived. The fresh air helped clear away some of the morning sickness that started to ease earlier in the day.

"How long are you going to stay there anyway?"

Dakota had been asking herself the same question. "I have another appointment with the OB doc next week. If the blood pressure is still down I'll probably come home."

"And if the blood pressure is still high?"

Dakota sighed. "I'll probably stay. Even if everything continues to go well with Walt and I, he could be called away at any time. At some point he needs to start his new job and that will mean two weeks in Florida."

"How are *things* with you two?"

"Good."

"Just good?" Mary asked. "Not crazy wonderful, amazing? Just good?"

Dakota snuggled into her blanket, a silly smile spread on her face. She thought of how she'd fallen asleep in Walt's lap the night before while they watched TV on her parents' couch. She'd drooled all over his pants, and woke only when he attempted to slide out from under her sometime after one in the morning. He'd kissed her softly, quietly, and told her he'd see her in the morning. "He's almost always here, or taking me somewhere where we can talk and plan. It isn't like when we were first dating. This is deeper somehow. Comfortable, dependable. You know what's really crazy?"

"What's that?"

"We're not sleeping together."

Mary paused. "Really?"

"We're not. I'm not even sure why we're not. He holds me, kisses me, and there are times I think he wants to rip off my clothes and take me against the wall, but then he pulls away."

"Have you talked about it?"

"No. You don't think he's turned off by the pregnancy, do you?"

"Is that what you think?" Mary asked.

Gotta love Mary, the psychologist in her was always close at hand.

"He doesn't act turned off. I'm sure the opposite is true. It's not easy hiding an erection when I'm lying in his lap."

Mary laughed. "That's true. What is it then?"

"I don't know. Maybe he's afraid he'll hurt me or the baby."

"He's a doctor. That can't be it. He knows better."

"I don't know what it is. But I'm not going to push it. The pace is right somehow. It's like we're dating for the first time, getting to know each other better than we did before we started getting naked."

"Getting to know each other after the bun is securely in the oven. Sounds ass-backwards to me."

"Backwards but right somehow. I think he has something to prove to me and to himself."

"He does have to prove something to you. Like he's not going anywhere. Like he's going to put a ring on your finger and make an honest woman of you."

Dakota laughed. "Oh, God, not you, too."

"You know you're thinking about marriage."

"I know I'm thinking about next week, next month. I'm thinking about if I'm carrying a boy or a girl."

"And if Walt is going to make you Mrs. Walt."

"Marriage isn't on the table, Mary. I don't even want to hear about forever unless . . ."

"Unless what?"

"Unless he loves me . . . unless his world wouldn't be the same without me, and not just our child. Getting married to make me an honest woman is not going to happen."

"It sounds like you're thinking again. Thinking and not just running."

"I didn't like where I was when I left California. Coming here, even dealing with my mom's dirty looks, has done some good. I even started writing again. You know it's bad when I'm not writing."

"If you stop writing because of Walt, your fans are going to hate him."

"I just needed to find my happy place again, Mary. I think I've done that."

"Good. Get a clean bill of health, stay in your happy place, and get your ass home. I miss my BFF."

Dakota laughed and had a sudden need to pee. "It is *all* about you."

"It certainly is. Love you, Dakota. Don't get too used to that Southern air again."

"What?" she said with more accent than when she left California. "You don't like my Southern drawl?"

"If you put a rocking chair on your porch, I'm buying a male blow-up sex doll and sitting him there."

There she was laughing again. "I've gotta go. You're making me need to pee."

"That would be Junior jumping on your bladder, not me. But go. I have a client in twenty minutes. Take care."

Dakota hung up and all but ran to the bathroom.

———•———

Maybe something in the water was slowing him down, or maybe it was in the air. Walt knew it had to be contagious because everywhere he looked people moved a little slower, waved a little easier, and smiled a little longer.

Walt joined Dakota for her OB appointment. He hovered when the nurse took her blood pressure, frowned when he heard she'd lost weight.

When Dr. Fisher came into the room, Dakota introduced him and insisted her doctor tell Walt everything about her condition.

"I'm encouraged to believe you'll avoid preeclampsia throughout your pregnancy. Your pressure is down significantly since your last visit."

Dakota smiled, Walt hesitated. "The drop could be temporary."

"True, Doctor, but Dakota has been monitoring herself and it seems there's been a steady decline. You should both keep an eye on her pressure, but in my experience, pressure that drops this early is a good sign that everything will even out."

Dakota captured his hand. "I'm feeling much better."

Walt offered a grin, but knew he'd worry even if Dakota didn't.

Dr. Fisher pushed a portable ultrasound machine closer to the table Dakota sat on. "Are you ready to see your baby?" he asked.

Walt's heart jumped in his chest.

He found his smile and looked into Dakota's dark eyes.

Dakota leaned back on the table and lifted the gown enough to expose her flat stomach. It was hard to imagine their child growing inside her . . . then Dr. Fisher turned up the volume and placed the wand on her skin, Walt immediately heard the fast heartbeat of their baby.

"Do you hear that, Dakota?"

"A heartbeat?"

"Rapid." For good measure, Walt pressed two fingers to the pulse point on Dakota's wrist, felt her heartbeat at somewhere around seventy beats per minute. "The baby's heart beats much faster than yours."

"Oh my God."

She had tears in her eyes. Walt felt his own swelling.

The images on the ultrasound were minimal. Dr. Fisher pointed out a heart, a head . . .

He was going to be a dad.

He couldn't stop smiling.

When Walt finally tore himself away from her side and made his way back to the hotel, he spent much of the night filling out the paperwork that accompanied his new job. He logged on to his bank site and paid a couple of bills . . . early. Progress, he thought.

Now he sat beside Dakota, dressed in costumes she insisted on, and driving to a Halloween party.

"Tell me again why we're dressed like this?"

Dakota was smiling. She wore the equivalent of a Catholic schoolgirl uniform. A plaid skirt that stopped above her knees, boots that left only a gap of three inches around her knees peeking through. She had on a white blouse unbuttoned enough to show the creamy white of her breasts, breasts that had grown when she had yet to show any real sign of pregnancy. Thanks to the morning sickness, she'd lost a few pounds, something the doctor wanted to see change if she in fact returned in a month. Even if she didn't, her reports would fly home with her, figuratively speaking, and her doctor in California would be harping on her to gain weight.

"Because everyone will be asking, so there's no reason to hide anything."

Dakota had slicked back Walt's hair with gel, placed a plain white T-shirt two sizes too small on his shoulders, and rolled up a fake pack of cigarettes in his sleeve. Dakota had the shirt made just for him . . . on the back it said *Dr. Baby Daddy*. He'd laughed when he'd seen it. He didn't tout his title often, but he thought it might prove to be the right move on this night.

"If you say so."

"They're my people. I know what makes them tick. Louise hasn't said two words to me since she started spreading the news. If she or Missy think I'm hiding at home, they forgot who I am."

"You don't have to prove anything to anyone, hon."

Dakota offered a smile. "I'm doing this for me. When I first got here a part of me was embarrassed, insecure . . . not anymore." She covered her abdomen with the palm of her hand and smiled. "We're going to be parents. We might not have planned it, but we're doing it on our terms. No societal restrictions saying we're doing it wrong."

Walt lifted her hand to his lips, kissed the back of it. "Save that speech for my parents."

She cringed. "One set of chaos at a time. Tonight is about the harvest festival and Halloween party. I have it on good authority there will be cotton candy. Have I told you how much I need cotton candy in my veins?"

"A time or two, yes. I almost called Mary to have her make a trip to a theme park back home just to bag some up."

Dakota cringed. "Hot cotton candy. I need *hot* cotton candy."

"And hot cotton candy you will have. I'm taking pictures and blackmail isn't beneath me."

Dakota's smile lit the car. "I don't care. Just give me gobs of that shit."

"Says the woman who won't eat a doughnut when she's not pregnant."

She lifted one eyebrow. "Doughnuts . . . hot doughnuts."

Walt rolled his eyes. "Oh, Lord."

Dakota licked her lips.

"Remind me to check your blood sugar when we get back home."

Costume-wearing kids, adults, and pets filled the harvest festival. Dakota pulled him from the car and headed straight to the cotton candy vendor. "You sure you don't want to toss a dart into a balloon first?" he asked.

"If I don't get some cotton candy there might be dart tossing, but it won't be at any balloons."

Walt pulled her close, kissed her head, and moved up in line.

When it was their turn, he told the kid wearing plastic hair-dye gloves and a cap to keep rolling the tube in the flaky sugar. When he looked like he was about to pull the tube away, Walt kept rolling his hand around, indicating he wanted more. Only when the swab of cotton candy reached giant-pumpkin proportion did Walt toss the kid ten bucks and walk away.

The pink of Dakota's tongue snaked a wad of sugar and she moaned . . . a moan he had wanted to hear since they'd started this pregnant dating dance. "It's *that* good?" he asked.

She moaned again and his body tightened, everywhere. "You have no idea."

"No, I don't," he mumbled.

A sparkle in her eye met his and she delivered a smile that matched her sexy voice. She pinched off a piece of cotton candy and brought it to his lips. The sweetness hit his tongue with a jolt of something sinful. Before she moved away, he caught the tip of her finger in his teeth for one brief second. Her eyes flashed as she removed her fingers from his mouth and licked them clean.

Walt groaned. "You're killing me."

"Good," she told him. "Maybe I can convince you to have me for a sleepover."

"You don't have to convince me."

She continued to eat the cotton candy, the entire picture of her wearing a provocative schoolgirl outfit, high color on her cheeks, and red lipstick worked perfectly with the kid candy on a stick.

Her body brushed his and she lifted her lips to his ear. "This platonic crap is for teens."

Walt pulled her body close to his, felt the skin at the small of her back. "Makes it better when we get back there."

"Promises, promises."

"I never renege on a promise," he told her. He kissed her then, sealing his promise with a taste. Just as Dakota softened in his embrace, the sound of someone clearing their throat pulled them apart.

Dakota recovered first, twisting her head in the direction of the interruption. "Sis!"

"I thought that was you."

The woman Dakota called Sis was dressed as a pirate, the man at her side copied the costume complete with a patch over his eye. Walt stood back while Dakota hugged her friend. "You guys look great. Hi, Billy." Dakota moved her hug to the man.

"So do you. Perfectly Dakota."

Dakota laughed and flipped her hair. "Sis, Billy, this is Walt."

Walt shook Billy's hand while Dakota offered the CliffsNotes version of their relationship. "And before you ask . . . yes, I am, and yes, he is."

Walt turned so they could see the back of his shirt.

"Perfectly Dakota," Sis said a second time.

"And who is this?" Walt asked at the toddler peeking behind his father's leg.

"That's Junior, say hi Billy."

Billy Junior managed a wave but didn't detach from his parent.

"You sure have grown fast," Dakota said.

"They do that," Sis told her. "We were on our way to the carnival booths. Junior wants Daddy to win the big gator."

"Congratulations," Billy managed when the women moved ahead of them.

"Thanks," Walt said.

Little Bo Peep and a man dressed as a deck of cards followed them with their eyes as they walked by.

"Dakota always did have a way of twisting heads."

"Did you go to school with her?"

Billy lifted his son up onto his shoulders. "Yes and no. She and Sis have always been friends. I only knew her through my wife. Sis tells me you were on the girl's shit list when Dakota first got here."

"The list only got longer once her parents realized we were having a baby."

"Can't blame them there." Billy pulled the patch up from his eye and nodded to a passing couple. "So when are you two getting married?"

Walt knew those questions were only just beginning. "We haven't discussed it."

"Are you guys moving here?"

"Couldn't tell ya."

Billy laughed. "Man, Sis is gonna be ticked."

Walt sidestepped a running Little Red Riding Hood. "Why's that?"

"Because she's going to quiz me on this conversation and I have nothin' to tell her."

Walt grinned.

Dakota had burned through the cotton candy before they managed one round of dart tossing.

Sis had skills with the ping-pong balls in floating cups, where Walt showed off his free throw with a basketball. The giant gator didn't happen, but Junior dragged around a smaller one with a toothy smile. As dusk turned into night, many of the kids started making their way home with grandparents or friends. Having stuck together most of the night, Dakota and Walt drove Billy and Sis to the adult party, which was under way across town.

There was already a busy crowd with loud music spilling from the bar.

"We haven't had an adult night out in forever," Sis said as they all climbed out of the car.

Billy snorted. "Says the woman who will be calling her mama within an hour to make sure Junior isn't crying."

Sis hugged her husband. "You're just as bad."

Walt stepped back to hold Dakota's hand as they walked inside together. "Guess we have that to look forward to."

"Diapers, sleepless nights. Yeah, I've been getting all kinds of details."

"The easy stuff. I'm thinking of ear infections and stitched-up foreheads."

Dakota cringed. "My details are better than yours. Let's live in my head for a while." Ahead of them, Sis and Billy jogged up the steps of the massive wraparound porch where the party had oozed out.

"So they really named their child Billy Junior?"

"Yep. Happens a lot around here."

"Do they realize he's going to be called BJ at some point?"

Dakota laughed. "See why Junior is off-limits? No undesirable nicknames. Ever."

"Glad we're on the same page."

———

The costumes were brilliant. Dakota congratulated herself. She forced an awkward *yes, I'm pregnant and single moment* into a *let it go* moment with a simple shirt. Carol Ann and Kevin showed up, excusing their absence at the carnival because Tanner was sick.

Seemed everyone wanted to talk about the trials of parenthood. Or maybe Dakota was hyperaware of the information.

"Are you guys going to be here through the holidays?" Carol Ann asked.

Dakota met Walt's gaze. "I don't think so."

Walt winked. They hadn't discussed where they should settle, or what the next step was. Now that she was in her second trimester and her body seemed to be adjusting better, it was time to plan the next six months.

Carol Ann offered a pout. "I was hoping you'd move home."

Dakota looked around the room. "There are more places out there, Carol Ann. You know I'm not one for small-town politics and gossip. Do you know how many people have come up to me asking if I was Elaine's pregnant daughter?"

"I'll bet Mom loves that."

"It's eating her up. I'd make her suck it up if I needed her to." Dakota patted Walt's hand that rested on her thigh. "I think I'm going to be OK." The way Walt was looking at her assured her she would be.

Her bladder had been knocking for the past quarter hour, and she stood to find the ladies' room. "I'll find the bathroom," she told Walt. "Can you order me a club soda, skip the vodka."

"Sounds good."

"Want me to come with you?" Carol Ann asked.

"Nawh, why don't you interrogate Walt. He hasn't had nearly enough of that tonight."

Walt rolled his eyes. "Way to throw me under the bus, hon."

She leaned over, kissed him. "It's OK, Baby Daddy. You can handle it."

He slapped her ass as she walked away. "Careful," she said over her shoulder. "I might like that."

"Dakota!" Carol Ann scolded with a laugh.

The line into the bathroom was ten minutes long and filled with a couple of familiar faces. After repeating the mantra of the night, *yes, I am*, and *no, I'm not married*, Dakota wiggled through the throng of women.

On her way out of the restroom, she found herself blocked by a familiar face. "Tommy."

Louise's husband stood toe-to-toe with her, nearly eye level with her heels. His eyes slid down her body and stopped on the way back up at her breasts. "Well, if it isn't Dakota Laurens."

Dakota might wanna take notes on how it felt to be violated with a look, and not in a good way.

"Hello Tommy."

"Mmm, mmm. You don't look all preggers." He moved a little too close and Dakota stepped back.

"How is your *wife*? Haven't seen her since I first came back." The *gossip girl* had seen her, spread the news, and disappeared.

Tommy waved a hand, his glassy eyes indicated the amount he'd had to drink. "She's around here somewhere. You always were damn sexy, Dakota."

"You're married, Tommy."

"And you're not." He had the nerve to reach out and run his hand over her arm before grasping it in a tight hold.

She pulled away, had to put some muscle in it to dislodge his fingers.

"You always were a prick. I see nothing has changed."

He offered a grin. "Feisty. Nothing like a girl with a little fight in her."

"Touch me again, and you'll see just how much fight I have in me."

He reached for her a second time only to have his hand gripped by someone standing behind her.

Walt pushed her aside.

The people standing around them grew quiet and stood back. "The lady said to back off."

"Who the fuck are you?"

"I'm the man who is going to wipe that smile off your face if you don't walk away."

Tommy stood taller, looked around, and pulled his arm from Walt's grip.

Just when the tension started to fade, Walt turned to her. "You OK?"

"I'm fine."

"So," Tommy said over the crowd. "You're the one she spreads for."

One minute Walt was beside her, the next he was swinging a fist and connecting it to Tommy's face with a sound crack.

Dakota was sure she screamed as Tommy came back with the same force.

Someone shoved her away as men jumped in to separate them. The fight didn't break up until several punches were thrown.

Louise, dressed as Marie Antoinette, ran to her husband's side, turned to Walt, and then noticed Dakota standing there. "What's goin' on?"

Dakota moved next to Walt, ran a hand over his red jaw.

"That bastard just up and hit me," Tommy said.

Dakota sent what she hoped was a deadly look. "You're a piece of shit, Tommy. Next time you wanna try and score with another woman, make sure she doesn't know your wife."

"What are you saying?" Louise yelled over the voices in the crowd.

"Let's go, Dakota." Walt wrapped an arm around her waist.

Dakota couldn't remember being this pissed. She didn't move, just glared at someone she once called her friend. "I'm saying you're married to a two-timing asshat that couldn't spell the word *monogamy*, let alone practice it."

Sure enough, one look at Tommy's face while he was trying to process her insult proved the man wasn't smart enough to be offended.

Dakota let Walt guide her away.

Behind them, she heard Louise shout, "At least I'm married."

Dakota lifted one finger and waved it.

Sis, Billy, Carol Ann, and Kevin met them in the parking lot. "And here I thought Dakota was the one to watch out for," Billy said. "Nice right hook there, Doctor."

Walt shook out his right hand, flexed his fingers. When she caught his gaze, she noticed the dark shade covering his normal warmth inside his eyes.

Dakota took Walt's hand in hers and examined his knuckles. "Ouch."

"I've wanted to punch that man for years," Kevin said.

"Did he really hit on you?" Sis asked.

Dakota ran a hand over where he'd grabbed her and looked down. Sure enough, his grimy fingers left a mark. Walt brushed her hand away. "He did this?"

She started to nod and Walt turned back to the bar.

Kevin and Billy stopped him.

Dakota rushed in front of Walt, placed both palms against his chest. "Let it go, Doc. He's not worth it."

"No one hurts you. Not while I'm breathing."

There wasn't much more he could say that could have been better. "I appreciate your chivalry more than you know. But one bar fight a night is my limit."

Thirty minutes later, Dakota was placing an ice bag over Walt's hand in the suite at the hotel. "You might have to take up kickboxing, Doc. This hand isn't going to be of much use in the ER if you keep bashing in faces."

"He deserved it."

"No argument there."

"I don't like how he looked at you, Dakota."

She shrugged. "Men look. It's in your nature."

"He said some ugly things."

"He's an ugly person."

Walt stopped her hands as they brushed over his, forced her eyes to focus on him. "Maybe we should get married."

A small part of her wanted to jump on his suggestion, but her head kept her from following her heart. "The words *maybe* and *married* shouldn't be in the same sentence."

"Fine. Let's get married."

She loved that he was so willing to jump in the fire, make decisions based on what he thought she needed. "Walt," she said with a sigh. "There will be more Tommy No-Nuts out there spewing crap to cover up their own. We're too smart and too determined to make the right decisions to let people like him have any effect on us."

"What if—"

She placed a finger over his lips, stopping him. "You jumped into marriage once to do the right thing. I can't let you do that twice."

He covered her hand with his, pulled it away. "I'm not jumping."

"Yes, you are. I know you're feeling the pressure. The fight tonight proves it's time for us to leave. This isn't where we need to be. As long as we're here, the pressure is only going to intensify until we're fighting about what the right thing to do is."

"It feels like we're running."

"We're circling the wagons, not running. We really need to focus on what we want and not what others want of us under the current circumstances. You're not running for president, and my fans aren't going to stop reading my books because I'm not married. We have all the time in the world to make a decision that will affect the rest of our lives."

He tilted his head and searched her with his eyes. "I don't ever want anyone to look at you the way *he* did because you're pregnant and not married."

A big part of her heart melted in that moment. Her head kicked in and her mouth stated the obvious. "And if I'm a single mom down the road because we jumped . . . where will you be then?"

"That isn't going to happen."

Dakota offered a smile, let his hands go, and hiked her plaid skirt up to straddle his lap. "You're right." She kissed his forehead. "I might be single." Her lips followed the side of his face, down his jaw to hover over his lips. "But I'm not alone."

He took her lips and wrapped his arms around her hips. Dakota wasn't sure what felt better, the expanse of his hands on her ass or his mouth, his tongue searching out hers.

For the first time in weeks, this wasn't a good-night kiss, a parting good-bye. His hands found the skin under her shirt and inched up, his thumbs tracing the outline of her underwear and tickling the fullness of her breasts. The sensitive skin under her bra had her gasping with the contact. "I've missed you."

He held her with one hand, pushed away from the couch with the other. "I'm right here."

Holding on with her legs wrapped around him, Dakota kissed the outside of his ear while he walked to the bedroom. Inside he sat her on the bed and pressed against her.

Perfect. The feel of his weight as she tugged the shirt from his shoulders and tossed it to the floor. Nothing would be better than this.

Walt's lips met with hers before detouring south. The buttons over her breasts didn't stand a chance. They popped and at least one flew as Walt explored her skin.

"This outfit has driven me mad all night."

Reaching around him, Dakota attempted to zip her boots down, only to find the task too difficult. Giving up, she ran her hands over his back and down his firm ass. "Serves you right for not making a move these past weeks."

He stopped exploring her breasts with his lips to look up. "You wanted me, too?"

"I did." She eased her hand inside the waist of his jeans. "But I think it's sweet you held off."

He stared at her eyes and purposely pinched her breasts. "Sweet?"

"Sugary goodness."

Walt dipped his head, pushed her bra aside, and nibbled.

There was nothing sweet or delicate in how he brought her nipple to a peak and moved to the next. Heat rushed to her breasts with a tingle and took a swift downward spiral. She moaned, let herself enjoy the sensation of being in Walt's arms.

Her shirt went one way, her bra another. His lips moved down her breasts, her stomach, and hovered. Was he thinking of their child deep inside her?

Walt's eyes met hers, hot, and needy. Then he tugged the zipper of her skirt down and tossed it to rest of her clothing.

"Boots," she said.

"Keep 'em on."

With knee-high boots and nothing else, she moved up on the bed and crooked her finger.

Walt fell into her seconds later, his clothes on the floor beside hers.

He filled his palms with her butt and then ran them to the tops of her boots. The smoldering heat in his eyes pressed the right buttons, made her squirm under his stare.

His mouth started at her knee, trailed up her leg. She trembled as her head fell back and he used that sinful mouth on her, bringing her to a fierce, hot rush of release.

Weak and panting, Walt pressed inside, not giving her time to think.

"I'll slow down," he managed. "Next time."

Their bodies moved together, skin to skin, his lips fused to hers as he sucked the rest of her energy and swallowed her whole. Her body was ripe, open, and responding to every thrust.

She pulled her lips away, desperate for air, her second orgasm was close, just over the next plunge until it was on her. Walt moaned, took more until pleasure rippled through him and emptied into her.

He mumbled something that might have been in a different language.

"I think you killed me."

"Serves you right," he whispered next to her ear. "You've ruined me for anyone else."

The feeling was mutual . . . so in sync it frightened her.

The tender moments after making love left her vulnerable and weak. Even with Walt, she'd placed so much weight in these moments only to be left alone.

Walt pulled his weight off her frame, traced his fingers through her hair. "You're frowning."

She closed her eyes, unable to take the intensity of his stare.

"Talk to me, Dakota."

"I want this to work, us to work. In here, out there."

He traced her eyes until she opened them.

"I'm afraid I'll open my eyes and you'll be gone."

Walt rested his forehead against hers. "I put that fear in your head. If I could take it all back I would."

"I'm not trying to beat you with it. But I need to be honest. I have nothing to lose by being honest with you."

"I'm in this, Dakota. Whatever we want us to be, I'm in."

"I've never been this insecure."

He kissed her, let his lips linger. "I'm not going anywhere."

"I'm going to get fat." She wasn't sure where those words came from, but they were blurted out without a filter.

"Pregnant and sexy. I'll make love to you every night."

"You live in Pomona and I'm in Orange County."

"I'll move in with you . . . or you can move in with me. I don't care where we live."

She felt tears stinging her eyes. "I hate being so emotional. I feel like I'm crying all the time."

"Hormones are pesky things that muck up an otherwise normal day." He kissed her again and rolled onto his back, pulling her with him.

Dakota settled into his side and closed her eyes. "I think you should move in with me. Mary's across the street and I might need her around when you're in Florida."

"I'll take care of everything when we get home."

"Aren't you scared?"

"No, Dakota. It feels like we're doing the right thing."

It did. Baby steps to move life forward.

The weight of sleep closed in and she sighed. "I'm still wearing my boots."

Walt's chest moved as he started to laugh. "God, that's hot."

Chapter Twenty-One

They'd barely made it back to California, packed up Walt's life in Pomona, and moved it to her home before he had to leave.

Dakota dragged Mary from her bed early and forced her presence on a morning walk.

"You're pushing the friendship card."

"Suck it up. Walt has only been gone three days and I've gained four pounds. How is that possible?"

"You're pregnant."

It was cold, for Southern California, both of them wore sweatshirts and sunglasses. "But four pounds?"

"You haven't gained anything yet. Are you even wearing your fat clothes?"

Dakota rubbed her belly. "My waist is pushing past the first button."

"Reason to shop if you ask me."

"I think you're right. My sweatpants are only going to work for so long." Mary laughed and Dakota smiled. "I'm just happy I'm not sick every morning."

They rounded a corner and walked up another couple of blocks. "Have you guys told Walt's parents yet?"

"We? Ah, no . . . Walt said he'd take care of that this week."

"Walt, the procrastinator, will take care of it." Mary didn't sound convinced.

"He has to. I told Desi last week and I'm going to go public with the information before *Surrender* is released. His sister follows me online."

"Are you still going to tour?"

"I don't see why not. I'm going to skip Europe. Make a special trip after the baby is born. I'm told long flights in your third trimester are awful."

"Maybe you can hook a deal with the Fairchilds and score some of that private plane action."

"Have you been talking to Walt?"

"No, but if that's what he's planning, I'm totally going with you."

They reached their normal walking turning point and headed home. "Speaking of the Fairchilds, whatever happened with you and Glen?"

"What do you mean, what happened? Glen lives a zillion miles away."

"He flies his own planes."

Mary grew silent.

"What are you *not* telling me?"

"Not everyone wants to date a psychologist."

"Oh, Mary . . . you didn't."

Mary moved faster. "I analyze people. It's what I do."

"How many times do I have to tell you to leave the clinician at home when you're getting to know someone? It's amazing you've ever gotten laid."

"I'm not that bad."

"Yes, you are. Glen was seriously hot and his eyes were all over you in Florida. Even long-distance booty calls are better than nothing."

Waving a finger in the air, Mary said, "Battery-operated boyfriends don't need to be analyzed."

"You're right. They don't talk back and they never let you down. Might as well get yourself a half a dozen cats and live happily-ever-after."

"I don't like cats."

They both jogged across the street, slowed their pace once they hit the last hill.

"Fine, dogs, or birds . . . collect raccoons for all I care."

"This is classic," Mary told her. "You're hooking up, have a baby on the way, and you think I need that, too."

"I wouldn't wish an unplanned pregnancy on anyone, least of all you. So get that out of your head. I'm coming to terms with it, but it hasn't been easy. What I'm talking about is sex for sex's sake. You might fall into a great pattern of release and relaxation if you hooked up with, let's say, Glen, once in a while. In order to do that you'll have to stop asking about his parents and past relationships . . . his childhood."

Dakota knew Mary was thinking about it. She also knew that it would take a miracle for Mary to loosen the hold she had on her uptight life.

Instead of offering one word of agreement, Mary mumbled, "No one has a pet raccoon."

Dakota was sitting in the middle of her bed, packages spread all around her. She pulled a pair of maternity jeans from a bag and held them up. She and Mary had laughed at the elastic waist until a woman well past her seventh month walked into the store. Dakota placed three on the counter.

Giving in, she shrugged out of her too-tight pants and pulled on the new ones.

"So much better." She turned to the side in front of her full-length mirror and tugged her shirt across her belly. "Might as well get used to the new baggy look."

After going to her closet and pulling several hangers, she returned to her bed when her phone rang.

She answered without looking at the number. "Hello."

"Dakota?"

"This is."

Dakota paused, certain it was some kind of phone solicitor.

"It's JoAnne."

Not a solicitor.

Dakota swallowed the edge of panic, and steadied her words. "Hello, Mrs. Eddy. How are you?"

The woman's voice was stone-cold. "I understand my son moved in with you."

"He did. He's not here right now."

"I know that. He just got off the phone with his father and me." JoAnne's words were clipped with an edge of agitation that proved she was only a breath away from losing her composure.

Walt didn't procrastinate. "I see."

"Do you? Do you see the terrible position you've put our son in?"

"Mrs. Eddy—"

"No, you listen to me, young lady. My son had been tricked into marriage once before and I said nothing. I will not be silent now."

"Mrs. Eddy—"

"I'm not finished."

Dakota sat on the edge of the bed and prepared herself for the hate that would come.

"Our son is much too responsible to walk away from his mistakes."

Dakota actually found herself flinching.

"That doesn't mean he should give up his life. I think what you've done here is highly suspicious. What grown woman *accidentally* gets pregnant?"

Dakota opened her mouth to respond and was cut off before she uttered one syllable.

"Now he has given up his job, moved to a different city. What was it, Dakota? You found yourself pushing thirty and decided it was time to have a baby? Waited for the first decent man to enter your life and accidentally forgot a pill?"

Dakota wanted desperately to blast JoAnne Eddy and all her accusations against the wall, or perhaps tell the condescending old bat that she nailed it. Dakota was looking for a baby daddy all along, and boy, did Walt fit the bill.

"If my son wanted to marry you, you'd already have a ring on your finger. You do realize that, don't you?"

The woman went for blood. "Are you finished?" Dakota asked in a voice so calm and slow even she didn't recognize it.

"I don't like you."

That almost made her laugh. "I figured that out, Mrs. Eddy, but thank you for the clarification. I'll be sure and take you off the potential babysitters list."

"I am not raising your child."

"Oh, bless your heart, did you think I would ever let that happen? If you did, you're highly mistaken. After this conversation, you'll be lucky to see our child."

"Are you threatening me?"

"Mrs. Eddy, if I was threatening you, you'd know it. I will tell you this before I hang up. I'm going to try and dig real deep inside of me to understand what possessed you to come off on me like this. I'm not the gold-digging, life-ruining woman you're painting me to be."

"You listen—"

"No, you listen. Our child will grow up in a loving home, one free of hate. If you ever want to be a part of that, you might call in a priest to exorcise the disgust from your heart, because I will not stand for it." Dakota took a solid breath, forced a smile. "Now you go and have a wonderful day, Mrs. Eddy."

Dakota hung up the phone. "Witch."

—•—

Dakota brought her laptop to bed and plugged away at her manuscript that was flowing like water in her head. Maybe it was her real-life drama fueling her muse, or maybe it was skill, but her work in progress was kicking ass in her head.

This time when the phone rang, Dakota checked the number before she answered. "Hey, Baby Daddy."

"It's so good to hear your voice."

She glanced at the clock on her computer. "You must be exhausted. That or you're out partying."

"Dinner did involve a couple of drinks."

He talked about his day, some of the details flew well over her head, but she listened and added a comment when she could. "And by the way . . . I talked to my parents today."

"I know."

"Oh?"

"Yes, your mother called me."

"Oh, no."

"Oh, yes. I don't think she's happy with our news."

"She had little to say when we talked."

Dakota shook her head and debated for the hundredth time that day on what she should reveal to Walt. Too many details would probably just make matters worse. "You're the blessed one then; she had plenty to say to me."

"What? What did she say?"

"You don't want to know. I'm sure she's just shocked. Hopefully she'll come around."

Walt's voice dropped. "You don't have to protect her. I know she can be difficult."

"Believe me, I'm not protecting her. I'd have to like her to want to protect her. Right now she's on the generic Christmas card list, you know, the one you have to send even though you don't want to."

Walt paused. "You still send out Christmas cards?"

Laughing, she moved the computer off her lap and left her palm over the baby bump. "You need me."

"Yes, I do."

She liked that. "Guess what I bought today?"

"A minivan."

She cringed. "Lord no. But an SUV of some sort might need to make the list. My tiny Beemer will be a pain with a car seat."

He laughed. "What did you buy?"

"A new wardrobe. Guess who started looking pregnant this week?"

"Really?"

"I kept thinking, *no way, it's too fast*, but then I looked at the calendar and realized that we're nearly at the halfway point."

"Little Horance isn't giving you trouble, is he?" They'd started saying the most ridiculous names in an effort to spark the right one.

"Philomena is fine. Not one headache. I started moving stuff out of the guest room."

"Wait until I get home. I don't want you lifting anything heavy."

She sighed, snuggled into the three pillows she had behind her. "When are you coming home?"

"I moved my flight up two whole days. I'll e-mail you the confirmation."

"You mean you didn't use Fairchild again?"

"He offered, I said no. Oh, guess who I heard from?"

She liked this, the day-to-day anything and everything about a committed relationship. This she could get used to, even if Walt had to be away once in a while. "Who?"

"The FDA. Looks like the Eddy nasal foreign-object extractor has made it through their system. I've already had two competing companies asking for a contract."

Walt was following his father's example in some ways. No, it wasn't with a cardiac clamp helpful for a cardiologist, but something every ER doctor came across in his or her career. Kids were notorious for shoving crap up their noses. Walt had used every device available at work. Some were successful, but his own modified paperclip device worked the best.

"That's awesome. I'm so excited for you."

"I'm pretty stoked myself. After four long years, it looks like I might have use for my dad's lawyers after all. I don't have the first clue about how to negotiate this kind of deal."

"Have you talked to him about it?"

"No. I thought maybe if we visited over Christmas I could bring it up then."

They'd talked about the holidays but hadn't made any commitments. "Let's get through Thanksgiving first." And discuss Christmas and his mother later.

"OK." He yawned.

"You need to go to bed, Doc."

"I do."

"I miss you."

"Call me crazy, but I like knowing you do. I miss you and little Sebastian."

Sebastian . . . good Lord, that was not going to happen. "Beatrice is right here when you get back."

"Sleep well, Mama."

"We will, Daddy."

After hanging up the phone, she placed a hand over her belly. "We'll find the right name for you, don't worry."

She picked up her laptop, placed it back on her legs. That's when she felt it. A flutter deep inside her womb. She'd heard of butterflies in her stomach, but this was low and deep. "Oh, baby." Dakota sat up and waited, when it happened again, she knew. Her child, their child, was saying hello for the first time. The desire to pick up the phone and call Walt passed and she grinned. "This is just you and me right now." And that was perfectly fine. Walt wouldn't be able to feel anything anyway, even if he were there.

Putting aside her work for the night, Dakota sat in the dark waiting for another flutter, another wave. Even though she was alone, she wasn't. There was someone an entire country away thinking of her, and one much closer depending on her.

Life wasn't so bad.

Thanksgiving plans changed the minute Walt realized how awful his mother had been with Dakota while he was in Florida. Neither one of them wanted to endure the drama of family, and luckily, they had friends who embraced them.

Walt helped Dakota and Mary with their luggage for the week-long stay on the East Coast. Monica and Trent were doing the traditional turkey along with ball games. When they sent a plane to pick them up, Dakota jumped at the idea.

"Besides," she'd told him after Monica offered, "my publisher scheduled a couple of interviews and New York is only a two-hour drive from Monica's."

"And we can go shopping," Mary chimed in. "I love it when we go to New York without a conference. And then there's ice skating . . ."

"I think I'll take a rain check on the ice skating this year," Dakota said.

The plans were sealed after that. Thanksgiving, New York, and shopping . . . the girls were happy and Walt could spend some of his time working out contract details with the Fairchilds when it came to Borderless Doctors. The job was paperwork heavy, lots of recruiting would happen after the holidays, lots of international travel. The good news was, Dakota was willing to travel with him, before and after the baby was born, so long as his destinations didn't involve contagious disease outbreaks. As she said, she could write anywhere.

Now they were parked in an auxiliary lot and shuffling luggage from his car.

Like every time Walt had flown with Fairchild Charters, a man stood holding a sign with his name.

Mary giggled like a schoolgirl as they were valeted through security and led straight to the tarmac.

"Are you our pilot?" Dakota asked as they walked through the hoards of holiday travelers.

"I'm the copilot, Miss Laurens. The pilot is still on board."

Both Walt and Dakota spotted the plane the moment they stepped onto the pavement. The familiar Fairchild name was written over the wing of the airplane, but unlike the others they'd been on, this one was massive. "Holy cow," Dakota whispered.

"Is that it?" Mary asked, her eyes wide.

"Yes, ma'am," the copilot offered. "Nothing but the best for the Fairchilds' personal friends."

Walt stood back and let the ladies walk up the steps and into the jet. He heard their reaction long before he saw what they gasped at.

Then he saw it.

"Holy shit."

Dakota turned, her grin tried to fall but failed. "This is too much. We can't accept this."

It was beyond too much. Unlike the other charter planes he'd been on, this one had sofas and a huge big screen, a bar, and if he wasn't mistaken, an entire bedroom suite through a door in the back.

"Trump called and wants his plane back," Mary mumbled.

Dakota laughed and moved deeper into the luxury jet. "See, this . . . this is why I write. Who knows, maybe someday we can own something like this."

Walt watched as joy stretched over her face and she sat on the lush leather sofa and placed a hand over their child.

We, she said we. Those words were fuel to his soul.

"Keep writing, babe. Who knows."

A woman emerged from the back of the jet. "Welcome aboard," she said. "I'm Mai and I'll be taking care of you." The tiny woman offered a full-toothed smile.

"Hi, Mai," Mary said.

Mai looked directly at Dakota. "There's a suite in back, if you need to rest." Her eyes drifted to Dakota's protruding belly.

"Thank you."

Mai offered her smile again.

"There you are!"

From the cockpit, a familiar voice filled the cabin.

"Glen!"

Walt moved in for a handshake and man-hug. "What are you doing here?"

"Trent said we needed a plane, and my pilots were already scheduled."

Walt glanced around his friend, looked into the cockpit. "You're flying this monster?"

"She's a beauty, isn't she? A Falcon 900 completely remodeled on the inside to accommodate a family of ten comfortably. I heard the bed in the back is like sleeping on a cloud."

Dakota moved behind him. "Hi Glen."

"Hey, Dakota. When Monica said you were expecting, we knew we had to bring a plane with a bedroom."

"I would have been fine without it."

Glen shook his head. "That's how we roll, Dakota."

Walt started to comment when he noticed Glen's gaze move beyond Dakota.

Glen stared toward Mary and an awkward moment of silence filled the plane. Walt glanced to Dakota, who was watching the others.

"Hi Mary."

"Glen." She paused. "I . . . I wasn't expecting you."

Glen's eyebrows went up with a smile that bordered on cocky. "I'm a pilot."

"You own the company."

"I still fly . . . as often as I can."

The moment of silence from before tripled.

"Mr. Fairchild," the copilot interrupted.

"Yes, Ian?"

"We've been given clearance. Ten minutes."

Glen clicked out of whatever trance he'd been in and smiled. "Make yourselves comfortable. We'll be in the air shortly."

Chapter Twenty-Two

They were less than two hours into the flight, Mai served them drinks, was preparing a meal within the hour, and Dakota and Walt were stretched out on the sofa, and all Mary could think about was the pilot.

What in the world was Glen doing flying *this* plane?

Dakota shifted on the sofa, looked toward the bedroom. "I feel like a balloon."

"Flying and pregnancy do that," Walt said.

She offered Mary a sympathetic look. "Would you mind?"

Mary nodded toward the back of the cabin. "Go on. You know you're dying to check out the bedroom." To help her friends move along, she tilted the deluxe seat she was sitting in to a reclining position and closed her eyes.

Walt and Dakota disappeared into the bedroom and closed the door.

The cloudless sky offered a great view of the earth below, but Mary didn't concentrate on it.

Maybe Glen had a camera on the interior of the plane, or perhaps it was a coincidence that he made his appearance from the cockpit within a minute after Dakota and Walt disappeared. Still, Glen emerged from the small pilot space once she was alone. Even Mai ducked back into her private space.

"Are Walt and Dakota resting?"

She nearly rolled her eyes. "Nice deduction, Watson."

Glen placed his six foot three frame into the seat across from her and smiled. It was bad enough the man towered over everything on the plane, his white uniform and pilot cap did something to her insides she didn't want to identify. She didn't have a uniform fetish. Broad shoulders tapering to a narrow waist and tight ass . . . yeah, that could be a fetish worth having.

She forced her gaze outside the plane.

"A bed in a plane is hard to resist."

Mary wanted to think her friend and her baby daddy were actually sleeping, but who knew? "I'm sure you'd know all about that."

When she looked, she found a crooked smile on Glen's clean-shaven jaw. "Jealous, counselor?"

"I most certainly am not!" She managed to push her chin in the air.

Glen laughed. "A therapy couch is more entertaining than a bed on an airplane?"

"I didn't say that." Didn't mean that. Instead of defending her answer, she diverted his attention. "Shouldn't you be flying the plane?"

"Autopilot . . . copilot." He glanced out the window. "The weather is perfect."

"Isn't that like driving a car with your knee? It works but it isn't safe?"

He laughed. "Not quite the same."

She refused to smile.

"I called you."

He had and damn it, she wished he hadn't reminded her.

"I appreciate your quick blow off. We do live far away," Mary said.

His brows drew together, eyes narrowed. "I don't believe I blew you off."

That wasn't how she remembered it. "It's OK, Glen. I understand."

The space between his chair and hers was separated by a fixed table, a table he only had to lean over to demonstrate how small it was. "You think too much."

He was too far into her personal space for comfort. "You don't know me well enough to know that."

His breath was minty, like he had some kind of candy in his pocket, or maybe gum . . . Glen moved his gaze from one of her eyes to the other. "I'm going back to fly the plane," he said. ". . . make sure you arrive in Connecticut in once piece."

"Way to make your passengers feel safe."

He looked at her lips, then looked away. "I try."

The prickles of awareness rolled over her skin for another hundred miles before she shook them off and closed her eyes. Then all she could see was the depths of a certain pilot's eyes.

———

Friends like the Fairchilds were better than family. At least Dakota's and Walt's.

"I've never cooked a turkey in my life," Dakota said as she and Mary stood in the kitchen early in the morning on Thanksgiving Day.

"Aunt Bea!" Monica said as she pulled a giant turkey from the refrigerator and set it on the granite counter.

Dakota wrapped the apron Monica made for her around her waist. It had a picture of a baby over her belly wearing pilgrim garb. Mary donned a white doily thing that looked like part of a French waitress fantasy for men. Monica, bless her little ol' heart, wore an apron that stated *I'm a nurse not a cook . . . complainers will be shot.* There was a picture of a syringe with green liquid inside.

This Thanksgiving would either be epic or a complete failure.

"You have an Aunt Bea?"

"No. My sister married into Aunt Bea. The woman has serious skills in the kitchen. Most times when she brings me into the kitchen she offers wine and suggests I watch and learn."

Mary groaned. "We're screwed."

"It's a turkey! And with Aunt Bea's instructions it can't go wrong."

Dakota flat-out laughed. "We're screwed."

Monica shook her head. "Have faith, ladies. Mary," she instructed, "start shredding the bread, Dakota, cook up the sausage, and I'll get this bird ready."

While Monica pulled crap from inside the bird, Dakota cooked a good pound of sausage.

"Who is this Aunt Bea and how is she going to help us?"

Monica shoved the turkey under the flow of water in the sink as she explained. "Aunt Bea is Beatrice Morrison, sister of Gaylord Morrison. That would be Jack's dad . . . Jack is Jessie, my sister's, husband."

Dakota was certain something inside her brain short-circuited.

Monica paused and tried again. "My sister's aunt through marriage."

Dakota met Mary's gaze. They nodded. "Aunt Bea is the cook in the family?"

"She's amazing . . . makes it look easy." Monica patted down the turkey and started rubbing spices over the outside. "Thanksgiving always meant burnt or undercooked turkey in my childhood home."

Mary moved from shredding bread to chopping celery. "I had a slew of foster homes growing up. Depending on the ethnicity, Thanksgiving changed every couple of years."

Monica paused, looked over her shoulder. "Really?"

Dakota had heard parts of Mary's story over the years and knew what was coming. "Yep. There was the Von Goosens, I don't remember much of them. Thanksgiving wasn't a part of their culture, I know that. Then there were the Beckers, they tried the whole turkey thing but spent most of the time drinking and we would end up with grilled cheese." Mary sighed, moved on to the onions. "The Mendez family, they celebrated with traditional Mexican flair."

As much as Mary tried to hide her childhood pain, Dakota saw through it.

"Suddenly my mother and all her posse of boyfriends feel much more stable," Monica said.

Mary shrugged. "Friends are often more important than family. I'm not sure if my real parents were just kids, dead, or not willing to take on another liability." She looked at the both of them and offered a smile. "Stop looking at me like that. We all have a past."

Dakota moved the pan of cooking sausage off the flame and hugged her friend. "I'm so glad you're here."

"We can all ruin Thanksgiving together. Now that's love."

They moved through the kitchen at that point, chopping, seasoning . . . and following Aunt Bea's recipes as if they knew what they were doing.

When everything was cooking, or at least at a standstill, Dakota found her way to the den, where Walt and Trent were watching a football game.

With the silly apron still wrapped around her protruding waist, she sat next to Walt and kicked her feet up on the coffee table.

"It smells good in there."

"I have no idea if anything will turn out. It's the blind leading the blind in there."

Walt pulled her in and kissed her forehead. "I have faith."

"I'm a writer, not a homemaker."

A tired writer who wanted a nap and it wasn't even noon.

Walt ran his hand along her and rested it over her belly. "I'll take ya anyway."

She closed her eyes and smiled. "Good thing."

Sure enough, the butterflies in her belly were becoming more frequent, she felt them now and placed her hand over Walt's.

"Feel that?" she asked.

He shook his head but kept his palm flat.

The game continued, not that Dakota was paying attention, and then Walt stiffened by her side.

"Oh . . . shit. Did you feel that?"

"What?" Trent asked as he sipped from a beer.

Walt flattened his hand, paused. Their child moved and Walt beamed. "Was that . . . ?"

She nodded. "Looks like Junior is wishing you a happy Thanksgiving."

Walt sucked in his lower lip, smiled when their baby moved again. "Wow."

Dakota squeezed his hand. "So here's the deal, Baby Daddy. I get the first nine months of carrying little Junior, and you get the next. Deal?"

Walt couldn't look more like a kid with a giant lollypop. "Deal."

Trent cleared his throat. "Do I need to leave the room?"

Smiling, Walt twisted toward his friend. "I can feel the baby moving."

Trent's eyes moved to their joined hands.

Walt waved his friend over. "C'mere."

Before Dakota knew it, Trent was placing his hand on her stomach and waiting. When he felt it, he jumped. "Holy crap."

After that Mary and Monica made their way into the den and Dakota's body was no longer her own.

—◦—

Somewhere between halftime and turkey time, there was *toss the ball* time. Walt stood in Trent's front yard with Glen and Jason, Trent's oldest brother, and the four of them paired off for a friendly game of football. The temperature outside was just above freezing but that didn't stop them from pretending to be younger than they were.

Walt passed the ball to Trent and watched as the older brother took out the younger. Another pass around and Walt felt the hard edge of the earth meet his shoulder. If the men didn't push each other to the ground, Trent's dogs, Ginger and Gilligan, were all too happy to trip and tackle the players.

Jason and Glen were strutting, up by seven points. But when Walt tackled Glen, some of that strut turned into groans. Walt wasn't sure what hurt more, tackling or being tackled.

"Next point wins," Trent offered, rubbing his shoulder.

"I can go with that." Glen ran a hand over his ass.

"There's a reason alcohol is a favorite food group during the holidays," Jason said.

Trent and Walt had possession and made a run for the goal.

Trent hit the ground as Jason made an attempt to capture him before the ball went over the invisible line. They came up grinning with two Irish setters licking their faces.

"It's actually a tie," Glen said, helping his brother up to his feet.

"Fine, a tie. Call it what you want. One more knock to the ground and I'm going to need Walt's services."

They did the *patting on the back* thing followed quickly by the *guzzling the beer* thing.

"So, Walt?" Trent asked. "What are you waiting for?"

Walt swallowed. "What do you mean?"

"With Dakota. Looks like you guys are playing house well together. You're obviously into her."

Walt grinned. "You sound like her dad."

Glen shoved his brother's shoulder. "Trent wants all his friends to settle now that he's paired up."

"Hey, marriage has perks. Something none of you know anything about."

They enjoyed a good laugh and Walt finished his beer. "We've talked about it. She doesn't want to rush into anything because of the baby."

"What do you want?" Glen asked.

"We'd already be married if it were up to me."

"Sounds to me like you have some schmoozing to do, Doc," Jason said with a smile.

"While the girls are enjoying some retail therapy in the city, I can hook you up with a certain jeweler I know."

Glen shoved his brother. "Pushy much?"

Trent held up his palm. "Just offering."

Walt pushed off the porch, turned toward the house. "Never hurts to look."

Glen shook his head. "Another one bites the dust."

Trent slapped his hand onto Glen's back. "I'm not dead, brother."

———

They waited until Saturday to invade the shops in Manhattan. After their first successful turkey, and only a slightly disappointing pie disaster, Thanksgiving was one of the best in recent memory.

"You do know normal people don't land on rooftops for shopping trips, right?"

Mary had a point, but Dakota wasn't complaining. Traffic into the city would have sucked and she'd never flown in a helicopter before.

Monica twisted in her seat to look at the three of them tucked in the back. "Have you met my husband?" They all wore earphones so they could talk to each other in-flight. Trent was navigating over rooftops as he made his way to the building where Fairchild Charters headquarters were located. "Believe me," Monica continued, "I'd much rather drive."

"Oh, you love it," Trent said.

Monica shook her head but smiled when Trent looked her way. "I do it for you, Barefoot."

Dakota found it highly entertaining that Monica had a fear of flying when her husband was one-third owner of the largest chartering company for private jets and helicopters. According to Monica, Trent would fly everywhere if he could just get clearance to land.

Trent set the helicopter down without so much as a thump. They waited until after he'd powered off the engine and the blades stopped rotating before they all jumped out.

The cold New York wind was blowing, making Dakota duck farther into her down coat.

Trent guided them to the elevator and down to the ground floor.

The building was virtually empty over the holiday weekend. Security watched them as they walked by.

"I have a car waiting to take you ladies wherever you want to go."

Dakota grinned. "What, you guys don't want to join us?"

Walt lifted one eyebrow. "For manicures and endless shoe shopping? How about we meet up with you for lunch?"

"Dinner at Bar Mesa. Lunch is only a couple of hours away and who knows where we'll be."

"So we'll meet at the hotel by six?" Trent asked.

They were staying in the city until Monday so Dakota could take care of her publisher business and deliver a surprise package to her agent and editor.

They stepped back out into the cold and Walt pulled Dakota close. "Careful, the sidewalks are slick."

"I'm a big girl."

He kissed her briefly and touched the end of her nose. "You're a tiny girl with precious cargo who might make you off your game. Be careful . . . for me."

With a request like that, she was helpless to do anything but nod. "What are you guys going to do?"

"I think there's a nudey bar on the east side," Trent teased.

Monica, not missing a beat, said, "You enjoy that, Barefoot."

"Any other woman would be jealous."

"Of heroin-addicted anorexic bodies twisting around a pole? I don't think so."

Dakota laughed. "Sounds appetizing."

Mary, in true Mary form, added, "I'm sure they're not all addicts."

Dakota shivered against the cold and laughed. "OK, Miss Literal. Let's get our minds out of the stripper bar and on to some serious Christmas shopping. I have goals, ladies, and they don't involve freezing my butt off out here."

They climbed into the back of a limousine and drove off.

"Can I just say, for the record, that I seriously love the style in which you guys live." Dakota sat back and stretched out her boot-laden feet.

"I still pinch myself," Monica told them. "My sister and I grew up without much of anything. It's taken Trent a few years to get me used to having money and spending it."

The long car moved along the New York streets, horns blaring and pedestrians trying to outmaneuver the cars. Even though the temperature dipped into the twenties and snow was in the forecast, the city buzzed with energy and droves of people filled every cement corner.

"We had all we needed." Dakota added her own experience with money. "Both parents, a house, food, and discipline but there wasn't anything excessive. We took family vacations, national parks, big attractions, stuff like that. That's all I really want for my kids."

"But this is so much better," Mary said.

"It doesn't suck."

The driver's name was Nathaniel, and he knew his way around the city and managed to get them curbside for every store they wanted to patronize. Window shopping in New York consisted of real windows. Some of the most recognizable department stores decorated their windows with massive holiday displays. Bell-ringing Santas stood on every corner.

They walked passed Bulgari and Monica paused. "Let's go in."

Mary rolled her eyes. "Why?"

"I wanna look. Besides, Trent likes buying me stupid expensive stuff. I might as well figure out what I like and lead him in the right direction."

They stepped into the warm jewelry store and Monica huddled close. "I have an idea."

"Oh?" Dakota removed her gloves and rubbed warmth back into her fingers. Her thin California blood was showing.

"We distract them with you looking for the perfect ring, and I can shop in peace."

"The perfect wedding ring?"

"Sure. Not a stretch with Junior on board." Monica looked down at Dakota's belly, which seemed to be expanding daily since she shopped for maternity clothes.

"Perfect idea," Mary said.

Dakota rolled her eyes. "Fine."

Monica laughed like a schoolgirl and headed to the wedding sets like a woman on a mission. "I'm telling you, this is the only place Trent shops."

A very tall, very stacked, very attractive brunette approached them with a smile that spread for miles. "Might I help you, ladies?"

Monica took over. "Is Gill here?"

The lady's smile waivered. "Of course."

As Miss Plastic turned to leave, Dakota whispered, "You know someone who works here?"

Monica shook her head. "No, but Trent does. Talks about this guy all the time."

"Why am I not surprised?" Mary asked.

"So here's what we'll do. Dakota, you look, play, fiddle. Mary and I will tag team at your side while I check out a few things in the store. Sound good?"

"How am I supposed to fiddle?"

"You're a writer . . . you can figure it out."

Mary chuckled while a tall, extremely attractive man stepped from the back of the store.

"Ladies?" He stopped in front of them and Dakota was sure the sound of Mary dropping an egg was heard over their collective gasps. "I understand you're looking for me?"

"We are?" Mary asked.

"We are."

Dakota leaned into Mary. "You like Glen."

Mary shook herself and the temporary insanity created by masculine beauty eased.

"I'm Monica Fairchild," Monica announced while she placed her hand in the jeweler's. "My husband shops here . . . or so I'm told."

"Trent. Yes, he does. We went to school together."

Monica smiled. "Is that right? He didn't tell me that."

"Some secrets are meant to be held close, don't you think?"

Monica's eyes grew wide and looked Dakota's way. "Well, we're here to help my friend."

Gill focused on Dakota and practically dismissed Monica.

"Maybe you know her. Dakota Laurens."

Gill offered a blank stare, not that Dakota expected anything different. Men in particular weren't her reading public.

The brunette who had searched Gill out lit up. "The author?"

Monica smiled and Dakota studied the floor.

"Yes, the author. She's looking at rings."

The entire idea started to give Dakota chills. "I don't know about this, Monica."

"C'mon. Gill is the best in the business. Trent only deals with the best. If there isn't something you like here, they can have it made . . . right, Gill?"

Gill offered a thousand-watt smile. "We do custom work all the time." He walked around the counter and shook Dakota's hand. "I've never met an author."

She smiled, shook his hand, and loosened the scarf around her neck. "I hope we're not wasting your time."

"Any friend of a Fairchild is a friend of mine."

Funny how a jeweler wanted to be friends with a gazillionaire's lady friends. "I really don't know what I'm looking for."

He led her to a counter and offered her a chair. "Monica said a ring."

"She writes romance novels. The sexy kind that always end with big diamonds and lots of glitter," Monica told him.

Gill laughed and pulled a platform of rings from the showcase. "A lady such as yourself must have an idea of what she'd like to see on her own hand."

Dakota glanced at the rings sitting in front of her and sighed. "Actually, I've no idea. Every character has her own ideas of the perfect setting. Personally, I've never given it much thought."

"Well then, we have some work to do."

Monica and Mary stood close while Gill showed her several settings. Most of the solitary-diamond, traditional two-band settings did nothing for her taste buds. Only when she shooed her friends off did Gill bring out the more glittery rings that Dakota didn't mind saying she liked.

He placed a large round diamond with double bands of smaller diamonds intertwined on her finger. "We can change the shape and quality of the stone," he told her.

"This is lovely."

"You have an eye for quality," Gill told her.

Dakota knew how to read between the lines.

"Quality means money. Do I even want to ask what this costs?"

He smiled. "Probably not."

She shrugged out of her coat and pulled her hair behind her. Dakota looked over her shoulder, noticed Mary and Monica looking at earrings.

"Should we talk budget?" Gill asked.

"Probably not," Dakota mimicked his words. "But a girl can dream . . . right?"

She looked at the ring one last time, removed it, and set it on the counter. "What else do you have?"

—————

Trent slapped a well-placed hand on Walt's back. "Gill and I go way back."

Walt watched Dakota on video.

Gill paused the video. "This is the only one she actually wore for any length of time and sighed when she took it off."

Walt peered closer. "I know nothing about diamonds."

Gill removed a box from his pocket and placed it in front of Walt.

"It's three and a half carats GIA certified . . ." He went on to spout numbers and letters. None of which made any sense to Walt. "The minute I started talking budget, she took it off and asked to look at other rings."

When Gill told him the cost, Walt understood Dakota's hesitation.

Chapter Twenty-Three

A buzzer . . . a bell. No, an earthquake.

Dakota shook herself awake and recognized a phone ringing. It took several seconds to orient herself.

The Manhattan Morrison, a shared penthouse suite . . . and an annoying phone ringing in the dead of night.

She heard Walt's sleepy voice as he answered the phone. "Hello? . . . This is."

It's insane how one can go from comatose to the world to wide awake in the blink of an eye. The way Walt spoke into the phone put Dakota on alert. She sat up and turned on a bedside light.

Walt was sitting up, his cell phone cradled to his ear, his eyes wide. "What was his Troponin level?"

She reached for his hand and held tight when he squeezed.

"I'm in New York. It's going to take me a few hours to get there. All right. Good-bye."

"What happened?"

Walt's face was a shade of white she never wanted to see. "My father had a heart attack."

Dakota blinked, felt her heart drop. "Is he . . ."

"Alive, in the ICU."

"Oh, Walt." She wrapped her arms around him, wished she could take some of the burden draping over him like a cloud.

"I have to go."

Dakota leaned back. "We. We have to go. I'll wake the others, you pack."

Between arranging a flight and driving to the airport, it took them nearly seven hours to land in Denver. Walt had little to say as he held her hand and walked through the doors of the hospital.

They were led to the waiting room of the ICU, where they found Brenda curled up, her head in Larry's lap.

Larry noticed them first. "Hey."

Brenda woke slowly, her eyes were swollen, her clothes rumpled. "Oh, Walt." She uncurled from the couch and moved in to hug her brother.

"How is he?"

"Sleeping. Mom is in there with him. It was awful, Walt."

Walt kissed the top of his sister's head and turned to the locked doors of the ICU. "Wait out here for me?" he asked Dakota.

"Of course."

After announcing himself to the staff, they buzzed him in.

Dakota dropped her purse into a chair. "How are the two of you doing? Have you eaten?"

Brenda shook her head, her gaze moved to Dakota's hand resting on the baby.

"So my mother was telling the truth."

It was hard to find a smile. "Walt and I are having a baby."

Without warning, Brenda pulled her into a hug. "That's awesome. I'm so happy for you."

Larry hugged her next, patted her belly the moment he let go. "For everything bad that happens out there, something good is there to take its place."

—◦—

Familiar beeps and dings filled the ICU as Walt walked through. Antiseptic mixed with more scents than should be possible filled his nose.

He thought he was prepared. It wasn't like he didn't know what a man in a hospital bed recovering from an MI looked like. Still, Walt hesitated at the doorway, feeling as if someone sucker punched him in the gut.

Walter Eddy II had aged ten years overnight. His face was drawn, his color matched the white of the sheets. Walt's mother sat sleeping in a chair by his father's bed, her head drifting to one side.

When his foot scraped the floor, his mother's head snapped up. "Walter," she whispered.

She unfolded from the chair and stepped into his arms. They stepped out of the room in an attempt to keep from waking his father.

"How is he?"

"Stanley said he's stable. You remember Dr. Altman?"

Stanley Altman was a longtime consultant with his father. A man they both looked up to and trusted. It would make sense that his father would want Stanley to take care of him, and vice versa if their roles were reversed.

"Of course. Has he been in this morning?"

His mom nodded. "Before office hours. He's waiting for you to arrive, said to call him when you got here."

Walt glanced back inside the room, noticed the cardiac monitor, his father's rhythm and basic vital signs. *Stable* was a relative term when someone was hooked up to as many drugs as his father was. Probably best the man was sleeping, Lord knew how he was going to react when he had enough energy to bitch.

Walt approached the nursing station and asked to speak with the nurse caring for his father. Millie was a tiny Filipino woman with very little accent. After he introduced himself he asked to see his father's chart, requested she call Stanley and let him know he was there.

As luck would have it, Stanley had cleared Walt to look over his father's chart.

He started with the ER report and traced the events. An ambulance arrived twenty minutes after 911 was called. Snow on the mountain and the remote location of his family home would always prove a problem for timely emergency response time. According to their records, his father had collapsed, crushing chest pain radiating down his left arm. All the classic signs of a heart attack. What surprised Walt was the record of medications his father was taking according to the triage report. From what he could tell, his father knew he had a predisposition for a heart attack.

"Dr. Eddy?"

Walt looked up, found Millie standing over him. "Dr. Altman is on the line."

"Thank you, Millie." Walt took the phone and turned the page in the chart. "Hi Stanley."

"Hello Walt. I'd ask how you are . . . but . . ."

"No need for pleasantries. Thanks for taking care of my dad."

"I'd do anything for him. You know that."

With the niceties aside, Walt dove in. "So he went to the cath lab?"

Stanley told him about his blockages, the ones they had to open in the cardiac catheterization lab . . . and the ones they still needed to attack. "He needs bypass, Walt. I've been harping on him for over a year. Maybe now he'll listen."

"Jesus, Stanley, he never said a word to me about this."

"We're surgeons, Walt. Hard to take it when something goes wrong with our own bodies."

"Hard to admit, you mean."

"Very hard. Maybe you can convince him. Of all people he knows the risk and the gain. Your dad is stubborn."

"You don't have to tell me. I'll do my best. When do you think he'll be able to go under?"

"I'd like to see him stabilize, get a couple nights' rest. Of course if he turns we'll want to go right away."

Emergency surgery was never an optimal choice. "I'll talk to him."

"You know where to find me. And make sure your mother goes home. I can't kick her out, but she's not doing him or her any good sitting there."

"Got it. Thanks."

Walt ran a hand over the stubble on his chin and closed his father's chart.

He encouraged his mother to join him outside the room.

"Looks like Dad is going to be here for a few days."

"That's what Stanley said."

"Did you know about his heart?"

His mother's jaw came up and part of her normal mask reappeared. "We didn't really talk about these things. He said something about taking medicine, but he didn't offer any details. I assumed he would have said something if it were serious."

That sounded about right. JoAnne liked her perfect world perfect, and his father often kept certain truths from her to keep her sheltered.

"He needs surgery."

She offered a blank stare and blinked several times. "Open heart?"

"Yes."

There was a pause. "And if he doesn't have it?"

Walt glanced into his father's room. "More of this. Hopefully the medics continue to arrive in time."

"Then what are we waiting for?"

Sounded like his mother was ready to move forward with the right decisions. "We need him a little healthier first. A couple of days if we can hold off."

His mom rubbed her forehead.

"You're tired."

"I've been tired before. I'll survive."

Walt placed an arm over his mother's shoulders. "You need some sleep, a good meal."

"I need to be here."

"You're of no use to anyone exhausted. Besides, Dad needs his sleep. When he has surgery, you'll want to be close by. I looked at his chart and Stanley agrees, he's stable. Let me take over for a while."

He shoulders slumped. "You're right. I know you're right."

She retrieved her purse from the room and followed beside him as they exited the ICU.

He found Dakota sitting alone in the lobby. She stood when they walked out and offered a smile.

His mother stiffened beside him. "I didn't know you brought *her* along."

How his mother could be anything but humbled, Walt would never know. Instead of honoring her words, he looked around the lobby. "Where did Brenda and Larry go?"

"Home. Larry said he'd be back in a few hours. They needed to recharge."

Walt turned to his mother. "Is your car here?"

"It is. But I can't go home now. I'm too upset to drive." She turned back toward the ICU and Walt jumped in front of her.

"I can call a cab."

"I don't think so, Walter."

"I can drive her," Dakota offered.

Walt would have refused if it weren't in Dakota's best interest to avoid hospital lobbies. The last thing Dakota needed was to catch something hanging out in a hospital. As much as he wanted her by his side, Walt knew to diminish Dakota's exposure to anything floating in the hospital. The fact she was pregnant and not able to combat simple bacteria or a virus would compromise her health. He had enough to deal with . . . Dakota becoming ill would gut him.

"You should both go to the house and get some sleep."

JoAnne started to refuse and Walt raised his voice. "Mom. Please. I need to focus on Dad and not on arguing with you."

She released a long-suffering sigh and walked out of the lobby.

Walt moved to Dakota's side. "Thank you for taking her home."

"Not a problem. How is he doing?"

He shook his head. "He's sick. Needs surgery. It's going to be a long week."

"Let me know what I can do to help."

Walt dropped his lips to hers. "Being here helps."

"I'm a phone call away."

"Text me when you get to the house."

"OK."

He kissed her again and watched her walk away.

Back inside the ICU, Walt took over where his mother left off.

When Millie came into the room to change his father's IV solution and check his vitals, his father finally opened his eyes. "Leave me alone, Millie," he told the nurse.

Walt laughed.

"Can't do it, Dr. Eddy. I let you sleep an extra half an hour, but that's it."

"I'm going to remember this," he threatened.

Walt met the eyes of the nurse and grinned. "He's all bark, Millie."

Walt's father turned his head. "Well look who showed up. Thanksgiving was a few days ago." He paused, pulled himself up higher in the bed, refusing Millie's help. "You're late."

"If it meant this much to you, Dad, you could have just said so. Faking a heart attack to get me to fly in the dead of night is overkill." He was smiling, enjoying the half smile on his father's face.

"Good God," Walter sighed. "A cardiac surgeon having an MI. What are the odds?"

"Really good according to your doctor. What the hell, Dad. You had to know this was coming."

Millie took his dad's temperature, and adjusted the amount of solution his father was getting in his IV. "I wanna see my lab work," he told Millie. "Make sure Stanley isn't overdosing me with Heparin."

"He uses the same titration for his patients as you do for yours, Dr. Eddy."

"Still wanna see my labs."

"Of course, Doctor."

Poor Millie. Walt made a mental note to deliver a bottle of good wine to every nurse having the *privilege* of caring for his father.

Millie finished her work and moved from the room.

"She's one of the best nurses in the unit," his dad said after she left the room.

"And yet you treat her like crap."

He scoffed. "I send candy at Christmas."

Far be it for Walt to explain hospital politics to his father. "Whatever works for you, Dad. I learned during my residency to respect the nursing staff and you'd never be jostled awake at two in the morning because your patient spiked a whopping 99.7 fever."

"I need to know that stuff."

"No, you need the nurse to order cultures and present them to you in the morning. A good nurse knows when to call, a nurse worried she'll be reprimanded for doing the right job will call and second-guess everything they do. I bet you never get a good night's sleep."

Instead of commenting, Walter picked at the tape covering his IV line. "Where is your mother?"

"I sent her home. You didn't tell her about your heart."

"I didn't want to worry her."

"Too late."

His dad dropped his head against his pillow. "I don't like being on this side of the chart, Walter."

"None of us do. Sucks being human."

His dad offered a half smile. "I'm going to have to have surgery."

Walt picked his words carefully. "You're always telling me how routine bypass has become."

"It is . . . it is."

"... But?"

"Wrong side of the chart. I can't control anything while I'm under."

Walt leaned forward, patted his father's hand. "You're a control freak."

"Lotta good that's doing me."

"You and Dakota have a lot in common."

His father glanced up. "How is your girl?"

"Fine. Driving Mom home."

"Alone?"

Walt nodded. "Yeah, why?"

"You're braver than I am. Your mother isn't happy with her."

"Hence the reason why we stayed away this week."

Walt noticed the monitor beeping as his father's pulse increased. It was time to change the subject. "Brenda and Larry just left to get some rest. Do you want them to bring anything back with them?"

"No. But when your mother returns tell her to bring my pajamas. I'm not letting any of these people see my ass."

His pissy disposition was proof positive he was on his way to recovery.

Chapter Twenty-Four

JoAnne's silence from her side of the car forced insecurity up Dakota's spine.

The drive up to the Eddy property was slow, slippery, and quiet. After only two comments about a California girl driving in the snow, JoAnne rested her head on the window and drifted off.

Good thing, too. Dakota wasn't as secure behind the wheel as she'd like to believe. It didn't take long to feel like she had some control over the car and the road. Still she inched up the hill and didn't pay a lot of attention to the locals who buzzed around her like she was a sixteen-year-old who'd never driven before.

She breached the Eddy gate, pulled in front of their home, and turned off the engine. Only then did JoAnne stir.

"We're here," Dakota offered.

JoAnne blinked a few times and then pushed from the car without a word.

Inside the house, JoAnne moved into the kitchen and poured a glass of water.

Dakota followed, not certain what to do with herself. "Would you like me to make you something to eat?" Dakota asked, steeling herself for whatever words were coming her way.

The last time JoAnne and she had spoken, they were less than friendly.

"I need to sleep." With that, JoAnne Eddy turned on her heel and left Dakota standing in the middle of the kitchen . . . alone.

Dakota watched Walt's mother retreat and blew out a slow breath.

At least she didn't have to add another ugly confrontation on top of everything else. She placed the small bag housing an overnight's stay of belongings on the sofa in the den, and took in the scene beyond the windows.

The lake she'd tossed Walt in only a few months before was iced over . . . snow filled in the edges and made the scene something out of a movie.

On any other day, this picture might inspire something moving. Today it felt frozen.

Perhaps if Walt were beside her she could appreciate it. Only he was held up in a hospital looking over his father's care.

She placed her purse in her lap and retrieved her phone. A quick text to Walt told him they'd arrived in one piece.

The moment she kicked her shoes off and her feet up, Junior decided to dance. "You're something," she said to her unborn child. "Nothing for hours and now you wanna play."

Instead of searching out a bedroom and risking disturbing JoAnne, Dakota helped herself to a glass of milk and a piece of bread before finding a blanket and pillow on a couch. Even with Junior kicking up a storm, she fell asleep in minutes and didn't wake for hours.

Her head ached, her back wasn't right, but she woke feeling marginally better than when she'd fallen in a comatose heap on the couch. The sun was still high, which told her she'd not slept as long as she might have needed.

She found her cell phone and checked her messages like some might check the morning paper.

Walt let her know he received her text hours before, and then sent a message later to text when she woke.

Another text came from Mary, asking how everyone was.

Then there was her agent, Desi, asking if they could meet before their noon appointment with the publisher.

Overwhelmed, Dakota called Walt first.

"Hey," she said when he answered the phone.

"You haven't slept long enough." Sure enough, she'd looked at the time on her phone before she'd placed the call and she'd only been down a few hours.

"I could never work graveyard and sleep during the day. How are you? You sound tired."

"Remind me to never do this again."

She forced a laugh. "Like you have a choice. How's your dad?"

"Cantankerous, argumentative, and downright mean. So he's better than I thought he'd be."

Funny how a man being an ass could bring joy to her heart. "Good to hear. How are you? Did you manage any sleep?"

"I'll sleep tonight."

Translation . . . no. He hadn't slept. "Walt."

"I'm fine."

"Are you sure?"

He sighed. "How's my mom?"

"Sleeping."

"Was she awful to you?"

Dakota watched the wind blow snow off the treetops. "She was too tired for that. She's been in her room the whole time."

"That's probably a good thing."

Walt went on to tell her about his father's upcoming surgery and how the nurses were earning their Christmas bonuses putting up with him. Walt asked if she could order dinner and lunch for the staff in an effort to ease their suffering.

Dakota moved into the kitchen and wrote a note to herself to order something for the staff. "I'll take care of it," she told him.

"Have I told you how much I appreciate you being here?"

"You have, and you don't need to. I'll let you know when we leave to visit."

"OK. Drive safe."

"I will."

Dakota hung up the phone and moved about the kitchen. After foraging through the kitchen, she found the coffee and brewed a pot. From there she managed to heat up some soup, found a mug to bring some to Walt when they left.

For company, Dakota turned on the television, found the evening news.

The forecast told her the night would freeze and sometime during the next twenty-four hours a low would pass through. On the heels of that, another would sock in.

"Great," she mumbled. "Like we need bad weather to make things harder."

The thought, however, made Dakota consider what was in the Eddy pantry. She moved into it, noted the canned food, the water supplies. The central heater kept the house warm, but did they have firewood?

In full prepper mode, Dakota pulled on her jacket and checked the mudroom and porch outside the house.

Firewood was stacked alongside the house, giving her some ease.

They'd be driving up and down the mountain . . . so the question was what did the Eddys have in their cars?

Dakota cringed when she realized how little JoAnne had in her possession when driving.

Well, Dakota knew better, and she went about making sure any car she'd be using over the next week was prepared.

The drive back down the mountain was just as entertaining as it was going up. JoAnne didn't sleep, but conversation was limited to directions. Dakota was happy to drop her off at the front door of the hospital and search out a parking spot on her own.

She took a moment alone once she parked the car to call Desi. "You're going to have to make my excuses," she told her agent. A five-minute discussion explained where Dakota was and why she wasn't meeting with her publisher in the morning. "The good news is, my next book is done."

"What?" Desi's surprise matched the high-pitched tone. "You're kidding?"

"No. I was going to deliver it personally, but I'm sending you a file instead."

"You're two months ahead of schedule."

"I know. Call me inspired, or maybe it was the restless nights. I'm sure the pace won't be the same once Junior is born. Might as well put in the hours now while I can."

"It sounds like you're stressed out. How are *you* doing?"

"I'm good, actually. Walt and I have found our pace, I think . . . hopefully his father's blip in his health is only that."

"And what about wedding bells? Any of those ringing?"

Dakota shook her head to the empty car. "There are a lot of Hollywood movie stars who shack up, have families, and don't get married for years."

"You're not that woman."

"Yes, I am."

Desi offered a short laugh. "No! You're not."

Arguing with her agent was a waste of time. "I've gotta go. Tell Loretta I'm sorry and that I'll send the manuscript tomorrow."

"I'll tell her. You take care of yourself. Make sure that doctor of yours takes care of you, too."

Dakota bundled against the cold and walked into the hospital. She ran into Walt as he was walking out of the ICU.

He looked tired, a full day's growth of stubble on his face, his hair looked like he'd combed it with his fingers for hours. "Oh, Doc."

He pulled her into his arms and damn near collapsed.

She just held him for several seconds. "Is it that bad?"

He shook his head, talked into the side of her neck. "He's irritable and ready to yell at anyone who walks in the room."

"So he's feeling better."

Walt nodded, pulled away, and captured her face in his hands. "You look good, smell even better."

"I bet you say that to all the women carrying your babies."

He kissed her gently. Dakota folded into him and smiled somewhere deep inside. Yes, they were in a hospital in a crappy situation, but they had each other.

Dakota ended their kiss when the door to the ICU opened to let someone out.

"My dad wanted to see you," he told her. "Then I'd like to get out of here."

"Are we leaving your mom?"

He nodded. "Larry said he'd drive her home after visiting hours. Stanley is enforcing visiting hours between now and his surgery."

"So your dad agreed?"

"Yeah. He's on the schedule for Wednesday morning."

Dakota laid a hand alongside his face. "Then we should try and catch some sleep while we can."

They walked into the ICU together.

Dakota had been in her share of hospitals over the years, but never in an intensive care unit, where the sick teetered on the edge of life and death. It was hard not searching out the conditions of the patients as she passed by the glass-enclosed rooms. The scent unique to hospitals was stronger here. She'd have to ask Walt later what she was smelling. Right now, she didn't want to know. Her stomach wasn't too happy with the odiferous department.

Walt walked her into his father's room.

Unlike the other rooms she'd passed, this one had a couple of people inside. Walter Eddy I sat beside JoAnne. The patient was sitting up in his bed, his gaze went to them as they stepped in. "There you are," Walt's dad said.

"Hello, Dr. Eddy."

Walt's dad was so much more welcoming than his mother. "Well c'mere and give an old man a hug."

She obliged, careful not to upset all the wires and tubes he was hooked up to. "You're not old," she told him.

"Feel like I'm a hundred today."

She smiled and left the comment about how he only looked ninety inside her mouth.

"So where's that grandchild of mine?" he asked.

Dakota stood next to Walt and patted her stomach. "Right where Stud Muffin put him," she said with a wink.

JoAnne scoffed and Walt's grandfather laughed.

"As soon as I'm well enough to knock some sense into my son, I'm going to ask about those wedding plans."

"So, by the weekend, then?" Dakota asked, showing her optimism.

Walt's dad winked. "I'll give you until next week. Consider yourselves warned."

Walt's grandfather chimed in. "Well, I don't have to wait."

JoAnne turned to her father-in-law. "Not now, Dad."

He grumbled.

"Well, son. I don't have to tell you why you need to get your girl out of here. We don't need her getting sick."

Walt placed a hand to the small of her back. "We're leaving." He turned to his mother. "Larry will bring you home."

"I don't have to go home."

"Yes, you do. Dad needs his rest, and so do you."

JoAnne pinched her lips even closer together. It was amazing the woman could still breathe.

"I'll see you in the morning, Dad."

Dakota went ahead and placed a hand on his leg through the blankets. "Don't pinch any nurses' butts. Be professional."

He chuckled and the sound grew like the first flower in spring.

They turned to leave.

"Walt?"

"Yeah, Dad?"

"Thanks for being here."

Walt smiled as they left the room.

———

For two days, Walt juggled his father's care, his mother's snotty disposition, Stanley, and the nursing staff on the unit.

Dakota managed meals, not that she cooked much of them, but she found a caterer that packaged premade lunches and dinners so all they had to do was heat them up when they returned to the house. Dakota sent meals, and not just pizza, to the ICU staff during both shifts. She made notes of who took care of his dad and started sending boxed bottles of wine to each one of them. She even made sure Dr. Altman's staff in his office didn't miss out.

Dakota listened. She heard each of Walt's requests once and used her time to make everything better.

Walt kept her away from the inside of the hospital as much as he could. Made love to her when he had the energy and simply held her when he didn't.

The night before his father's surgery, the five of them exited the hospital and sat around a table at a local Italian restaurant.

"Dad looked ready," Brenda said once they were all seated and drinks were served.

"He did." Larry smiled at his wife and leaned into her.

"I know everyone will want to be at the hospital tomorrow, but visiting after surgery is no more than a glimpse of him before we're all shooed away," Walt explained.

JoAnne picked at a breadstick. "I'd worry more if I stayed home."

Walt couldn't argue that.

"There's no harm in staying long enough to know he's through surgery." Walt reached for Dakota's hand that sat on the table. "I really don't like the amount of time you've spent in the hospital as it is."

Dakota shook her head. "I doubt the pregnant doctors and nurses take nine months off."

"They're not you."

"That's sweet, Doc, but I'm still going tomorrow."

There was a pause and then Brenda changed the subject.

"So, Dakota . . . how did the two of you meet anyway?" Brenda asked.

"He was horning in on my room at a conference."

The memory of her squaring her shoulders and meeting his stare on that day made him grin. "You were teaching a class on . . . what was it again?" he asked.

"Crafting a satisfying sex scene."

Larry spit out the water he was attempting to drink and Walt's mom scoffed.

"Keep your voice down."

Walt looked around, didn't notice anyone within earshot. "Let it go, Mom."

"He made some crack about bodice rippers and I did everything in my power to one-up him."

"You did," he agreed, thankful their conversation had moved from hospitals and surgery. "But that's not when I first noticed you."

"Oh?" Brenda leaned on her elbows to listen.

"She walked into a bar wearing a Lakers cap, sat at the bar, and started eavesdropping on conversations."

Walt ignored his mother when she rolled her eyes again.

"I call it research."

"Did you hear anything juicy?"

Dakota grinned. "I was listening to the pickup lines at the bar. It's amazing what comes out of people's mouths."

"I'll bet."

"So you listen to personal conversations and then exploit them?" his mom asked.

"No. I study people. Try and figure out what makes them tick. It helps when I'm creating fictitious characters in my books."

"I can't imagine why that's needed when writing *your* books."

Brenda spoke out first. "Wow, Mom. Try not to hate so much. Besides, if you haven't read them you shouldn't cast stones."

Walt saw through Dakota's smile. Even though she didn't show it, he knew his mother's words stung.

"You and my mother would get along very well," Dakota said. "She says I write smut."

"There's nothing smutty about your work," Brenda said. "What are you working on now?"

Walt kept glaring at his mother, hoping she'd get a hint.

While Brenda kept quizzing Dakota on her next book, the waiter delivered their dinner.

———

Hours later Walt tucked Dakota into his arms as they snuggled in bed. "I'm sorry about my mom."

"Don't be. She's got to be under an enormous stress."

"We all are, but that doesn't give her the right to paint a target on you."

Dakota turned her dark eyes on him. He pushed a lock of hair behind her ear. "Your mom and I will work things out. You have enough to think about and our relationship doesn't have to be one of them."

She rested her cheek into his palm and smiled at him. A tsunami of emotion rolled over him. "I love you," he whispered.

She paused and sighed. "Walt, I—"

"I'm not telling you that to hear the words returned. I just can't keep them to myself anymore."

Her eyes softened, if that were possible, and he knew he wasn't alone.

Instead of saying a thing, Dakota reached for him, covered his lips with hers in a kiss that picked up his soul and intertwined it with hers.

"Make love to me," she said against his lips.

Walt smiled, pulled her under him, and loved her with every ounce of energy he had.

Chapter Twenty-Five

Dakota sat, stood, paced, walked the halls of the hospital, did just about everything other than relax for the hours it took for Walt's dad to come through surgery.

As the hours ticked by, each of them grew more silent, a little more humbled on how fragile life was.

When the hour that they should have heard something came and went, uncertainty wiggled its nagging little bone into Dakota's head. Each time the door leading into the surgery suites opened, they snapped their eyes to the door, hoping to see Dr. Altman.

"Walt, please ask someone how it's going?"

Walt placed a hand over his mother's. "Stanley knows we're all waiting. He'll be out as soon as he's done."

Yet even with his words, Dakota saw his eyes shift to the volunteer desk, the door to where his father was lying on a table.

She squeezed his hand, saying silently that she was right there with him. He kissed her fingertips and jumped when the door to the back opened.

"Stanley!"

They all stood only to have Dr. Altman wave them back into their seats. Dressed in scrubs from the top of his head to booties on his feet, Stanley Altman appeared just as stressed as they did.

He offered a smile and directed his attention to JoAnne. "He's resting, JoAnne."

"How is he?"

"He's a tough bastard. He gave me a little trouble but came through just fine."

Dakota felt tears in the back of her eyes as a collective sigh moved through all of them.

JoAnne grasped both of Stanley's hands. "Thank you."

"He's in recovery right now, on a ventilator for a little while longer." Dr. Altman ran through some of what Dakota thought were routine procedural steps Walt's father was going to have to endure.

"When can I see him?" JoAnne asked.

"Let me get him off the vent first. Then you can see him. After that, I want you to go home. I'm sure your son has already explained that there's nothing you can do. He'll be up for visitors tomorrow, even more in a day or two."

Walt shook Dr. Altman's hand and pulled away with him to talk privately.

Brenda called her grandfather and another friend of the family who was in charge of informing the rest of their extended family.

Dakota attempted to text Mary, and noticed her battery dead on her phone. She placed her phone into her purse and waited for Walt to return so she could use his.

"We have at least an hour's wait to see him," Walt said when he left Dr. Altman's side. "I could use some fresh air."

They left the others in the lobby and took the elevator to the ground floor. Walt's silence sparked her concern. "What's wrong?"

He waited until they were out of the hospital, and walking around the cold sidewalk of the hospital grounds. "He's doing all right, but not great. Stanley didn't want to worry my mom. There was a little more bleeding than he would have liked, and a longer time on the bypass machine."

"What does all that mean?"

"It means the next night is going to be touchy. More than normal."

Not good. None of that sounded good.

"You should stay down here then. I'll get your mom home."

"She'll figure out something's wrong if I stay."

"You're a doctor. You can actually do something, where all we can do is stand by and worry. Your mom might actually like you staying back."

"You have a point. We should know by midnight if he's going to have any issues."

Dakota shrugged. "So we make an excuse for you to stay behind a little longer, and work from there. I can endure another silent drive with JoAnne."

Walt shook his head. "I owe you."

"Big-time, buddy." She winked. As they moved back into the hospital, she lifted her palm. "I need to use your phone to text Mary. Mine died."

He handed it over, grinned. "You need me."

"Yep, I do."

"I know you're hiding something from me," JoAnne said ten minutes into their drive. They'd managed to crawl out of the city and were at the base of the mountain. It was past eight, black ice covered the road, and snow was going to be a factor if they didn't make it to the Eddy home before nine. The streets were deserted and the glittering of Christmas lights lit up the homes, making the winter scene bearable.

"Why would I hide anything from you?" Dakota turned the radio down, the heat up. The windshield wipers whisked away the falling snow seconds after it hit.

"Why did Walt stay behind?"

Dakota gripped the wheel. "He told you. The snow might make it difficult to come down early in the morning. He wanted someone to stay and since he's a doctor, he's the most practical candidate. Besides, hospitals always have beds for the doctors to sleep in if they're needed."

Dakota feathered the brakes as she came to a stop at a light, felt the car slip, and eased off and back on. Driving in the snow wasn't her strong point, but she'd grown more used to it since she'd arrived in Colorado. She couldn't help but think this trip up the mountain was going to test all her reflexes.

The light turned, the wheels to the SUV gripped the pavement, giving Dakota some encouragement.

"I don't believe you."

"Oh? What don't you believe? The part about your son being a doctor? I thought you knew that." Dakota's attempt to get JoAnne to smile failed.

"You think you're funny."

No, I know I'm funny.

Fifteen minutes later, they were only a couple of miles off the turnoff to the mountain road to the Eddy home. The road was in relatively good shape, but the snow was starting to pile over the tracks laid by other vehicles.

"Should we put on the chains?"

JoAnne rolled her eyes. "It isn't that thick yet."

Having never put on chains before, Dakota opted to go with JoAnne's words and continued on. As luck would have it, the more snow that fell, the easier the car gripped the road. As long as she didn't get in a hurry and hit the gas, she felt the car would eventually make it.

Dakota had to lean forward in the car to see the road signs, and even then, they were covered in snow.

"It's not this one," JoAnne said when Dakota slowed the car down.

She drove a little farther, listened to JoAnne tap her fingers against the armrest. "Can't we go a little faster? I'd really like to get to bed before midnight."

"Do you want to drive?"

"My husband just had open heart surgery. No! I don't want to drive."

Dakota took her eyes off the road for only a second to glare at JoAnne. "Then kindly be quiet and let me get us home safely."

"My home is not yours."

Dakota tried not to take offense. "You've made that painfully clear, Mrs. Eddy."

"Then please refrain from calling it *home*."

Her back teeth ground together. "Yes, ma'am, I'll do my best."

"Oh, now you're being sarcastic. Your accent always makes an appearance when you're trying to dig at me."

She glanced left, looking for the giant boulder that signaled the upcoming street. "It's a wonder as to how I don't sound like this all the time, don't you think?"

"I don't care for you."

Dakota was about to tell JoAnne the feeling was mutual, and then decided to try something different. "Well, that just sucks for you. I've actually grown fond of you."

JoAnne twisted her head to stare out the window. "Oh, please."

"No, really. You're a loyal wife, devoted in a way I didn't see coming."

JoAnne huffed, but didn't say a word.

"You raised two great children. Brenda's just a doll."

Dakota kept searching for the rock, didn't see it. Probably up ahead. Going as slow as she was, it was a wonder they had gone so many miles.

"Did you like Larry when he and Brenda first started dating?"

"Larry was always a gentleman." Yes, but Dakota knew that JoAnne had given him trouble at first.

"Bless his heart. A gentleman will always win a woman's devotion."

JoAnne scoffed, peered over the dash. "I think you missed the turnoff."

Dakota slowed the car, which didn't take much. "I did?"

There weren't any lights ahead or behind them. "Should I turn around here, or is there someplace wider up ahead?"

JoAnne sat back, crossed her arms. "There's another road a half mile or so up, we can go around the back way. Driving downhill in this isn't nearly as easy as driving up."

Dakota wanted to argue. Her shoulders were killing her for all the tension she was holding. Deep inside, the baby kicked her. *I'll get us home.*

The half a mile came and went, still no turnoff. "Is it farther up?"

"It must be."

They kept driving. Two miles later, Dakota took her time turning around. She put the car in low and crawled back down.

JoAnne pointed. "This is it . . . I think."

"You think?"

"This is it. I do live here."

Dakota stopped the car, looked down the snow-laden street, the tall pines were covered with snow and it was coming down so hard the windshield wipers couldn't keep up even at the highest speed. "Now is not the time for grandstanding, JoAnne. Getting lost out here isn't something I want to do."

"That isn't likely."

Everything was a blanket of white, all landmarks were gone, and the dark made it even harder to see.

Dakota turned down the road and watched the tracks behind her fill with new snow.

—·—

Walt checked his watch for the third time in fifteen minutes. He huddled over his cup of coffee and checked his phone.

He left a third message at home and still he hadn't heard from Dakota. The snow was coming down, which added to the anxiety crawling in his chest.

Finally, he called Brenda. "Hey, sis."

"Oh, no. Is everything OK?"

"Dad's fine. Stanley's right. He's a tough bastard."

His sister sighed. "Oh, good. How are you holding up? Did they find you a bed? Those foldout chairs kinda suck."

"No, not yet. Listen, have you heard from Mom or Dakota?"

"No. They left when we did."

"I know. It's just, they haven't called and it's been an hour and a half."

"You know how it is driving up there in the snow. Slow. I'm sure they'll call soon."

He needed to hear that. "Do they still plow the road?"

"Of course. There's been some new housing developments going in, so it might take them a little longer to make the rounds, but they go nonstop."

"Good. Well, if you hear something from Mom, call me."

"Why don't you just call Dakota's cell? The service up there isn't that spotty."

"Her phone died."

"Call Mom's then."

Good point.

He hung up and dialed his mother's number. When it went directly to voice mail, he started to panic all over again.

As the clock struck ten thirty, Walt woke Larry. "No one is answering. There's no way it takes two and a half hours to get up that hill."

"We're lost."

"We are *not* lost. I've lived here for thirty-five years."

"I don't care if you've lived here for sixty years. We're lost." Dakota stopped the car, put it in park. "The more we drive in circles, the harder it will be for anyone to find us."

JoAnne stared out the window. "Find us? You're not suggesting we just sit here."

"That's exactly what I'm suggesting."

"I'm sure the way back to the main road is just up ahead."

Dakota blasted the heat a little higher. "That's what you said a half hour ago. We almost got stuck, which is why I know we made a big circle." She pointed out the front window. "Our tracks are still here."

JoAnne glared out the window. "We'll just call Larry. He'll come and get us."

Dakota reached her hand out, palm up.

"What?"

"Your phone?"

"Mine is at home."

Dakota shivered.

"What?" JoAnne's word stiffened Dakota's spine.

"My phone lost its charge hours ago." She reached over, opened the glove box. The charger inside wasn't the one her phone used. *Freaking perfect.*

On the dash, north was behind them, but the information was close to useless. They knew the main road was east of them, but the path east was filled with forest and trees and not a road.

Dakota tried to calm her kicking baby, and tried even harder to ignore her bladder.

While the car idled, she turned the radio back on, found a news station.

For the first time in hours, JoAnne didn't question her as they both listened to the weather report. The report earlier said this storm wasn't going to come in until two in the morning, but instead it blew in early and seemed to be parking itself over the mountain.

"It's almost midnight. We have just under half a tank of gas. The more we drive around, the less gas we'll have to keep warm during the night."

"If we stay here, the car will get stuck."

"And if keep driving, we might *get stuck*. Getting out now to put on chains wouldn't be smart."

JoAnne wiped the condensation off the window with her hand. "We should try and find the road."

Instead of arguing, Dakota found a compromise. "We drive for another few miles. If we don't find it, we stop. Agreed?"

For once, JoAnne didn't argue.

Five miles later they stopped.

With the engine still running, and the heater still blowing, Dakota set the parking brake and managed to climb into the back of the car. She unfurled two blankets and handed the water bottles to JoAnne.

"What is all this doing in here?"

"I stocked the car the day after we got here."

"You thought this would happen?"

"I hoped it wouldn't."

For a woman who claimed to be tired hours ago, JoAnne sat with wide-opened eyes and fear all over her face.

"I have food back here, too. Not a lot, but enough for a couple of days."

"We can't survive out here that long. We'll freeze."

Dakota avoided panic by focusing on the positive. "We won't freeze. And someone will come looking for us before morning."

"Oh, God."

Dakota climbed over the seats and killed the engine.

"What are you doing?"

"Saving gas. Put your coat on, your gloves, wrap up in the blanket. Jump in the backseat. Try and get some sleep."

Dakota bundled into her ski hat and gloves and closed her coat around her tight. Then she reached for the door.

"Where are you going?"

"I just need to pee, JoAnne. Your grandchild has been kicking my bladder for two hours."

Dakota left the lights of the car on as she stepped out. Snow fell quietly; the fresh scent of the air would have been welcome from the porch of the Eddy home. She watched as her breath made the air fog with each exhale. She didn't move far from the car and proceeded to freeze her butt off as she emptied her bladder.

She barely zipped her pants before rushing back to the car and climbing inside. "Shit, that's cold," she said the moment the door slammed behind her.

JoAnne handed her the second blanket.

Several minutes passed, and Dakota switched off the lights of the car. The silence grew as the temperature in the car fell.

"We're going to be OK," she told Walt's mother.

"Of course we are."

Good, that fight would help as the hours ticked by.

Chapter Twenty-Six

The plows went all the way to the Eddy house.

Nothing.

No one.

By two in the morning, the police were looking, but an official search wouldn't happen until morning. Dakota and JoAnne weren't the only missing people caught in the storm.

The roads farther up from his childhood home became impassible with the exception of plows, and even then, they were waiting for daylight and a break in the weather to get ahead of the snow.

He couldn't sit, couldn't sleep, couldn't close his eyes without seeing Dakota on the side of the road, or worse, down the side of the mountain. What if they'd gotten into an accident? Were they hurt?

Larry made his way to the hospital, leaving Brenda at home to catch any possible phone call there.

At least his father rested comfortably, none the wiser.

Running on caffeine, Walt watched the sky lighten, but the snow kept coming.

With chains on his four-wheel-drive truck, Larry drove the two of them to the police station, where they were met with a lobby full of bundled residents and several sheriffs trying to calm and address each one.

When Walt met the whites of the clerks' eyes, he forced his attention on her.

"We have every officer out at this time, Dr. Eddy. We have a description of your mother's car. We're looking."

"Where are you looking?"

The phone rang, distracting her again.

Walt turned around.

Larry nodded toward the door. "C'mon. We'll look."

The plows had been through to his parents' turnoff, but the road to the house was covered in over a foot of snow. They'd been told that an officer had knocked on the door, but there was no evidence of a car passing.

That scared Walt even more.

Larry inched the truck to the house.

Inside was dead silent, the red light on the answering machine blinked.

He heard his own calls, felt his panic all over again with each one.

Walt grabbed the throws from off the backs of the sofas, piled a bag full of water and ready-to-eat food, and shoved them into Larry's truck.

"They could have missed the turnoff at night."

"Hard to believe Mom would have missed it."

"Unless she'd fallen asleep and Dakota missed it."

Walt agreed with Larry, and they headed farther up the mountain. The snow was even thicker, and the falling rate would give them another six inches before noon.

They made it to a blockade, indicating that the plows hadn't gone through in some time.

Each hour that passed killed part of Walt's soul. He called Brenda every thirty minutes only to learn that she'd heard nothing.

Some of the chaos at the police station had mellowed when they returned there just after noon.

Panic moved to anger and Walt made sure he had the attention of as many officers as he could.

When the clerk started in with the *we're looking* spiel, Walt lost it.

He slammed his hand on the counter. "My pregnant fiancée and my mother are out there. My father is recovering from heart surgery. *We're looking* isn't good enough!"

Finally, a sergeant came forward. "I'm Sergeant Mills. Let me show you where we're directing our search."

A map in a back room had colored stickpins dotting all over it. "We've been patrolling the main road, searched the road leading to your parents' home. The electricity is out all over the west side of the mountain, and we've been all over that area helping residents get out, or get in."

Walt studied the map, pointed above the turnoff. "The road is closed up here, when did that happen?"

"After midnight."

"Has anyone been up there since? We didn't get through."

"The plows are going through within the hour. If your family missed their turn, there is another one a quarter mile up. Could they have taken that?"

"Anything is possible."

Walt ran a hand through his hair.

"I know you're frustrated. We're using every resource right now. All emergency vehicles are out in the storm. Power is out everywhere, people have been stranded in cars overnight. We're hoping the snow slows down before sunset. If not, then first thing in the morning we'll start again, get a bird in the air and see if we can find them from above."

Walt thought of Trent, his resources. "How many choppers do you have?"

"Two."

"I can get more."

"We might not need them."

Might wasn't good enough.

He put a phone call in to his friend.

Both Dakota and JoAnne huddled in the front of the car when they turned on the car to heat it up. The sun might have been up, but the temperature was still bitter cold. Dakota had managed maybe an hour of sleep in the night. JoAnne did marginally better.

About the time the engine warmed enough to blow hot air, Dakota would blow the horn a few times. Three short, three long, three short. If there was one prepper code known, it was SOS. She only did it while the engine ran, afraid she'd kill the battery and they'd lose their ability to warm the interior of the car.

For the first time since Dakota had met JoAnne, the woman appeared her age. The makeup was long gone, her hair flat from the couple of trips outside the car to relieve herself.

When their teeth finally stopped chattering, JoAnn followed her blank stare with a shudder. "I really hope Walt doesn't tell his father that we're missing."

"Your son is smarter than that."

JoAnne sipped water and continued to stare out the window. "He was such a bright child growing up. Walter and I knew he'd be a wonderful physician."

"He is. Monica has told me plenty of stories. It takes a special human being to give of themselves as much as he does."

JoAnne actually cracked a smile, but kept her thoughts to herself.

"He thinks he disappointed you and your husband."

She snapped out of her trance. "What?"

Dakota wasn't sure if she should be saying any of this, but what could it hurt? "He didn't follow your husband into cardiology."

JoAnne's lips formed an *O*. She sighed. "Well. I suppose at first we might have been. But Walter and I knew by the way he craved travel and excitement that taking over the practice wasn't something Walt would do. We're not disappointed. Though I can see why he might think that. We worry that his quest to save the world will put him in danger."

Dakota rubbed their baby through her own skin. "I worry about that a little, too. I have to believe that he'll make the right choices when he's playing doctor."

JoAnne actually laughed a little.

"When he and Brenda were little, he'd play doctor. He'd diagnose every blemish on her skin, every sneeze. When they were in school, he'd tell his teachers he was playing doctor with his sister."

It was Dakota's turn to laugh. "Oh, no."

"Oh, yes. The phone calls came in. Everyone jumped to the wrong conclusions. Walter and I were mortified. Oh, we laughed about it later, but at the time, we about died of embarrassment."

"He didn't tell me that story."

JoAnne smiled, warmed into a thought she didn't share. "You have plenty of years to hear his stories."

Those weren't words Dakota thought she'd hear from JoAnne Eddy.

Dakota reached for the key when she realized they were both free of chattering teeth. Sundown was only a few hours away. They'd need the heat more then. With the engine off, it was only their voices to kill the silence.

"On our first date, Walt took me bowling."

"That's nice. He always liked to bowl."

"I didn't think anyone bowled anymore. He seemed at home in rented shoes."

JoAnne shrugged. "He should. He has been on several leagues."

"No. Really?"

"He didn't tell you?"

"I guess he didn't want to embarrass me. My gutter balls must have made him cringe."

JoAnne leaned her head back, closed her eyes. "I can't bowl either. Walter dragged me to the alley all the time until Walt could join him."

"Does Brenda bowl?"

"Yes, actually." JoAnne opened her eyes, paused. "I'd do just about anything to bowl a few gutter balls right now."

"I'm right there with you." Dakota paused, looked out the window. "Walt told me you went to college."

"I did."

"What did you study?"

JoAnne actually smiled. "Interior design."

That made sense . . . the Eddy home had the hand of a professional in how it was decorated. "Did you want a career?"

"I thought I did. Then I met Walter. Seemed silly to juggle being a wife, mother, and an interior designer. After a while I stopped thinking about it."

"Your home really is lovely."

JoAnne accepted the compliment with a smile.

Dakota rubbed the small of her back.

JoAnne watched her. "Are you OK?"

"Just a little stiff." Her stomach growled. "And hungry."

They'd eaten protein bars for breakfast followed by a few crackers.

"How much food do we have back there?" JoAnne asked.

"A couple of days' worth, if we're careful."

"Then you should eat something," JoAnne said.

"I'm all right."

Not five minutes went by and her stomach growled again.

"Dakota, please eat something. Think of your baby."

Giving in, she tilted the seat back to crawl into the back of the SUV. Her limbs protested as she squeezed into the back. To give herself more room, she folded the backseat onto itself and leaned against it as she dug through the bag. She lifted two cans. "Canned chicken or tuna for an early dinner?" she asked JoAnne.

"Surprise me."

The can of chicken was larger, easier to split. Dakota dropped the tuna back into the bag, only to have it roll out and under the seat.

She reached around blindly to find it. Instead of a round can, she came in contact with something small and square.

She settled back on her heels and looked at what was obviously a jewelry box.

"What did you find there?"

"Looks like a jewelry box. Are you missing anything?"

JoAnne turned in her seat. "I don't misplace my jewelry."

"It's probably empty." Dakota was looking at JoAnne when she opened the box.

She gasped, nearly dropped it when her eyes settled on what it contained.

Sitting on a bed of black velvet was the ring she'd admired while shopping with Mary and Monica. "Oh my God."

Walt! It must have fallen out of his luggage, his pocket, something.

"What is it?"

With tears in her eyes, Dakota turned the box toward JoAnne. "Oh, my."

Dakota ran her fingertips over the ring, what it meant sank in. "I love your son. I love him so much it hurts."

Using the back of her hand, Dakota tried to dry her tears. Why had she not told him her feelings when he'd whispered his love for her?

Fear.

Fear of letting him in, which was stupid since he was already sitting on her chest laying claim.

If she made it out of this car, she'd drag him to Vegas the second they could catch a plane.

"Let me see it." JoAnne wiggled her gloved fingers.

Dakota let go of the box, wanted it back the moment it left her hand.

JoAnne whistled. "My son has excellent taste." She removed the ring from the box, tilted it in the light. "Lovely." She admired it a little longer and handed the ring toward Dakota. "You really should put this on. We wouldn't want Walt to lose it twice. I love my son, but he is sometimes a little absentminded with things like his bills, and engagement rings."

Dakota frowned, not sure she should since he hadn't yet given it to her. "I don't know."

JoAnne rolled her eyes, braved an open door, and tossed the empty box out of the car. She once again handed Dakota the ring.

With little left to do, Dakota removed the glove on her left hand and took the ring from her future mother-in-law. She slid it on and felt fresh tears.

I love you, Walter Eddy the Third. Now find me so I can tell you in person.

She sent her silent words to the Universe and hoped someone listened.

Mary's words assured him, even though he heard a tremor in her voice.

"Dakota's a prepper. She will have food, water, extra blankets. If they got lost, she'll park the car and wait to be found."

Night had fallen again, the snow let up right before the sun went down. They'd checked the roads about the house and didn't find anything. There were plenty of turnoffs, old campgrounds, a few abandoned houses.

Not that a lack of the sun was going to stop Walt's search. He and Larry were bundled and ready for another trip up the mountain. The police used the house as a base camp, plows would pick one of them up as they continued on up the road.

"I'm going to find her," Walt assured Mary.

"Of course you are. Trent and Glen are flying in tonight, so long as the weather holds. By noon tomorrow you'll be sipping hot chocolate and laughing." Mary choked on a cry.

"Have you called her parents?"

"I have. They're booking flights. I'll let your sister know when to expect all of us. We'll get to you, don't think about us."

"I don't have room in my head to."

"Dr. Eddy?" One of the officers waved him over.

"I've gotta go."

"Go find her."

"I will."

Walt climbed into another plow and watched as light sparkled off the snow. Instead of traveling the main road, they took the back one.

Even though the plow could chomp through the snow and ice like a teenager did pizza, they moved slowly and shed light on the side roads as they went. "C'mon, Dakota. Where are you?"

———

With the open skies, the temperature dropped below zero, or so the outside temperature gauge on the car said when they cranked the engine to heat the inside.

The gas in the car was still reading a quarter of a tank.

Dakota ran the flashers and honked the horn several times when she could. The fear of running out of gas and heat was a larger concern than food at this point. JoAnne was the one who suggested they move to the backseat and huddle together to stay warm.

Using the flashlight to keep a light in the car on, Dakota propped it against the front seat and helped JoAnne into the back. They bundled close, used the blankets to contain as much heat as they could.

"First thing I'm doing when we get home is filling a tub with scalding hot water."

Dakota agreed. "With scented bubbles. Rose or lilac."

JoAnne offered a dry laugh. "We do stink."

"I'll pack air deodorant in the emergency kit next time."

"Bite your tongue, young lady. We most certainly are not doing *this* again."

Dakota smiled, closed her eyes. "Yes, ma'am."

They were both quiet for a while, yet neither of them slept.

"I'm scared, Dakota."

Dakota reached for JoAnne's hand, squeezed it. "We won't run out of water, we can survive for several days without food."

"What about freezing to—"

"Don't! We're cold, not frozen. We're fine."

"But—"

"JoAnne, I just started to like you. Don't go blowing it with *buts* and death talk."

Dakota felt JoAnne's hand squeeze hers. "You're a pushy one."

"Damn right. A trait you'll learn to love."

JoAnne leaned her head against Dakota's and her breathing evened out.

Dakota shook herself awake sometime later, noticed ice forming on the inside of the window. Easing out from under JoAnne's sleeping head, Dakota uncurled from the heat of the blankets and wiggled into the front seat. She turned the engine over, panicked a little when it took a moment to start.

"So cold." She heard JoAnne mumble in the back.

"Heat is coming." Dakota blew the horn, signaled SOS, and checked the time. After three. According to the temperature gauge, it was minus five degrees.

She would never again curse Southern California for all the windy, hot weather it provided.

She hit the horn again, followed it with a flash of the headlights. Once the chill was out of the air, she cut the engine.

They only had one-eighth of a tank left.

Tomorrow she'd have to figure out how to keep them warm without the use of the engine.

———•———

Walt's plow met up with Larry's. "Anything?" Larry yelled from the cab.

"Nothing. You?"

"We thought we saw tracks leading farther north. Didn't want to risk the road alone."

"Let's go," Chance, his driver, said.

They found the tracks, or what Larry thought were tracks. Looked more like big circle. Like maybe kids got out there and did doughnuts in the snow before it really hit hard. The road from here led off in three directions, the one they came in on, and two others.

"Do you know where we are?" Walt asked his driver.

He peered out the window. "Think we're at an old summer camp site."

That would explain the open road and several turns. "Any idea where it dumps out?"

"Main road is five miles away. But we know they didn't find the road."

Walt tried yelling at Larry over the noise of the engines. "It's an old campground."

"That explains a lot. Think they could have gotten turned around in here?"

"Maybe."

Something out of place sounded behind him. Walt turned toward the noise. "Did you hear that?"

Larry shook his head. "What?"

"Chance, kill the engine."

Walt made a cutting motion with his hand to the other driver.

With the noise down to nothing but the bubbling liquid inside the engines, Walt tilted his head.

The hope that had filled him a moment before drowned as he heard nothing but silence.

"Now I'm hearing things."

Larry cursed. "We'll find them."

Walt was punchy, tired, and so fucking scared he couldn't see straight. "You circle around east, we'll take the west, meet back here."

"Sounds good."

Chance started the engine again when Walt heard the noise. "Turn it off," he yelled.

Every hair on his arms stood. A horn. Weak but clear. He caught three short honks, three long, three short.

"Holy shit," Larry yelled.

"Where's it coming from?" The noise bounced off the trees, making it sound like it was behind them, then in front of them.

Walt thought he saw a flash of light, only to look over his shoulder to notice the flashing lights of the plow.

He pointed behind them. "I'm going that way, circle the back side. Someone is out here."

Larry smiled for the first time in two days.

———

Dakota once again huddled next JoAnne, and forced her eyes to close. Sleeping while she was mostly warm was safer than doing so while freezing.

Slumber knocked on the backs of her eyelids. She imagined the warm breeze off the ocean, the gentle waves. Didn't Monica say she and Trent had a vacation home in Jamaica? God, that sounded really good.

The hum inside her head had been there for hours. She didn't want to acknowledge the headache or the possibility that her blood pressure might be taking a hike on the high road.

She ignored the hum and snuggled deeper under the blankets.

The hum grew and Dakota jumped.

She peered outside the car and screeched when she noticed a distant fading light.

"Oh, God." She jumped over the seat, sent JoAnne flying.

She hit the horn, let it blare. When she turned on the lights, they faded.

"What is it?"

"Help." Dakota pointed out the window. "They can't hear us. Grab the flashlight."

JoAnne scrambled out from the covers, grasped the flashlight, and waved it out the window.

Dakota opened the door, ignored the biting cold, and ran to the back of the car.

The lights connected to the hum moved farther away.

She dug in her bag, found the flare, and flinched when she sparked it to life.

With the red glow sloshed in three feet of snow, waving it. "Here! Hey!"

JoAnne laid a palm into the horn.

"Oh, God, no."

The vehicle moved away from them.

Dakota screamed.

She tried to run, fell flat on her face and nearly doused the light of the flare.

The horn lost its power but that didn't stop JoAnne from yelling out the window.

Dakota turned to look at the car, noticed a second light.

Changing her focus, she waved at the second set of lights, the ones moving closer. "Look!" she yelled and pointed.

JoAnne turned, flashed the light in a new direction.

The lights on the plow turned off and then on again.

They see us.

Dakota moved to JoAnne's side. They hugged each other. "They found us."

"They did."

The plow stopped feet from the car, and someone from the passenger seat swung down from the cab.

"Dakota? Mom?"

"Walt!"

"Walter."

They crawled over the snow and met somewhere in the middle. Bundled and hardly recognizable, Walt pulled them both into his arms.

"Thank God."

Joy came in the way of heat as it spread all over her limbs. Tears, the good kind, fell down her cheeks.

JoAnne was laughing with nerves. "About time you found us."

Walt laughed and soon Dakota joined in.

He pulled away and looked in her eyes. "Are you OK?"

"I am now."

He kissed her, as if she were a lifeline and he was on his last breath. He stopped long enough to hug them both again, then ushered them inside to the warmth of the plow.

Chapter Twenty-Seven

Calls were made long before they arrived at the house. Walt didn't let go of Dakota's gloved hand the entire trip down the hill.

His mother's story kept him from needing to ask anything.

"It's my fault really. I shouldn't have distracted Dakota. We got turned around. I thought I could get us back to the house the back way."

"We looked there."

"We obviously didn't get there. We drove in circles until Dakota put her foot down and we stopped."

Walt kissed Dakota's forehead.

"She'd filled the car with water and food. Such a smart girl you have here, Walter."

Dakota glanced over Walt's shoulder at his mother. "We bonded."

"It seems that way."

His mom laughed. "I suggest a spa weekend if we need more bonding. I think it might be time for your father and I to find a second home in Arizona. Do they call that snowbirds? Living in one place during the summer and a warm place in the winter?"

Walt couldn't remember another time when his mother rambled so much.

"Yes. That's what they call it."

"Besides, Arizona is closer to you two. Once the baby comes I'm sure your father and I will want to be more involved than just holidays."

Walt placed a hand on his mother's head, peered closer. "Did you hit your head?"

She shooed his hand away. "Don't play doctor with me. I'm just fine."

Beside him, Dakota laughed and his mother joined in.

His mom placed a finger in front of her lips. "Shh!"

Dakota winked and made a zipping motion over her lips.

"Secrets? You two have secrets?"

"What happens in snowbound cars, stays in snowbound cars."

His mom took a deep breath, blew it out. "How is your father?"

"Restless. We told him you were both snowed in at the house and waiting to get down the hill. I don't think he bought the lack of phone service, but he was too tired to argue that much."

They arrived at the house with a rush of activity. Brenda grabbed a hold of her mom and didn't let go.

The police took a statement and eventually left.

Walt forced Dakota to sit through a simple blood pressure and blood sugar test before he allowed the EMTs to leave.

They shed their coats and shoes before the massive fire in the fireplace and sighed.

Walt took their coats, placed them on a drying rack.

Brenda was already warming up hot soup, and Larry was calling family.

Walt turned to see Dakota rubbing her hands over his mother's. "Let's not do that again, OK?"

His mom grasped her hands and held them. "Thanks for keeping me sane."

Dakota smiled and they both looked down at their hands.

His mom patted her hand, and that's when Walt noticed the shine coming from Dakota's ring finger.

"I think I'll find that bubble bath before I eat."

JoAnne walked by his side, patted his arm, and smiled before walking away. "Brenda, honey, can you bring that to my room? I must shed these clothes."

Walt heard the others exit the great room. He moved to Dakota's side and took her hand in his.

The ring was perfect, and the fact that it sat on her ring finger made him smile like a kid on their sixteenth birthday. Car keys in hand.

"I thought I lost that."

She stretched out her hand, admired the ring. "Oh, is this yours? I found it under the backseat while searching for canned tuna."

Walt lifted her chin to meet her eyes.

"I thought I lost you."

Dakota shook her head, slowly. "Takes more than a little snowstorm to get rid of me. Besides, I have some seriously unfinished business to take care of in this life."

He smiled, loved that she could laugh in the face of what had to have been a harrowing experience. "What's that?"

She searched him with a look. "I need to tell the man who bought this ring that I love him."

The words were music, like a breathing child, like a heartbeat where there once was nothing. They filled him, she consumed him.

"I love you, Walt. I really hope this ring is our next step."

He stepped closer, felt her body against his. "Are you ready for the next step?"

Her smile was ear-to-ear. "I need a little sleep, a long shower, and some food, but after that I'm ready."

"So we're getting married."

"Oh, we're getting married, Doc. We are *so* getting married."

He brushed his lips against hers. On a sigh, she melted into his touch.

Their child, not quite ready to say hello to the world, kicked him.

Dakota pulled away laughing. "We'll get your father healthy enough to wear a suit, make sure my parents and sister can be here. Fly Mary in, get Trent and Monica here . . . maybe even my agent."

"Sounds like forever."

"Not quite forever. I'm thinking this weekend will work. Gotta snag ya while your mom still likes me."

Walt scooped her up, spun her around. "I love you."

He kissed her again, felt his heart sing.

"I need food, a bath, and a bed," she told him.

"You got it."

She stopped him before they headed up the stairs. "Wake me in the morning with a kiss."

"I'll wake you every morning of our lives with a kiss."

Epilogue

She felt him long before he slid into the space beside her, placed his lips against her ear, and said, "Please tell me that ring doesn't mean you're married."

Dakota pulled her hair aside to feel the warmth of his breath on her neck. "Oh, I'm married." She laid a hand on her belly, felt Junior stretch to the point of rearranging one of her lungs. "But you might convince me to stray."

The woman sitting at the bar beside her looked Dakota up and down, and then swung her gaze to the man trying to pick her up.

His breath tickled the lobe of Dakota's ear, made her lean into him. "I'm in the penthouse suite," he murmured.

"Tempting." Dakota sucked in her bottom lip, gave it a little chew.

The eavesdropping woman clicked her tongue, grabbed her drink, and left the bar in a huff.

They both started laughing as Walt took the now unoccupied seat.

"Is everything all set?" she asked.

"The room is filling, the books are stacked, even our moms have added their own personal flavor to the event."

Dakota groaned. "Should I be worried?"

Walt took her hands in his, kissed them. "No. This idea of Mary's is just short of brilliant. What better way to show our families how respected you are, than to bring them here?"

The holidays were behind them, as was their brief honeymoon in the western Caribbean.

The New York Morrison was hosting her release party and book signing of *Succumb to Me*, the final chapter in Mathew and Cassidy's story.

"Tell me our mothers are getting along."

Walt tossed his hands in the air. "If they're not, they aren't bogging me down with it."

"How's your dad?"

"Loving the attention. He and Dennis are sitting in the back of the room, watching the show."

Dakota wasn't even sure what the show was. She'd been told to stay clear of the ballroom where she'd be giving a speech about her latest book, and plugging her new one that would be out in late fall. With the exception of the hotel, and the guest list for the after-signing party, Dakota was clueless. "What show?"

Walt winked, not giving her anything. He checked his watch and stood. "Showtime, Baby Mama."

She held his hand as they walked through the hotel, down a long hall, and into a holding room beside the ballroom.

A high rumble of excitement came from the many voices inside the ballroom, an occasional bit of laughter leaked through the doors leading in.

The door opened and Mary popped out. "There you are." Her blue eyes sparkled when she smiled. "I love this part."

"I know." Mary had been at her side for much of her success, and release events like this were always so full of life and energy it was hard going for long stints without them.

Dakota glanced down to see what Mary was wearing. It was a pink T-shirt with Dakota's website on the left shoulder. "Cute shirt."

Mary giggled and turned around. On the back, the shirt said, *Baby Mama's BFF*.

"I love it."

Mary kept laughing. "Wait until you see the rest."

Dakota turned to Walt.

He smiled and took his jacket off. His shirt was blue, on the back it said, *Dr. Baby Daddy*, below that it stated . . . *Inspiration for Chapter Thirteen.*

Didn't matter that Dakota didn't know Walt when she wrote chapter thirteen, the implication would be clear. Chapter thirteen was sexy hot, and well worth a Walt mention. She let out a squeal and was laughing as Mary led her into the fray.

The ballroom was a sea of pink and blue, with dashes of black and white, which were the colors on the cover of *Succumb to Me*. At the door, Glen stood beside Trent, they both wore blue shirts. They turned around to show her their personal graphic: *Baby Daddy and Mama's Personal Pilot.*

Mary pulled her past Glen and avoided the man's gaze.

Dakota noticed a smirk on Glen's face before she took in the room.

There were balloons, flowers, and rows of women who were slowly noticing that she stepped into the room.

The pink-and-blue theme went throughout the family. *Dr. Baby Daddy's Mom, Baby Mama's Sister, Baby Mama's Agent.* If the person in the room knew Dakota or Walt personally, they were wearing a shirt describing their relationship.

It was funny, personal, and so thoughtful Dakota was grinning to the point of pain.

"Whose idea were the shirts?" she asked.

"That would be Walt's," Dakota's mom told her. "I thought it was silly, but your fans seem to love them."

"You're a sport for wearing it," she told her mom with a half hug.

Elaine smiled when JoAnne approached.

"If you need to rest, you just let us know," JoAnne said.

"I think I'll be fine."

Dakota smiled at her new in-laws, winked at Walter II. "How are you feeling?"

"Never better." He'd taken the past couple months away from his practice, didn't plan on going back full-time. He looked damn good, and Dakota hoped that expecting his first grandchild was fueling his quick recovery.

With Walt's hand in hers, she turned to the sea of pink and blue. "I can't tell you how much I appreciate you all being here."

Carol Ann stood beside Brenda, the two of them having hit it off from the day of the wedding. "I've been telling Mom for years how she was missing out. Now she knows."

Dakota's mother caught her gaze and held it.

For a brief moment, there was silence in their group.

"I've been less than supportive. I want to change that."

Tears tickled the backs of Dakota's eyes.

Walt's arm came around her, her anchor, her support.

"I love you, too," she said, brushing away a fallen tear.

Mary sighed, patted her on the back. "You ready?"

"Yeah."

Mary took to the podium to introduce her. Her BFF did her justice, repeating her accolades and achievements.

Dakota let her belly lead the way, accepted the audience's enthusiastic applause.

When they settled, she glanced over the crowd, saw her family and her husband, smiling from the eaves.

Before she uttered a word, Junior gave a solid kick, making her hand grasp her belly. "Oh," she said. "This baby thing . . . I'm sure some of you will understand if I suddenly run off to the loo." Using the English term for bathroom always captured the American audience by surprise.

Laughter rose and several hands clapped.

"How about these shirts?" she asked, accepted more applause. "We've purposely waited to find out if Junior here is a boy or a girl, but my husband is a doctor." She winked across the room. "He's looked at those ultrasounds a little too much for someone who says he doesn't know the gender of our child."

She waved a finger Walt's way, made sure several heads turned to look at him.

Walt shrugged, looked at the ceiling, but didn't say a word.

"I know this day is about celebrating the next chapter . . . the next book. None of that has been more true to me personally that being here with my family."

She waited for the applause to die. "Imagine an author . . . one who makes her living writing happily-ever-afters, never having found everlasting love. Then one day, the love of her world walks into her life and redefines everything."

Walt tilted his head, listening to her words.

"Imagine what that author will be able to bring into her next book, her next chapter?"

She took a long breath and pushed the air out in a sigh.

"I believe you'll all love Mathew and Cassidy's happily-ever-after. God knows I do. They brought me face-to-face with the love of my life." She raised her hand to Walt, waited for more than half the audience to turn. "He's mine, ladies. The inspiration to my every chapter thirteen . . . or chapter fifteen, eighteen . . . or maybe even chapter two."

The audience laughed, Dakota pulled herself back.

"Give it up for Dr. Baby Daddy, the inspiration to my chapter thirteens and all my happily-ever-afters."

As complete as she might have felt the last time she addressed a gaggle of fans, none were like this.

Dakota captured Walt's gaze, mouthed the words, *I love you.*

He blew her a kiss, told her he loved her, and Dakota began the next chapter in her life.

Acknowledgments

There are so many people in my life that came to mind while writing this book. Every author, reader, editor, publisher, and agent I've ever met filled the pages of this book. While writing is a very solitary art, interacting with readers and other writers is not. When attending conventions, we invade hotels, take over restaurants, overfill bars . . . and we create memories that will last a lifetime. For all my writer and reader friends . . . I won't list names, for that list would be way too long and I'd undoubtedly forget someone or misspell a name. You know who you are. Thank you for being a part of my life.

As always, thank you Jane Dystel and everyone at Dystel and Goderich Literary Management. If I ever get bumped up to the penthouse suite in New York, drinks are on me.

My editor, Kelli Martin, and everyone at Montlake for believing in every book I write. Let's order some champagne at the next convention . . . OK?

TJ MacKay, my partner in crime who I have a hard time rooming without. Love ya, babe.

My critique partner, Sandra/Angel . . . so happy you're writing full-time now.

For all the doctors I've known that inspire my every Dr. Eddy.

And finally . . . I round back to Angelique. A sister through marriage, but more importantly, in my heart. You defended and supported me early on, strengthening a bond usually reserved for blood relatives. I will never forget those first months in California. Ever.

You've gone on to carve a career from nothing, and are raising beautiful children on your terms. For reasons I'm sure you can see . . . this book was dedicated to you.

I love you,
Catherine

About the Author

Photo by Lindsey Meyer, 2012

New York Times bestselling author Catherine Bybee was raised in Washington State, but after graduating high school, she moved to Southern California in hopes of becoming a movie star. After growing bored with waiting tables, she returned to school and became a registered nurse, spending most of her career in urban emergency rooms. She now writes full-time and has penned the novels *Wife by Wednesday, Married by Monday, Fiancé by Friday, Single by Saturday,* and *Taken by Tuesday* in her Weekday Brides series and *Not Quite Dating, Not Quite Mine, Not Quite Enough,* and *Not Quite Forever* in her Not Quite series. Bybee lives with her husband and two teenage sons in Southern California.